Spud – The Madness Continues ...

John van de Ruit

Spud–The Madness Continues…

RAZORBILL
Published by the Penguin Group
Penguin Young Readers Group
345 Hudson Street, New York, New York 10014, U.S.A.
Penguin Group (USA) Inc., 375 Hudson Street, New York, New York 10014, U.S.A.
Penguin Group (Canada), 90 Eglinton Avenue East, Suite 700, Toronto, Ontario, Canada M4P 2Y3
(a division of Pearson Penguin Canada Inc.)
Penguin Books Ltd, 80 Strand, London WC2R 0RL, England
Penguin Ireland, 25 St Stephen's Green, Dublin 2, Ireland (a division of Penguin Books Ltd)
Penguin Group (Australia), 250 Camberwell Road, Camberwell, Victoria 3124, Australia
(a division of Pearson Australia Group Pty Ltd)
Penguin Books India Pvt Ltd, 11 Community Centre, Panchsheel Park, New Delhi – 110 017, India
Penguin Group (NZ), 67 Apollo Drive, Rosedale, North Shore 0632, New Zealand
(a division of Pearson New Zealand Ltd.)

Penguin Books (South Africa) (Pty) Ltd, 24 Sturdee Avenue, Rosebank, Johannesburg 2196, South Africa

Penguin Books Ltd, Registered Offices: 80 Strand, London WC2R 0RL, England

10 9 8 7 6 5 4 3 2 1

LIBRARY OF CONGRESS CATALOGING-IN-PUBLICATION DATA IS AVAILABLE

Printed in the United States of America

For Barry Emberton, a man of mirth, who mastered the art of casting backwards

and

For Barbara Jean Ellis (my Wombat)

ACKNOWLEDGMENTS

My thanks to all the wonderful Penguins, who march relentlessly. My thanks especially to my editor, Alison Lowry, who led me along the stony path like a chilled-out honeyguide and made sure that the Madness didn't continue forever. To Sue Clarence for her help on the London adventure. To Anthony Stonier for a classic Wombat story. To my family and friends—my deepest apologies for the times when I didn't return your calls or respond to your e-mails. To Benny V for his friendship, support, and creative energy. Thanks also to Patrick Bond, Mickey Moegoe, and the gentlemen of the Pimp's Paradise. Also the wildcats—Strangely Grey, Two-Tone, and Godot—who allowed themselves to be gentled, and to Zog, Potato, and family, who made me laugh and feel like a child again. Thanks to my old school for seeing the funny side and to Dionne Redfern for her support. Once again, apologies to Guy Emberton, who continues to get menacing looks from old ladies in his hometown, and to Richy (the royalties are in the post, China!). To Julia: Thanks for your love and laughter and for reading *The Madness* . . . in nightly installments. My thanks also go out to Ben Shrank, Jessica Rothenberg, and the marvelous gang at Razorbill who have taken a chance and made me feel special. Finally, I would like to thank all of you who read and laughed and remembered. You reminded me that in this beautiful country nothing is impossible.

TOWN HILL (THE BEGINNING . . .)

Tuesday 15th January

13:35 Dad sat back in the driver's seat, surveyed the road in front of him, and then screamed so loudly that the keys fell out of the ignition. Once the screaming had died down, a long and disturbing silence descended on the infamous lime green Milton station wagon.

Dad had been playing his Carpenters tape at full blast and hadn't felt the terrible shuddering as our un-trusty old Renault chugged up Town Hill toward school. Suddenly, halfway through the second chorus of "Top of the World," an earthquake struck the green machine. The back-right tire was so flat that the rim was sticking through the rubber. Dad did his usual whistle, nodded at the shredded tire, and announced that we had a puncture. He then grinned at me and said he'd been changing tires since he was "knee high to a grasshopper."

With a skip and a whistle he popped open the boot with an unhealthy creak and lifted up the carpet cover. His eyes glazed over and his lips moved without making a sound. Sensing a nasty turn of events, I moved in to get a closer look. Instead of a spare tire there was a crate of Castle Lager. On top of the beer crate was a faded handwritten note that read:

Pete you old crab stick, hope you don't mind, but I needed the tire. Here's some jungle juice to keep the old engine purring. —Frank

And then it said:

PS Will return it by Monday

Underneath the date was written:

24/7/1988

Dad cracked a Castle and reread the note. He didn't seem at all concerned that Frank had borrowed the spare tire for a weekend and hadn't returned it for two and a half years. In fact, he seemed to be far more impressed that the Castle Lager still tasted good after spending nearly three years in the station wagon. My father held out the beer can like it was the Cullinan diamond and said, "The taste that stood the test of time." He then grabbed two six-packs, returned to the driver's seat, and switched on the Carpenters again.

13:45 Dad drained his beer and crushed the empty can on his forehead (a skill he has perfected since New Year's Eve, when the same stunt ended up with Mom rushing him to Addington Hospital for stitches). My father burped loudly, shouted, "Gesundheit!" and immediately cracked open another beer. In a voice that could have grilled a steak, Mom instructed Dad to put his beer down and find help. Dad clearly wasn't picking up Mom's mood because he spread his arms out and said, "We must trust and believe that help will find us."

Mom then said that the only thing that would find Dad were divorce papers.

Dad shook his head and grumbled to himself. He then grabbed a six-pack and started striding up the emergency lane of the freeway. Mom jumped out of the car and ordered my father to leave the beers behind.

Dad returned to the car and offered Mom fifty bucks to go and find help. Mom was appalled that Dad thought so little of her that he would bribe her in an emergency.

After more shouting and some serious haggling, a bribe of sixty-three bucks was agreed on.

Mom strode out into the truck lane of the freeway, waving her arms above her head, and soon managed to flag down a PPC cement truck. After some lengthy discussions she drove off in the truck with a sweaty man in a white undershirt called Larry. Dad looked at me, shook his head, and muttered, "Women." He drained his Castle and began singing sadly along to "We've Only Just Begun."

I opened my new shiny red diary.

Year 1991
Name .... Spud
Comments .... The Madness Continues . . .

HOLIDAY REPORT

HOME

I guess overall my holiday gets a six out of ten, which, although a bit disappointing by most standards, was still pretty decent for a Milton. The first two weeks were a bit rough, and I mostly slept and watched videos. Dad tried to get me out of the house to play some cricket in the garden, but that was called off after he clobbered my first ball through the dining room window. Blacky (my deranged Labrador) had to have an emergency operation after he swallowed the hose nozzle. Fatty called me once and asked if I wanted to go with him to the Stellawood cemetery at midnight to look for ghosts, but I lied and told him I had diarrhea. He said if I ate a pound of chocolate and drank three teaspoons of cooking oil, I'd be fine in a day or so.

MERMAID AND SPUD IN THE WILDERNESS

The Wilderness is a splendid seaside holiday place near George on the Cape Garden Route. Unfortunately, Mermaid's folks fought solidly for three days before her dad finally packed up and left. Mermaid got all depressed again, although we still managed to go to the beach every day and take a few romantic walks.

CHRISTMAS

Wombat took us to lunch at the yacht club and soon caused chaos when she accused a four-year-old girl of stealing her Christmas cookie. Things were beginning to get a bit nasty, so the waiter brought out two cookies for Wombat as a peace offering. My grandmother refused to accept them, thumped her fish fork on the table, and called the little girl a thug. Eventually, our table was moved outside onto the balcony, Wombat's meal was on the house, and we scored a free bottle of champagne.

NEW YEAR'S

Dad's best friend, Frank, elected himself the DJ, got really drunk, and jumped in the pool wearing a pair of underpants that said NUTCASE on the front. Unfortunately, as DJ, Frank was meant to be responsible for the countdown and we only realized at about 1 a.m. that his watch wasn't waterproof. We all sang "Auld Lang Syne" at 1:03 a.m. and that's when Dad tried to squash the beer can on his forehead. The guests left, Mom took Dad to the hospital, and I was ordered to clean up and search for Wombat. I discovered Wombat in the lounge reading to a very confused Innocence, our housekeeper, from a book called *The Fundamentals of Contract Bridge* (*Advanced*).

Mermaid and I are in love and as soon as we leave school, she wants us to get married. I hope my balls drop by then—still no sign of anything and I'm fifteen in three months! Worried people are going to think I'm a freak.

Guess it's another year of being a spud.

BACK TO THE BEGINNING . . .

17:10 The security guard saluted as the station wagon pulled up to the school gate. Dad, who by now was well into his second six-pack, gave a dodgy salute out the window and shouted, "Viva!" The guard looked at him like he was a maniac and slowly closed the huge iron gates behind us.

I lugged my bags over my shoulders and staggered through the archway into the main quad. The old statue of Pissing Pete looked a little sorry for himself as he dribbled water out of his sword and down his leg. Suddenly there was a loud shout of "FORE!" followed by the sound of metal scraping against concrete. A huge army trunk roared through the house doors, raced across the cobblestone corridor, and came to rest in the gutter. I could hear the muffled sound of sobbing from inside the trunk. I approached cautiously and opened up the lid to discover a tiny boy with freckled skin and eyes red from crying. He looked utterly terrified. Then a gruesome face leered through the house door sniggering and guffawing. It was Pike. "Ahhh, Spud," he said. "Check—I've found you another Gecko to play with!" Pike sniggered again before forcing the new boy back into the trunk and resting his left foot on the lid. He didn't seem at all concerned that the small boy was freaking out and banging desperately against the sides of the trunk. Pike looked me up and down and said, "Welcome back, girly boy. Think you're a bit of a rock dog now you're in second year? Just remember I'm in matric and most probably a prefect." He spat a greeny on my cricket bag and strolled off back into the house.

I trudged up the stairs, turned the corner, and stopped for a minute outside the second-years' dormitory. I paused and took a deep breath. Then I threw open the door and there they all were—the Crazy Eight. (Minus one, of course.)

Fatty sat on his locker eating a large packet of salt-and-vinegar chips. Simon was perched on his footlocker knocking in his cricket bat with a mallet. Rambo was lying on his bed and obviously in the middle of telling Boggo a war story from the holidays. Boggo was listening to Rambo's story while popping a zit in the mirror. Mad Dog was half-way through engraving his name on the newly varnished windowpane with his hunting and filleting knife and had already made a spelling mistake. And finally, there was Vern, sitting on his bed having an in-depth conversation with Roger the cat. When Vern saw me, he began jumping up and down and pointing at the other bed in his cubicle. He then introduced me to his teddy bear, Potato. I shook Potato's paw and started unpacking. It seems that for the second year in a row, I'm sharing a cubicle with Rain Man. A bed in the far corner of Fatty's cubicle stood empty. It doesn't feel quite right without Gecko—I'm not sure it ever will.

HOLIDAY SCORECARD

RAMBO Went to Europe with his dad and his new stepmom. Rambo says his stepmom is hot and only twenty-seven years old. Rambo's dad is forty-six! Rambo reckons he wouldn't mind shagging his stepmom.

FATTY	Has put on five pounds since last year, which he says isn't bad since he's only keeping up with inflation.
BOGGO	Worked at his mom's boyfriend's betting shop. He also says he has a girlfriend but didn't seem to know what her name was or anything else about her. He just said that "a girl can't talk with her mouth full!" Unfortunately for Boggo, nobody believed his story and Rambo threw his alarm clock out the window.
SIMON	Went to America and made Fatty jealous by going on for ages about how delicious McDonald's burgers are. He went to Disneyland and the Grand Canyon but said Washington was freezing and boring.
MAD DOG	Had to go to extra math, English, and Afrikaans lessons because he failed all his exams despite being on standard grade. Apparently he's dyslexic, which according to Mad Dog means he reads words backward like the Chinese. The Glock has said he can enter second year as long as he drops to functional grade.
VERN (RAIN MAN)	It's unclear what Vern did in the holidays. All we could get out of him was

that he and his mom knitted a jersey for Roger. Rain Man said it's Roger's birthday on March 7th and he'll wear his new bright orange jersey then. Bad news is that Vern looks even crazier than last year.

Our new dormitory is far brighter and less spooky than the old first-year dormitory. There are no rafters and the walls are painted cream. I took a stroll around the deserted first-year dorm before lights-out and sat on my old window ledge for a few minutes. I then started feeling sad, so I returned to the new dorm and watched Mad Dog slicing off the ear of Potato the teddy bear while Vern groaned and cried on his bed.

Luthuli dropped by to switch off the lights and say hello. With his head boy's blazer and tie, he looked very smart and impressive. He welcomed us back and said he was thrilled that he was no longer responsible for the Crazy Eight.

I lay awake late into the night listening to Pissing Pete and thinking about the Mermaid. She left a pressed purple flower on the back page of my diary. It smells beautiful and mysterious—like her.

Wednesday 16th January

06:15 Bad news. The bloody rising-siren hooter is right outside my window! Poor old Roger screeched and leapt up in fright. Unfortunately, he must have forgotten that he was sleeping in Vern's locker, and he knocked himself out cold and ended up facedown in Vern's sheepskin slippers.

After breakfast, Spareribcalled the Crazy Eight (minus Vern) into his office. He glared at us with his wonky eye and welcomed us back to school before threatening us with barbaric punishment should we get up to anything as dodgy this year as last year. He also said we must accept the fact that Vern is a complete nutcase and that we must be prepared to give him some rope. (I would have thought rope is the worst thing you could give to a nutcase.)

Spareribthen licked his thin lips and winked at us (it could have been a wonky eye twitch) and said, "I'm not sure if you are all aware of this, but the so-called Crazy Eight seems to have achieved some sort of notoriety around the school." Rambo looked immensely pleased and nodded like a proud father. Spareribglared back at him and spoke in a menacing voice. "You so much as try another illegal caper, Mr. Black, and you'll feel my wrath, and believe me, I've been playing a lot of squash lately." Spareriblifted the short sleeve of his shirt and showed us his veiny bicep. Mad Dog then pulled up his sleeve and showed Spareribhis bicep. Spareribglared at Mad Dog with his wonky eye until Mad Dog put his bicep away.

"Twenty-four boys from other houses have requested a move into your dormitory because obviously . . . Henry . . . Gecko—no longer . . . er . . . due to . . . certain circumstances . . . we now have a vacancy there." Sparerib sniffed and looked sour. "Now, you may think that notoriety is something to be proud of, but in my book that's a direct insult to me and the proud discipline of this house. You're here to get educated, not horse around looking for ghosts and terrorizing people." This time Spareribglared at Fatty, who stopped chewing his rubber band and looked mildly ill. "So I have decided that your new dormitory mate won't be a joyriding thrill seeker from another house but a boy who will hopefully instill some good old-fashioned normality to proceedings." We all leaned forward in anticipation, but nothing more was said about who the new boy in our dormitory is going to be.

"Oh, and finally," said Spareribs, "you will under no circumstances attempt to corrupt, touch, or bully any of the first-years. They will be vulnerable enough, and I won't have you worsening the situation. I also understand that there is no love lost between you lot and Leonard Pike, but his brother Renton is a first-year in our house and I won't stand for any shit. You hear me?"

I've never heard Sparerib swear before—clearly the Crazy Eight has him worried! He continued to glare at us with his wonky eye before uttering in a cruel voice, "I'll be watching. . . ."

It was quite funny watching the new boys arriving and being led by their proud parents through our dormitory and into the dingy first-year dorm. We were all very polite, and Mad Dog made a point of bowing to every parent and calling them "ma'am" and "sir." Boggo pretended to be writing the new boys' names down but was actually making a list about which mothers he'd like to shag. Fatty kept a close eye out for new boys with a good supply of snacks, while Vern lay on his bed talking to himself and pulling out hair and was clearly disturbed by all the activity.

While all the new boys went off to meet The Glock and have lunch in the quad with their parents, Rambo convened our first Crazy Eight meeting of the year. He reckons that nobody can just join the Crazy Eight because they move into the dormitory. He said that whoever this new dude is, he'll have to prove himself to be a legend, a fine sportsman, or completely insane. Apparently the new guy is arriving tonight!

20:00 Sparerib called the entire house to a meeting in the common room. The poor new boys looked terrified, apart from Renton Pike, who was sprawled out in a chair looking like a millionaire. It was good to see Rambo accidentally kick him twice in the shins on his way past.

Sparerib announced our head of house and new prefects.

HEAD OF HOUSE

Greg Anderson

PREFECTS

Guy Emberton (Rumor has it his dad is now building a rugby pavilion on Trafalgar.)

Linley Perkins (weedy-looking guy whose nickname is Death Breath)

Julian (who is coming back to do six months of post-matric before heading off in August to the Royal College of Music in London. He's not back yet from a holiday in Thailand with Reg, former fellow prefect and least coordinated boy to ever pass through the school.)

The good news is that Pike and Devries have to carry their own laundry this year because they aren't prefects. The bad news is that Anderson has never forgiven me for insulting his crippled sister, despite the fact that he doesn't even have a sister. Emberton still blames me for ruining his chances with Amanda—and Death Breath has always looked at me shiftily in the showers.

After the house meeting I took a stroll around the school to find my new classrooms so that I don't look like a first-year and get lost on the way to class tomorrow morning. As I walked out into the quad, I heard a great booming voice shout out, "MILTON THE POET!"

The Guv strode up to me swinging his walking stick wildly and gave me a bear hug that lifted me clean off my feet. All I could manage in return was a very spudly squeak of "Sir." Once he'd plonked me down and given me a friendly crack on the head with his stick, he demanded to know what books I'd read in the holidays. I thought about lying but then confessed that I'd read absolutely nothing except for the Sunday papers. His eyes bulged and he let loose a torrent of swearing and general abuse in the middle of the main quad. A new boy carrying three cups of tea stopped and stared, his mouth wide open. The Guv told him to get lost, making the frightened first-year spill half the tea on himself. The Guv looked very healthy and impressive in his tweeds and said that he has a new lease on life. He reckons he's coaching the under-15A cricket side, but he's not my English teacher anymore. With that he shouted, "Exit, pursued by a bear!" and marched off toward the chapel.

23:00 The door creaked open and there was a loud scuffling sound as an extremely tall figure dragged his trunk and bags toward the empty bed in Fatty's cubicle. The new boy started unzipping his bags and packing things away into his locker. We were all awake, although for some strange reason we pretended to be sleeping. (Except for Vern, that is, who stood on his locker and shone his torch directly onto the new boy.) It felt a bit weird—like there was a trespasser in the dorm. I found myself resenting this tall shadow for taking Gecko's bed and forcing himself into the Crazy Eight.

I dreamed that Pike slit my throat in the night. I tried manfully to stop the blood by putting on my school tie, but then thankfully the rising siren screeched in my ear and pulled me out of my own murder.

Thursday 17th January

06:30 There was an uproar at roll call when the very tall new boy in our dormitory responded to the name:

Alexander Short

Alexander Short looks much better in the dark. He has a bad case of pimples around his mouth, which makes him look like the kind of person who frequently forgets to wash around his mouth after eating. I introduced myself to him, but all he said was an unfriendly "Howzit."

07:25 Wombat called to wish me happy birthday. I didn't want to confuse her, so I said thank you and tried to sound happy. She then started crying and said I must get on the first boat for Southampton as soon as the war ends. She then said an air-raid siren had gone off and she had to switch off the electricity and hide under her bed. I called home to tell Mom that Wombat was losing her marbles but got Dad instead. There was a lot of shouting and commotion in the background and Dad kept screaming, "Straighten up! Straighten up!" Then there was a huge crash and the line went dead. Mom phoned back to say that the builder's truck just smashed the gates clean off! Dad's building what he calls a "safe house" behind the garage with a concealed door. He says it's for safety reasons, but Mom and I reckon it's because Innocence and Dad need more space to brew their liquor.

We have a whole lot of new teachers; most of them are really boring. Luckily we still have Lennox for history. Our English teacher, Norm Wade, is wickedly dull and never changes the tone of his voice when he speaks. He also has a mean stare and a bad stutter. Boggo thinks Norm could have the makings of a seriously good poker player providing he doesn't have to speak. His official nickname is Salamander because he has long legs and very short arms. Eve is now the school counselor and no longer teaches drama. (Not sure if this is because of her affair with Rambo last year or because of Dr. Zoo leaving.) Boggo says he heard Dr. Zoo is now doing experiments on people in Zambia. Viking is teaching us drama, which should be scary. I'm also doing art with Mr. Lilly and something called Adventure Club with Mr. Hall.

11:00 There was an awkward moment in the main quad when Eve abruptly walked out of Sparerib's office and nearly bumped into Boggo, Rambo, and myself. Rambo stepped forward as if he wanted to hug her, but Eve marched off without even greeting us properly. Then Sparerib came out and ordered us back to the house. He didn't look at Rambo once, and clearly there's still tension in the air. The soap opera continues!

I asked Fatty about my nightmare last night. He said having a black cat sleeping in my cubicle is bound to create bad karma. He suggested poisoning Roger or drinking a quart of water before sleeping to cleanse my bed of evil spirits.

Friday 18th January

08:00 The Glock was all fire and brimstone at the first assembly of the year, although most of the school were trying to hide their sniggers at our headmaster's ridiculous sunglasses tan. Obviously the big man had fallen asleep on his tanning bed again. The first-years looked terrified of The Glock and he made a point of glaring at them the whole time. Hard to believe I was just like them a year ago.

11:00 I have been selected for the under-15A cricket team! The only change from last year is that Rambo has replaced Steven George, who has quit cricket and taken up canoeing instead.

17:30 Anderson forced Mad Dog, who forced us, to co-apologize to Alexander Short in the san for hitting him in the back of the head during cricket trials. When Sister Collins saw our faces at the door, she shouted, "Oh, Christ!" and stubbed out her cigarette in a potty, which she now seems to be using as her ashtray. She reluctantly let us in and showed us to Alexander's bed. The new boy looked very funny with his neck in a brace and his feet dangling off the end of the bed. Vern pointed at the patient and squawked with laughter. He then realized that everyone was staring at him, so he produced a very fake cough before moving across to the window and hiding behind the curtain.

Short reckons he has concussion and should be out of the san by Monday. Mad Dog apologized without really meaning it and told him that he deserved to get bounced because he didn't wear a helmet. Alexander looked insulted and said he didn't expect his friends to try and kill him at cricket practice. Rambo's eyes bored into the new boy and he said, "Who's talking about friends; we don't even know you yet." Then there was an awkward silence, so we all said we had to go and left the new boy in peace.

Fatty reckons any boy who tries to replace Gecko will be cursed by his ghost and he said it was no coincidence that the new boy had ended up in the san, Gecko's old haunt, just a day after his arrival. Fatty then said that Mad Dog had also broken Gecko's arm at the beginning of last year so this was definitely a sign from Gecko's ghost. Nobody was particularly impressed with Fatty's theory, and a loud and abusive argument began and lasted until about a hundred feet before we reached the dining hall. That's because Fatty was walking too fast for the rest of us to catch up.

20:30 House elections for captains and representatives.

Fatty was voted in as the house catering rep, Boggo the AV rep, and Vern won a crushing win over Devries for his second term as bog (toilet area) monitor. (In fairness to Devries, he was set up by Pike, who proposed him as a joke and then voted for Vern.) Vern punched the air with his fist when he heard the news of his victory and asked Sparerib if he could leave the house meeting immediately for a thorough bog inspection. Even Sparerib couldn't contain himself and the entire house erupted once Vern had pulled out his notepad and pencil and marched off to the bogs.

23:00 Rambo announced that the time had come for the Crazy Eight to introduce themselves to the first-years. Boggo refused point-blank. (If anybody so much as looks at a first-year sideways before their week of grace is over, they are guaranteed to be expelled.) Rambo accused us of being gutless cowards, so we all backed down and made our way to the first-years' dorm.

We stood in silence in our creepy old dormitory. After a long pause Rambo spoke in a deep voice. "Which one of you is Junior Pike?" There was a groan and then a tired voice said, "Um, I'm here. . . ." Rambo spoke again. "Junior Pike, I have bad news for you."

Junior Pike staggered out of bed and into the harsh gleam of Vern's torch. He blinked like a mole and asked, "Wha . . . what's happened?" There was a pause. Rambo cleared his throat and then spoke in an icy deep voice. "Your mother's dead."

Junior Pike was struck dumb. He just stared helplessly into the light, opened his mouth, and then closed it again.

"Your mother died in a skydiving accident," Rambo continued. "She jumped out of the plane but forgot to put on her parachute. . . ." Pike shook his head and tried to say something, but Rambo told him to keep silent.

Then Boggo joined in.

BOGGO Obviously stupidity runs in the family.

RAMBO	Pike, your mom crashed down to earth at twice the speed of sound.
BOGGO	Half the speed of light.

And then Mad Dog joined in.

MAD DOG	Quarter the speed of my bowling!

A loud guffaw. Junior Pike was by this stage beginning to look distraught.

BOGGO	She was lucky to survive the fall.

Relieved again.

JUNIOR PIKE	So she's okay?
RAMBO	Her fall was broken.
BOGGO	And so were her legs.

More elbowing and some sniggers.

RAMBO	By the power lines.
BOGGO	Do you have any idea how many volts of raw un-pasteurized electricity pass through those wires?
JUNIOR PIKE	No, I—
BOGGO	Well, neither do I, but I heard it's a shitload!
RAMBO	The power lines didn't kill your mother, Pike.

JUNIOR PIKE	Look, there must be a mistake. My mom doesn't skydive.
RAMBO	Shut up. The power lines broke her fall.
MAD DOG	And her legs.
RAMBO	And her legs.
BOGGO	They both fell off.
RAMBO	Pike, I hate to tell you this, but your mother was legless.

By now there were loud cackles and sniggers. I think Junior Pike smelled a rat, but he was still looking half asleep and completely disoriented.

RAMBO	She fell to the ground.
BOGGO	And landed safely on the freeway.
JUNIOR PIKE	Look, I don't know what you—
MAD DOG	Where she was run over by a rhino.

More giggling and elbowing.

BOGGO	Incorrect. She was run over by a Greyhound bus.
RAMBO	They found her head in Bloemfontein.
BOGGO	And her arms outside a lesbian club in Lesotho.

Vern enjoyed the lesbian-in-Lesotho bit and started shrieking with laughter and stomping his foot in the dustbin.

And then the lights flicked on. Anderson looked a little disturbing, dressed only in striped underpants and looming over us brandishing a sawn-off hockey stick. He glared at Rambo. "What do you think you're doing?" Rambo didn't answer. I have to admit the scene didn't look good. Mad Dog was armed with his hunting and filleting knife, Rambo carried a cricket bat, while Vern was madly pulling out hair with one hand and clutching onto Potato with the other.

Next Emberton sauntered into the dorm munching away at a stick of sugarcane and looking smug. "Friday night and the shit hits the fan." He grinned at me and took another munch of sugarcane. The two prefects circled slowly like sharks at an aquarium five minutes before feeding time. By now other new boys were peeping over their lockers to see what the commotion was all about. Junior Pike scrambled to his feet and leapt back into bed.

Anderson and Emberton led the Crazy Eight back to our dormitory. In the meantime Rambo had thought of a plan and he launched into a long story about breaking down barriers and becoming friends. Anderson let him finish and then grinned. "What a load of horseshit! You may have fooled Luthuli last year, but I'm no fool. I know you scavengers. Give you a fingernail, you take the whole flippin' arm!"

We were ordered to line up outside Anderson's room. One by one we took our thrashings (two strokes with the sawn-off hockey stick). The only bonus was that I got to stare at a naked centerfold on Anderson's wall while he was thrashing my bum.

Emberton lay on the bed and continued noshing his sugarcane while the floggings were dished out. He looked especially pleased after I started running on the spot before I could get out of Anderson's room.

I lay in bed with my bum on fire listening to Junior Pike sniggering triumphantly in the next dorm. Sometimes I wish Rambo would just die peacefully in his sleep! (Make that shockingly run over by a rhino!)

Saturday 19th January

THE BOG DISASTER

20:10 Saturday night movie was *Kramer vs. Kramer* with Meryl Streep and Dustin Hoffman (the real Rain Man). It was good to see Hoffman speaking normally again. Unfortunately, the first ten minutes were very slow moving, so I ducked off for a drink of water. I heard one of the first-years sobbing in the toilet. I tried to talk to him, but he ignored me. Then Vern charged in to see what was happening in his beloved bogs and ordered the first-year out of the toilet. Rain Man was dead set on reporting the poor homesick first-year to Sparerib. He seemed appalled that someone should be grief stricken in his bogs without permission. Vern wrote a warning on his pad and slid it under the door. I kept trying to stop him, but he threatened to report me to Sparerib for bad form in the bogs and surrounds. (I can't believe bad form in the bogs and surrounds is a real offense, actually.)

Then Vern started banging on the toilet door before scribbling down a second warning and sliding it underneath it. Unfortunately, he slid the warning into a puddle of stagnant toilet water. While Vern was furiously writing the second draft of his second warning and muttering angrily to himself like Gollum, Boggo strode in from the common room and asked us what was going on. Vern told him there was a criminal hiding in the bog. Boggo said that the only way to drive a rat from its lair is by an airborne bogwash.

"Bogwash," gasped Vern, like Boggo had given him the cure for cancer. Boggo filled a bucket of water and hurled it over the toilet door. There was a crash and a splash and then silence. Vern banged viciously on the door again and demanded that the criminal emerge from his hiding place. Then the latch clicked and Eunice, the African lady who cleans the bogs, staggered out crying her eyes out and holding a drenched letter in her shaky hands. My heart sank. I felt like crying. I heard Boggo saying, "Oh, shit!" Vern and I said nothing as Eunice shuffled past us and disappeared out through the house door. There was a loud thunk as Vern ripped out a knot of hair. The only other sound was the hum of the neon bog lights.

As if all the guilt isn't enough, Anderson was hanging around outside the house drinking tea and saw what happened, so now we're in serious shit as well. Anderson says we have to apologize to Eunice in writing. (Vern started right away on his notepad.) We also have to do an hour of hard labor in Eunice's vegetable garden at a time that suits her best.

I returned to the common room to watch the movie. It was all about divorce, which made me think of Mermaid. I ducked out again and called her, but Marge said she was out with friends. Then I imagined her out with other boys and got insanely jealous, so I told Death Breath I had a headache and went to bed.

Sunday 20th January

After chapel I sprinted across the quad in an attempt to get to the dining hall before Fatty. (Halfway through Reverend Bishop's sermon on fish and wine, Fatty announced that he was ravenous and that he was planning to eat our table's entire bacon ration.) I was stopped in my tracks by a loud screech, followed by a squeal of joy. Our choir leader, Julian, is back!

Julian galloped over to me with a look of horrified panic on his face. I said, "Hello." Julian squealed again and jumped for joy because my voice hasn't broken yet. He reckons the choir is touring Johannesburg at Easter. He waved his finger at me, rattling the bracelets on his arm, and said, "May God help you if your balls drop an inch!"

Monday 21st January

The morning headline read:

SHORTFALL!

The entire front page was devoted to Alexander Short's dad, who has been arrested for fraud, embezzlement, and money laundering. The newspaper said that further charges against Hugh Short would be added once further investigations have been concluded. They also mentioned Alexander and the school and made his dad sound really dodgy. When Rambo read the story, he thumped his hand onto the couch and said, "This is exactly what we need. The Crazy Eight now has a criminal!" Boggo and Fatty were so excited about the idea of hanging out with a criminal's son that they led us all down to the san after breakfast. Sister Collins came to the door waving her arms and shouting, "Too late! Too late!" She wouldn't let us in.

We only discovered at break that when Sister Collins was shouting, "Too late!" she didn't mean that visiting hours were over. It was because Alexander Short has left the school because his father has been liquidated. Fatty said liquidating is some kind of Chinese water torture, but he was lying because I overheard Death Breath saying it had something to do with freezing money.

After spending four days at school and one night in the dormitory, Alexander Short was gone but not forgotten. He already had three nicknames and was famous throughout the school. He is now known as:

Alexander Short of Cash

Alexander Short Stay

ASS

Rambo said that Alexander Short Stay would always be an honorary Crazy Eight member and that he had added yet another mystery to the Crazy Eight.

Once again Gecko's bed lies empty.

12:00 Had our first double drama lesson with Viking, who is as wild and scary as ever. He made an aggressive speech where he compared the theater to the Mafia. He said the director is the drug lord of the theater while the actors are the mules that smuggle the drugs overseas. Boggo got excited and asked Viking if he was a drug addict. Viking hit him on the head with a *Guide to Greek Theater* and locked him in the costume room for over an hour.

Still no news from Mermaid—she hasn't returned my call or written me a letter. I hope she hasn't given up on me because I'm nearly a fifteen-year-old spud! I wonder if she thinks I'm a freak or a transvestite or something?

Tuesday 22nd January

Called Mermaid, but there was no reply.

Boggo says Sparerib is livid that Alexander Short Stay has left the school and thinks the Crazy Eight is cursed. He's said to be furiously looking for a replacement for our dorm.

14:00 For the second time in just over a year we had cops in the Crazy Eight dormitory. This time it was investigators who had come to search through Short Stay's clothes and belongings. Most of his clothes were still in his trunk and they didn't find any clues. (Fatty and Boggo had already searched his stuff last night, although they were probably looking for food and porn.) The detectives under the wonky eye of our housemaster smashed open Short Stay's locker.

Everything that belonged to ASS has been removed by the detectives. It almost feels like a bizarre dream that never really happened.

The first-years' period of grace is now over. Poor bastards have to start slaving! Unfortunately, Anderson says the Crazy Eight have to keep away from them for at least another week or he'll beat us all to death.

Wednesday 23rd January

Feeling homesick. Called home, but Mom said she was on her way out. In desperation I phoned Wombat for a chat, but she thought I was a Jehovah's Witness, so she told me she was Jewish, shouted, "Yom Kippur! Yom Kippur!" and hung up.

Had our first Adventure Club class today with first-team rugby coach Mr. Hall. He outlined our missions for the first two terms. These include rappelling, mountain climbing, survival techniques, cooking, and first aid. In the second term we are all going on a three-day adventure hike unattended by teachers! Mad Dog reckons it will be the first time he passes a subject on higher grade.

14:30 Choir auditions. I've been made head of the spud (treble) section. The bad news is that I have no responsibility whatsoever except for sitting at the end of the row. Further embarrassment is that I'm now the only second-year in the spud section and the only member of the Crazy Eight in the choir. (Fatty auditioned but didn't make the cut again. He looked quite upset, so Julian told him he could be a reserve in case one of the tenors died.)

21:45 Rambo held Vern down while Mad Dog cut off Potato's other ear. Poor Vern was so distraught he burst into tears and spent half the night trying to tie Potato's ears back on with fishing line. I was too homesick to feel sorry for him.

I dreamed about saying goodbye to Mermaid at a train station. (I hope this doesn't mean that she's leaving me.)

Thursday 24th January

06:30 I GOT A CALL FROM MERMAID!!! Just when I thought it was all over, she phoned to say she loves me and that she's been really busy with stuff. She said her friends had entered her in the Miss Teen Durban beauty contest but that she didn't think she would go for it. She loved my letter about Alexander Short Stay and promised to send one back today or tomorrow.

Speaking to my Mermaid made me a lot happier, and suddenly I wasn't homesick anymore. Rambo said I needed to stop being so pussy-whipped. I nodded in agreement although I didn't have a clue what he was talking about.

Friday 25th January

Double art class with Mr. Lilly turned into a complete circus. Poor Lilly is terrified of Rambo, Boggo, and Fatty, so he seems to direct all his teaching at me. I'm afraid art isn't one of my specialties (I can only do stick figures), but I tried to look as professional as possible with a good selection of sharpened pencils carefully placed out on my desk. Lilly instructed us all to draw a picture of something we loved. Fatty drew a hamburger, Boggo drew a huge pair of breasts, Rambo drew himself, and Vern did a splendid picture of Roger. I tried to draw the Mermaid, but halfway through I realized that my picture didn't look like the Mermaid or any human, for that matter, so I changed it into a strange-looking tree with big boobs. Lilly was thrilled to see that Vern has a talent for drawing and asked him to sketch a self-portrait.

Vern set off with his pencils and his tongue sticking out of the side of his lips and drew another picture of Roger. Lilly didn't know what to say, so he applauded and told us that Vern was an impressionist. Not sure if Vern can only draw Roger or if he genuinely thinks he is Roger—either way it's a worry.

Spent the whole afternoon practicing my bowling in the nets. The Guv told me to place a handkerchief on the spot where I wanted the ball to land and see how many times I could hit it. Unfortunately, after about half an hour of nonstop bowling I hadn't got near the hanky once (except for a ball that hit it on the third bounce). I decided to try a swimming towel instead of the hanky to build up my confidence, but I missed that ten times in a row so gave up and went back to the dormitory, where Fatty was trying to eat an entire loaf of bread without using his hands.

Saturday 26th January

Today we had to travel to Westwood College for our cricket match. Mad Dog was so excited that he pulled one of the windows out of the bus, making it easier for him to bark at people on the road. We were all intrigued to see if Westwood's opening bowler (the one with a car) was still playing for them or whether he had died of old age.

We arrived to find the Westwood opening bowler (the one with the car) sitting outside the change room reading the *Weekly Mail* while a small boy sandpapered his bat. Dad was there. He did a war dance around the front of the bus as it came to a halt. Unfortunately, it was the under-fourteen bus in front of us and all the first-years looked terrified and refused to disembark until Dad had moved off to a safe distance.

I glanced across at the green station wagon and saw four deck chairs laid out. (Usually there are only three.) My heart did a triple somersault as I suddenly thought that the folks had brought the Mermaid with them, but then my fantasy exploded as a great shock of purple hair emerged from the back seat. Wombat!

I tried to look the other way and duck off to the change room, but there was a loud screech of "David!" so I thought it best not to ignore her in case she followed me into the toilets. I felt everyone staring as I skulked up to her. Wombat's face fell as I approached, and she turned to Mom and said, "Oh, dear. He's looking more and more like his father. Isn't there anything we can do?"

Back in the change room, everyone wanted to know why Wombat had purple hair and called me David. I told them she was certified mad in 1977 and that she had murdered her brothers and sisters when she was a child. (This was a lie, but I needed to try and prevent anyone going up and talking to her.) Mad Dog looked wickedly impressed that my grandmother was a psychopath.

Thankfully, I didn't have to bat or bowl and Simon and Mad Dog thrashed Westwood single-handedly. The folks left soon after lunch because Wombat was getting drunk and disorderly.

Sunday 27th January

The choir sounded brilliant during the morning Eucharist. While disrobing in the vestry afterward, Julian complimented me on how fabulous my spud section sounded. He then slapped St. John Lyle (the tenor leader) on the bum and told him the tenor harmony on "How Great Thou Art" was a disgrace and that the tenors would not tour unless they became radically less diabolical. St. John Lyle (who everyone calls Sin-gin) looked terribly upset and stuttered and stammered in protest while his glasses steamed up.

I called Mermaid to find out how her beauty contest went. Her mom said she was out with friends celebrating her being crowned Miss Teen Durban '91! I was so excited my hands went all shaky. My girlfriend is a beauty queen and a supermodel. I must be the luckiest guy in the world!

I called again after supper, but Marge said Mermaid was sleeping at a friend's house.

20:00 African Affairs (AA) Society meeting. There were no new people at the AA meeting, so I'm still the youngest. Luthuli was voted in as chairman. Linton Austin, who's back for post-matric until he goes to Cambridge in August to study economics, was made treasurer. Gerald nominated himself for everything but didn't win anything. Obviously the society hasn't forgiven him for his blunder last year when he said apartheid wasn't such a bad thing before denying that he'd ever said it.

I was very pleased when I was voted in as AA secretary. This was until I discovered that my job is to keep the minutes. (Basically, I have to write down what everyone says and read the previous week's minutes back at the next AA meeting.) This is my second leadership position that requires absolutely no leadership. At least Vern can report people for wasting toilet paper!

Monday 28th January

Mermaid was on the front page of the morning paper. She looked beautiful, with a small crown on her head and her big blue eyes filled with tears of joy. The caption under it said: DURBAN'S SWEETHEART. Boggo stuck a copy on the house notice board. Underneath he wrote MRS. SPUD with an arrow pointing at Mermaid's cleavage. Boggo then made another copy, which he said was for his personal files. I charged off to call Mermaid, but her brother said she was being interviewed by the *Northglen News* and couldn't come to the phone. I called Mom, who had already heard the news and was in the middle of a celebratory champagne breakfast with Dad.

Tuesday 29th January

Mermaid called and sounded happier than I can ever remember her being. She said she won a thousand bucks' worth of shopping vouchers and free access to the Aquarium whenever she wanted. She also got flowers, jewelry, and some designer clothes. Then she told me she loved me and said she had to go.

Give us five years and we'll be a Hollywood glamour couple like Richard Gere and Cindy Crawford!

21:30 Greg Anderson said we were now allowed to see the first-years, thereby declaring first-year hunting season open, but said he would be watching us like a hawk. He then switched off the lights and slammed the door. We all marched straight to Rambo's bed. Rambo told Vern that he was allowed to take Roger along but had to leave Potato behind in his locker because it sent out dodgy signals.

One by one we slipped into the first-year dorm. Fatty lit his candles on the floor and burned two sticks of incense. Rambo ordered the new boys to get out of bed and sit on the floor in front of the candles.

"We are the second-years. My name is Rambo and I am your king. If anything happens in this place, it goes by me first. You will not refuse or disobey me under any circumstances." He then moved to Simon. "This is Simon. He is the finest cricketer this school has ever seen." And then to Fatty. "This is Fatty, the greediest schoolboy the school has known. He weighs three hundred pounds, can fart for half a minute, and also has supernatural powers." Fatty eyed the new boys solemnly and lit yet another candle. Rambo then moved to Boggo and slapped him on the back. "This man is Boggo—the greatest pornographer since Hugh Hefner. If your mom posed naked with a horse, believe me, Boggo's got the proof." He then ambled up to Mad Dog, who took out his hunting and filleting knife. I could see the first-years' eyes widen in the candle-light. "This is Mad Dog, a savage, brainless killer. Whatever you do—never look him in the eyes!" Mad Dog barked loudly and pegged his knife into Gecko's old locker. And then Rambo came to me. "This is Spud, actor, singer, and his girlfriend is a supermodel. Unfortunately, he's a homo, so keep away from him in the showers." My jaw dropped. I tried to say something, but Rambo glared at me, so I stopped. "And this is Rain Man. Last year he ran away from school, stole a hundred and fifty pairs of underpants, and ripped half the hair out of his head. He is the craziest of the Crazy Eight, so stay away from him at all times, particularly after dark." Vern grinned like a psychopath and ripped out a small clump of hair. The first-years stared at him openmouthed. Rambo then introduced a wild-looking Roger before asking Fatty to open the ceremony with a supernatural ritual.

Fatty took the floor for half an hour, lighting more candles, humming strangely, and generally being weird. He then went on for ages about Gecko dying and said it had happened directly after a visitation by the school ghost. Throughout his lecture on paranormal dormitory activity, the first-years were dead silent and wide-eyed. Except for Junior Pike, who had a cheeky grin on his face like he didn't believe a word that Fatty was saying.

Rambo took the floor again and said, "Our housemaster's nickname is Sparerib, and he's married to Eve, who's the school counselor. I can have sex with Eve whenever I want." There were a few raised eyebrows among the Crazy Eight, but nobody said anything. Then Rambo said the time had come to officially nickname the first-years. There are three boys who look very similar, and bizarrely, two of them are called

Michael and the other Mark. It turns out they aren't related, although Boggo said that one of the moms could be a slut and responsible for the whole litter. Rambo decided to call them all Darryl, after the brothers Darryl in *The Bob Newhart Show*. I christened another J. R. Ewing because he looks exactly like the actor from *Dallas*. The boy's real name is Roy, and he didn't look very impressed with his nickname. He's also far bigger than me, so I'm now regretting getting involved at all. Mad Dog called the new Gecko impersonator Runt.

Junior Pike was initially named Dickhead by Simon, but this was later changed to Spike. And finally, the tallest first-year was then named by Fatty, who decided to call him Thinny. Vern asked if he could call one of the three Darryls Roger instead, but Rambo said he liked the consistency of three Darryls. We agreed that the first-years needed a group name, so we called them the Normal Seven.

THE NORMAL SEVEN

The three Darryls
J. R. Ewing
Runt
Spike
Thinny

Wednesday 30th January

The Guv shouted at me in the quad this morning because I forgot lunch with him on Monday. He said he was dropping me off his Christmas card list and called me a "delinquent vermin." He then shouted, "Monday the eighteenth, Milton! And if I have to reheat that Christmas turkey once more, there will be an outbreak!" I promised him I'd remember next week. He straightened his green hunting hat, pointed his walking stick at Pissing Pete, and said, "Exit, pursued by a bear!" And off he went.

12:15

ADVENTURE CLUB

Mad Dog said he hardly slept last night because he was so excited about Adventure Club. Fatty is terrified—he reckons he'll die if he has to rappel because the ropes won't hold him. Nobody's too sure how heavy Fatty is. Rambo says two hundred pounds, but I'm not so sure that's possible. Fatty reckons he broke his mom's scale, which only goes up to 264 pounds. Anyway, it's possible that Fatty is three times my weight and could potentially eat me in my sleep.

Mr. Hall led us across the athletics field and out into the great outdoors. He was disgusted to see Fatty doubled over on the fence gasping for breath. Bad news for Fatty was that we hadn't even reached the dam yet! Mr. Hall carried a long case, which Mad Dog reckoned had a double-barreled shotgun in it. Once we were out of the school grounds and had finally made it to the forest, Mr. Hall unzipped his case and Mad Dog was right. Mad Dog whistled and whispered with awe, "She's a beauty, sir."

"Right," said Mr. Hall in his gruff voice. "Which one of you rotters can throw the furthest?" Vern's hand shot into the air as did all the others. Mr. Hall considered the situation for quite a while and then announced that we would have a throwing competition. Fatty staggered into the clearing sounding like he was on the verge of an asthma attack but was unable to enter the throwing competition because he needed both hands to hold himself up against a tree. We all hurled stones into the trees and Mad Dog won by miles. Mr. Hall then led us to a ridge above the dam and pointed out a flock of Egyptian geese bobbing happily in the middle of the dam. "Now listen up, Mad Dog," he said. "I want your rock to land near those geese in the middle there. Is that too far for you?" Mad Dog grinned, ran back about thirty feet, and then charged up and let rip. The rock sailed over the geese and over the dam, crashing into the reeds on the far side. We all applauded Mad Dog, who barked loudly and showed off his bicep. Mr. Hall lit his pipe and considered the situation for some time. He blew out a huge puff of smoke and told Mad Dog to try again.

Mad Dog then let fly with another rock, which nearly landed right on the geese. They squawked loudly and flew toward us. Mr. Hall cocked his shotgun and took aim. Then there was a massive bang, a loud gasp, and a dead goose floating in the middle of the dam. Mr. Hall passed his shotgun to Mad Dog, took another suck on his pipe, and looked at us sternly. After some time he exhaled and said, "Right. Now which one of you can swim the furthest?" Only Vern put up his hand.

Friday 1st February

We had to paint a still-life picture in art class. Mr. Lilly had a huge drum of fruit, vegetables, logs, and leaves from which we could make up our own still life. Boggo drew two plums and a banana and made them look like two balls and a willy. When Mr. Lilly saw Boggo's effort, he blushed, giggled, and blew his nose. Rambo drew a picture of himself eating an apple and Vern drew Roger again. Mr. Lilly's seriously worried that Vern can only paint Roger and tried again in vain to get him to sketch something else, but Vern refused.

23:00 Rambo and Mad Dog woke up the first-years and told them to go night swimming. One of the three Darryls refused to go and started blubbing. Rambo held him down and Fatty loosened his pajamas and threatened to fart on him. Darryl then said he would go and climbed out the window, sniffing and shuddering. Thinny was the last to leave and Fatty warned him about getting stuck in the chapel window. We watched the Normal Seven disappear into the chapel and then returned to our beds to wait for something to happen.

Within a minute our dormitory door swung open and Anderson led in a mob of prefects and matrics. They marched through our dormitory and into the first-years' dorm.

After about half an hour the Normal Seven returned, panting and giggling and in a general state of terrified excitement. One by one, they scampered through the window and back to their beds. And then suddenly there were shouts and screams and the lights were switched on. It was all a setup! Boggo couldn't contain himself and charged into our old dorm with the rest of us following. Anderson was already prowling around with his sawn-off hockey stick and looking smug. Emberton arrived with his stick of sugarcane, which has now dried into a nasty yellow stalk.

Two of the Darryls were sniffing and the other was sobbing while Anderson marched around and gave them a grilling for being irresponsible and poor ambassadors of the school. Emberton thrashed his yellow sugarcane into a locker every time he felt it necessary.

Then Runt stupidly raised his hand and said, "Sorry, sir, but Rambo forced us to do it. . . ." He then started sniveling. Unfortunately, that started Vern off and he began sniffing and snuffling next to me. Vern realized that everyone was now looking at him rather than at Runt so he announced, "Night swimming!" rather loudly and then began stroking Roger in a furious manner. Anderson wasn't quite sure what to make of Vern's general madness so he allowed a long pause before continuing, "So, Runt, you are accusing Rambo over here of forcing you out the window and all the way to the dam and back?" Runt nodded and sniffed. Rambo stepped forward, looking mean. Runt then began sobbing, as did Vern. Roger howled a terrible moaning sound and we all stared at the weirdos around us.

Anderson gave the first-years a choice. Either they could be thrashed by himself and Emberton or be run in to Sparerib and take their chances with him. Anderson gave Rambo a high five on the way out of our dormitory. He then paused at the light switch and said, "It must be quite a weird feeling. There's shit going down and for once you've nothing to do with it. Let's keep it that way." Then our head of house plunged us into darkness.

I learned two things tonight:

1. The first-years' night-swimming bust is a house tradition. (Wish I'd found that out a year ago!)

2. None of the first-years had wet hair, which tells me they didn't make it to the dam and certainly didn't swim.

As my dad says twenty minutes into every episode of *Matlock*: "The plot thickens!"

Saturday 2nd February

We drove for over an hour in the bus, only to arrive to find that Arlington High had forgotten to prepare a pitch. I don't know if the coach was lying or not, but he told us not to worry about getting off the bus because his team had already been sent home. The Guv was outraged and accused their coach of cowardice, malpractice, and poor form. Their coach marched off in a huff after calling us a bunch of snobs. The Guv was furious and ordered the bus driver to take us to the Royal Hotel for tea and biscuits. En route to the Royal, The Guv spotted a pub called The Greasy Goat and asked the driver to halt for a pit stop. We never made it to the Royal Hotel.

20:00 The Saturday night movie was *Dead Poets Society* and it nearly caused a riot. It's an amazing film about a teacher called Mr. Keating who arrives at a private school and inspires the boys with some interesting teaching methods. (A bit like The Guv, except without The Guv's swearing, drinking, and mad behavior.) At the end, when Keating is forced to leave, Vern jumped up and shouted at the TV, sending Roger fleeing off his lap and out through the common room window. Vern soon realized that everybody was staring at him, so he said, "Night swimming," and then sat down. The end of the movie is seriously moving, when the boys all stand on their chairs as a way of saluting their teacher. I must confess I was a little emotional and left the common room totally inspired to seize the day. Unfortunately, Death Breath said it was lights-out, so I had to go to bed instead.

Sunday 3rd February

Because of the choir singing at Evensong, it meant I had the whole day free. Still feeling inspired by *Dead Poets Society*, I suggested to Fatty that we do a day of exploring in Nottingham Road (a small farming town near school), so we borrowed two bikes and got ready to go. We were about to leave when Boggo said he was bored and wanted to come with us. Boggo took Thinny's bike without permission and we set off into the Midlands to carpe diem.

Fatty's bike really took strain under his huge weight. Boggo and I took bets on when his back tire would explode. Fatty didn't seem concerned about possible tire explosions and pedaled along at a furious rate. Unfortunately, we had to stop and rest after every hill so that he could get his breath back. Upon arriving at Nottingham Road, Fatty bought three packets of salt-and-vinegar chips. Boggo tried to buy a *Scope* magazine, but the man at the till asked him for ID. I bought a small orange juice.

We then moved on to the farmers' market, where people sell anything that's homemade. As we approached, we could see that a big crowd had gathered and loud music was being played. We chained our bikes to a fence and went in to check things out. A huge banner over the gate read:

Bite My Sausage

Underneath was a bad painting of a gigantic sausage smothered in ketchup. Fatty took one look at the banner and charged toward the crowd. When he found out that we had stumbled upon the annual Nottingham Road sausage-eating competition, he nearly fainted with joy. The bad news was that it cost twenty bucks just to enter and we only had about eighteen left between the three of us.

After groveling around in the dust for half an hour looking for spare change, we gave up. We then saw a brunette with huge boobs. Boggo smacked his lips together and said, "Watch this, I'll kill two birds with one stone." He marched up to the girl and said, "Hello, gorgeous, do you mind if I borrow two bucks and your phone number?" The girl looked Boggo up and down and replied, "Fuck off, spot face." She then tossed her hair back and stalked off toward the ladies' toilet. Boggo didn't seem fazed by the savage bat he'd received and said the brunette with big boobs was just playing hard to get.

The entries had to be in by midday, and with ten minutes to go, Boggo and Fatty finally decided the only way we could make money was for me to sing and for Boggo to pass a hat around. I refused point-blank, but then Fatty promised me and Boggo a third of the prize money each if I made him two bucks. (The sausage-eating prize is a hundred bucks and half a sheep.) We found a spot next to a stall that was selling lamp shades. I cleared my throat before letting rip with "Another Day in Paradise." Boggo stood next to me with his cap in his hand. Fatty said he needed to focus and collapsed against the fence and finished off his third packet of chips.

Before I reached the chorus, there was a crowd of about twenty people enjoying the singing and staring at the three of us like we were a bizarre circus act. At the end of the song everyone clapped and Boggo sent the hat around. He motioned for me to keep singing, so I tried "I Still Haven't Found What I'm Looking For." This seemed to hit the right note with my audience because soon there was a big crowd gathered, half of whom were singing along with me. At the end of the song there were whoops and cheers and Boggo sent the hat around again. He motioned to me to keep singing and handed Fatty the extra money needed to qualify. Fatty galloped off back to the Bite My Sausage caravan to enter.

Next I hit my audience with "The Final Countdown." (I know the words because my parents sing it whenever there's a special occasion.) Suddenly a funny-looking man with long hair and a wizened face arrived on the scene with a guitar and a bar stool. He sat down next to me and said, "Kid, let's make some rock and roll." A lady from a stall selling wind chimes then shouted, "Feel the love, baby!" The man shook my hand and said, "Peace out." I said, "Peace out," back to him. He slipped his cigarette under the strings at the end of his guitar and asked the crowd if they were fans of Janis Joplin. A drunken farmer in khaki cheered and the strange guitar man played a song that I'd never heard before.

Boggo looked flushed with excitement and told me that I'd made eighty-six bucks in just three songs! He then gave me a piece of paper that had been thrown into the hat. It read:

I can make you a star.
Errol (not my real name)

Phone 3663171
(Strictly after hours)

Boggo said I shouldn't get excited because he's most probably a pedophile. Looks like Boggo has elected himself my singing manager!

A fat man called De Wet (not sure if it's his first name or surname) got up and announced that a record thirty-five entries had been received for the sausage-eating competition before announcing the competition rules.

NATIONAL SAUSAGE-EATING COMPETITION RULES

1. No more than thirty-second breaks allowed between sausages
2. A sausage is only counted as eaten once the contestant has swallowed the last bite.
3. Vomiting = disqualification
4. In the case of a tie, the prize is shared. Not sure where De Wet found his sausages, but they were enormous—I reckon I'd battle to finish one!

Because Fatty entered late, he was only number twenty-eight on the list of thirty-five people. This gave us time to suss out the opposition. None of the first few contenders got beyond four sausages. But then a huge bear of a man called Russell got up and ate seven very quickly but then had to quit halfway through his eighth. Fatty began to get a bit nervous, so he decided to head for the toilet to throw up the salt-and-vinegar chips he'd eaten earlier to make space for the sausages to come. After a successful hurl, he settled himself down on a large wicker chair and got into one of his supernatural trances. Boggo looked worried and whispered to me that he reckoned Fatty wouldn't be able to make eight because he was too nervous.

Russell's seven sausages was by far the best effort, and the nearest challenger was a large lady who had managed five. Eventually it was Fatty's turn, and there was loud laughter when his name was called out. The big guy strolled onto the stage looking like he meant business. He then sat down at the table and didn't stop eating until he'd finished nine sausages. He then dabbed his mouth with a napkin, looked at De Wet, and said, "Thank you very much. That was a delicious snack." The crowd roared and clapped. Boggo was so excited that he jumped up and down and then hugged me. The rest of the contestants threw in the towel and Fatty was declared the 1991 Nottingham Road Sausage-Eating Champion, and De Wet handed over the prize of one hundred bucks and half a sheep.

There was quite a long debate about how to get the half sheep back to school. Fatty offered to stuff it in his shirt, but Boggo said it would put too much weight on Fatty's tires, which looked permanently on the verge of explosion. (I think Boggo was more worried about the half sheep becoming a quarter sheep.) Fatty then attached the half sheep to my handlebars, but that made my bike keep veering out into the middle of the road. I was already getting nervous because just about every car hooted when they recognized Fatty, and I was then forced to wave with one hand and look for hot girls while trying to stay in the emergency lane and keep the half sheep between the handlebars. Eventually, the half sheep was untied from the front of my bike and Boggo bravely strapped it to his back with the help of six shoelaces and my T-shirt.

Unfortunately, the half sheep began to defrost on the way home and by the time we returned to school, Boggo looked like a victim of the Texas chain saw massacre. Further bad news was that the half sheep couldn't fit in the prefects' room freezer, so Fatty said we had to eat it by Tuesday and stored the carcass under his bed.

21:00 Feeling nauseous after watching Fatty eat half the half sheep, which looked badly undercooked on Mad Dog's gas cooker.

Wednesday 6th February

Boggo turned up at choir practice and told Ms. Roberts that I have turned professional and that she has to pay me if she wants me to sing in the choir. Ms. Roberts looked dismayed, but then Julian arrived on the scene and promptly grabbed Boggo by the hair and threw him out of the chapel.

Anderson dragged Fatty into his room and demanded to know why there was a rotting piece of mutton under his bed. Fatty tried to explain but was still beaten with the sawn-off hockey stick and ordered to write a five-thousand-word essay on personal hygiene.

Fatty then sent around a petition in prep whining about his brutal punishment for an innocent crime. One by one we signed the piece of paper and cunningly passed it on under the buzzardlike glare of Death

Breath. The petition eventually made its way back to Rambo, who read it and then stuffed the entire page into his mouth before nonchalantly returning to his geometry. Fatty hissed across the classroom to Rambo (who was now chewing happily on the petition) but was caught out by Death Breath and given finger tongs by pounding with a blackboard duster.

Fatty blamed the whole thing on the half sheep and said he was retiring from eating competitions if this is the thanks he gets for all his professional gluttony. He then shat all over Boggo and fired him as his agent. Boggo said that he couldn't be fired because he has a binding legal document signed by Fatty that says that Boggo is his agent for life. Fatty studied the document and then slunk off to his bed mumbling on about being stabbed in the back by his best friend.

I lay back on my bed and looked out through the open window at the full moon. I could hear crickets and the sound of a truck struggling up a hill in the distance. Poor Fatty kept groaning and whimpering. In that moment it didn't seem so bad being me. At least I haven't signed my life away to Boggo.

Thursday 7th February

I called Mermaid in the afternoon, but she said she was on her way out, so we couldn't chat.

I was awoken sometime in the night by the sound of Vern beating his laundry bag with my cricket bat. He soon realized that Roger and I were staring at him, so he stopped thrashing the daylights out of his laundry and said, "Night swimming." Not sure if anybody is aware of this, but Vern has now gone beyond mad and into the realm of the completely insane.

Friday 8th February

It poured with rain the entire day. By three o'clock there was a huge sign on the notice board saying that all cricket tomorrow has been canceled. We were scheduled to play Blacksmith College in Durban. I have to say I'm secretly relieved it's been canceled, because when we played them last year, Mom went out in her sundress to test the pitch and the whole Blacksmith team doubled over with laughter.

Next week is the big one—Kings College, and this time we are playing them at home. The Guv wants us to skin them alive! He calls Kings "the royal stain on our reputation" and has called us for a team meeting on Sunday night.

16:00 Mad Dog led the Normal Seven on a duck-diving mission. He sprinted onto the field and then took an enormous dive. He slid for about the length of a cricket pitch, jumped up, and howled like a wolf. I only slid about ten yards, but it was still an amazing feeling. Fatty embarrassed himself when he didn't slide at all and made a huge hole in the ground. He then called Mad Dog a fool and limped off to the san, complaining about his back. Soon we were completely drenched and having a great time until Mr. Hall drove up in his car and shat on us for destroying his field.

During prep Boggo passed around a note that read:

You are cordially invited to witness a first-year flogging massacre outside Sparerib's office at 20:00.

20:00 A huge crowd gathered in the main quad outside Sparerib's office to watch the first-years being thrashed. The major highlight was when Spike sprinted out of the office rubbing his bum and then slipped and fell in the gutter. He tried to make it look like he did it on purpose, but the jeering crowd didn't buy it.

21:45 There was a loud squeal outside our dormitory. Suddenly the door flew open and the lights were switched on. Julian had arrived for his first botty inspection of the year. He lined up the first-years and told them all to strip. After a series of photographs, he announced that Thinny was the overall winner before complimenting one of the Darryls on having a shapely backside. The poor first-years looked terrified as usual. Julian raised his forearm to his forehead like he was in the depths of despair and said, "Oh, to be young and smooth." He then shouted, "Good night, darlings," and switched off the lights.

Saturday 9th February

Still raining. Boggo reckoned it's officially a flood because the main quad is waterlogged. Fatty argued that a flood is only a flood if somebody drowns. Mad Dog offered to settle the debate by drowning a first-year. The scary thing is that he wasn't joking.

08:15 Mom called in hysterics to say that our house has been broken into! She says the whole place has been ransacked and the TV, video machine, and hi-fi are gone, along with her jewelry and clothes. She said that she and Dad had gone out to dinner and returned to find the door smashed off its hinges and the place in a mess. She then started sobbing and said she had to go because the police had come to take fingerprints.

During Saturday maths I suddenly felt my skin crawl and the blood rush to my head. What if they've stolen my 1990 diary! I raced back to the house after class and called Mom, who was still crying. I asked her to check if there was a silver box with a padlock under my bed. While she went off to check, I could feel a thumping in my chest. What if the burglars thought the box had money in it? I heard her footsteps down the passage and then her voice. "It's still there." I gasped with relief. I could hear shouting and screaming in the background. Mom said it was just Dad chasing Blacky around the pool. Apparently, Dad is blaming Blacky for the break-in and wants to thrash him within an inch of his life. There was a crash and a huge splash, then Mom said, "Oh my God," and hung up.

09:25 Wombat called in hysterics to say that her flat had been broken into as well. She said everything had been taken and told me to call the police.

WHAT THE HELL'S GOING ON?

09:28 I phoned Mom to tell her that Wombat had been robbed. Mom shouted, "Oh for God's sakes!" and hung up.

09:35 Mom phoned to say that Wombat had got caught up in the excitement and was confused.

09:38 I phoned Wombat to see if she was okay, but before I could say anything, she shouted, "I don't want to buy anything!" and hung up.

09:50 Dad phoned and told me to pack my trunk because we're leaving the country tonight. He then started swearing at Blacky and handed the phone to Mom, who told me not to panic. (I think I'm the only one not panicking!)

After all the madness I felt exhausted and went to bed wondering why the Miltons seem to have more catastrophes than everyone else combined.

Sunday 10th February

Mom called to say that everything was fine again and that the house had returned to order. Now Mom wants to emigrate and Dad still wants to drown Blacky in the swimming pool. Wombat has completely forgotten about the robbery and was playing Scrabble with Ethel (another old wombat who lives upstairs in Wombat's block of flats).

Monday 11th February

Thursday is Valentine's Day. I have decided to spend my singing money on a huge bunch of flowers for Mermaid. I asked Mom if she would mind buying and delivering twenty-four roses and a card that reads:

For my Mermaid Valentine. I love you.

Mom said she would do it and I handed over half my life's savings. I wish I could see Mermaid's face when the roses arrive at her door.

Everybody's buzzing about Valentine's Day. Boggo's convinced he'll receive something. He said he's never had a card and is way overdue. Simon looked smug all day—no doubt he'll fill his locker with cards. Rambo is sending one to Eve! He reckons it's a joke, but we aren't convinced.

Thursday 14th February

VALENTINE'S DAY

11:00 Just about the whole house waited anxiously for Julian to arrive with the post. Everybody pretended to be there by accident, but you could feel the excitement and tension in the air. Julian danced into the quad holding a huge box. He skipped across the grass and announced: "Love is in the air." He stood on a chair and everyone crowded around him, no longer pretending to be cool. One by one he handed the cards out, making sarcastic comments and squealing every time there was a present or pink envelope.

There was nothing for me.

23:30 Rambo woke us all up to say that he had just bonked Eve in the theater costume room. He reckons she dressed up as Mary Queen of Scots and ordered him to suck her big toe while fanning herself with a Chinese fan. Rambo said it was the sexiest thing he's ever seen or done. Nobody was quite sure what to make of Rambo's bonk story. I tried to imagine what our counselor would look like dressed as a queen with her big toe in Rambo's mouth. (I wouldn't have thought this was good form for a queen or a counselor.) Boggo tried to suck his own big toe but just wasn't flexible enough. He then woke up Runt and ordered him to suck on his big toe, but Runt sprinted downstairs in terror and locked himself in a toilet. Boggo eventually gave up after rupturing a muscle in his side and cutting his top lip open with his toenail.

Friday 15th February

06:00 I couldn't sleep last night.

13:30 Nothing from Mermaid.

15:30 Rambo has been walking round with a huge smile on his face. Everywhere he goes, people have been stopping him to shake his hand. Nobody has seen Eve all day and her door is locked. Not everyone believes the story, but the whole thing is very fishy. . . .

18:00 Still nothing.

21:10 Mermaid called and said she was breaking up with me. I was so shocked I nearly dropped the phone. I managed to stammer out, "W-why?" She said it wasn't about me, it was because of her. She then said I deserved better than her. (Is there anything better than her?) I couldn't talk, my mouth was dry and I was struggling not to cry. She thanked me for the flowers and told me I was special. My bottom lip was shaking violently. All I could say was, "Please don't." There was a pause and then she said, "I'm sorry, Johnny. I can't do this anymore."

The line went dead.

I sat there in the tiny little phone room holding on to the phone. I heard whispering and then laughter, but I couldn't see who it was because I had tears in my eyes.

Monday 18th February

Mom called with the news that we are all going to England in July to explore the possibility of emigrating. Good news is that Wombat is paying for everything; the bad news is that she's coming along. Dad got on the phone and said he couldn't raise an innocent boy with crime running rife in the backyard. Not sure if he was talking about the robbery or the illegal brewery. He didn't sound too keen on moving to England either but said, "You know your mother, once she gets an idea in her head . . ."

Had lunch with The Guv. I told him that Mermaid had dumped me. His eyes bulged and he shouted, "Frailty, thy name is woman!" He then opened a bottle of wine and said I needed a good book to see me through this rough patch. "I think it's about time I challenged your radical politics," he said as he thrust a book in my face and said, "You have two weeks, Milton. Thereafter I shall remove a limb a day until only your head is left."

The book is called *1984*, by George Orwell.

I couldn't sleep. Thinking about emigrating.

Tuesday 19th February

Today was cold and drizzly. I thought about calling the Mermaid but chickened out at the last minute. I then thought about my old friend Gecko and what advice he would have given me. He would have made me call her.

Read the back cover of Orwell's book.

Thursday 21st February

BOG DISASTER HARD LABOR

Spent the whole afternoon digging and weeding in the blazing hot sun. Vern had an absolute ball and spent most of the time imitating a chicken that was pecking around us. Boggo didn't say a word all afternoon except for muttering, "And to think my folks have to cough up twenty grand a year for me to dig around in a crummy garden."

Dad phoned to say that he was in the dog box again. For their seventeenth wedding anniversary he booked Mom into a three-week cooking course. Mom apparently threw the envelope back in his face and screamed, "If you don't like the food around here, then why don't you get off your arse and you go on a cooking course." Dad then blundered rather badly by saying that cooking classes were for homos and housewives and that the cooking course was cheaper than a month's supply of Immodium. Mom then blew her top and raced off down the road in the green machine. Dad reckons she's at Wombat's, but he's too scared to phone in case Wombat answers.

After some haggling I agreed to phone Wombat under the ruse of calling for a chat. This was completely ridiculous because nobody in their right mind would ever phone Wombat for a chat. In return Dad's gonna double my pocket money.

I called Wombat's, but Mom answered and screamed, "Go to the bloody Kentucky Fried Chicken or even better—find yourself a young floozy!" I didn't know what to do, so I hung up and then phoned Dad, who answered on the first ring. I told him what had happened. He refused to give me the pocket money raise that he'd promised because I'd hung up and now Mom thinks that it was Dad who phoned and chickened out. If Pike hadn't been waving his willy at me from the urinals, I would have argued. Instead I wished Dad luck and headed back to prep.

Friday 22nd February

Just before lights-out Sparerib entered the dormitory and told us that he was not bringing in another new boy to our dormitory after all. He didn't look very happy about this and told us he was keeping a sharp eye on us. Obviously, he wasn't referring to the wonky one.

After Sparerib had slunk out, Rambo gathered us around his bed and said, "For once I agree with Sparerib. That bed should be empty in memory of our Gecko." We all nodded in agreement. But then Rambo frowned and looked serious. "But guys, we've got a problem. We are famous for being the Crazy Eight. We will be spoken about for years to come. Especially with Fatty running the school archives." Fatty grinned proudly and licked the sides of his chip packet. Rambo continued, "The only problem is, how can we call ourselves the Crazy Eight when we are only seven?" There was a troubled silence until Boggo piped up and said, "Well, if we're crazy, then we'll get away with it." There was another silence broken by the sound of Fatty striking matches and lighting his candles.

Rambo stood up and announced that Roger should be made an official member of the Crazy Eight. Boggo, Simon, and Mad Dog sniggered. Vern stood up and stared at Rambo like he was the Pope. Rambo ordered a vote. Rambo, Vern, and Fatty voted yes and the others gave Roger the thumbs-down. For the first time ever I had the casting vote. I lifted my thumb and Vern hugged me so hard I was winded.

Vern dressed Roger in his pink frilly outfit and carried him to Rambo's bed. Roger then got a bit spooked by all the attention and tried to make a break for it. Vern grabbed him and held him up in the air. Poor Roger was so terrified that he froze and pretended to be dead. Vern placed Roger back on his bed and he immediately relaxed. Rambo stepped forward and placed his hand on Roger's head like he was giving him a blessing and said, "Roger, you are now a lifelong member of the Crazy Eight." Roger took the news rather casually and, without so much as looking at Rambo, set about licking his balls and purring to himself. We all shook Roger's paw—except for Mad Dog, who isn't allowed anywhere near him.

Seven boys and a cat. Boggo was right—what's crazier than that?

Sunday 24th February

Read all morning. Orwell's *1984* is very interesting but seriously bizarre. It's set in a futuristic world called Oceania and predicts what our world will be like in 1984. It was actually written in 1948 and is all about Big Brother, who runs the world in a vicious police state.

In the afternoon I couldn't get the Mermaid out of my head, so I decided to play poker with Boggo and Rambo and lost just about all my pocket money.

Monday 25th February

We are having extra choir practices every day now in preparation for the Easter tour to Johannesburg. The choir is sounding brilliant—except for the tenors, who, according to Ms. Roberts, are a little wobbly on the harmonies. (Julian was less complimentary and called the tenors "ball-bouncingly bad!") Julian asked me if I would sing a solo of "Dear Lord and Father of Mankind" for the tour. I told him that after singing it at Gecko's funeral, I'd rather not. He said, "Oh, my darling boy," and then hugged me passionately.

Received a letter from the Mermaid. It basically said exactly what she said to me on the phone when she dumped me. She reckons she loves me but doesn't want a relationship because her life is too busy and she's in a "funny place right now." I showed the letter to Simon to get his opinion. He read the first line and then burst into hysterical laughter. He then showed Boggo, Rambo, and Fatty, who also roared with laughter and slapped me on the back. They showed Vern, who also cackled with laughter and furiously banged his hand on his locker. Unfortunately, it was clear that he didn't know what was going on and only succeeded in looking like a cretin. I snatched the letter back and reread the first line. It said:

Dear John,

Just to rub salt in the wounds, my ex-girlfriend had sent me a Dear John letter!

Tuesday 26th February

SHROVE TUESDAY PANCAKE RACE

We all gathered in the quad for the traditional inter-house pancake race, where a boy from each standard and the housemaster run through the cloisters of the main quad flipping a pancake at every corner. From our house representing the Normal Seven was Thinny, who looked hilarious in very tiny running shorts, and this time Mad Dog was running for the Crazy Eight. Clearly Rambo was a bit miffed about not being chosen this year.

The Glock fired the starter's pistol and Sparerib screamed off to a big lead. (It must be noted that he was running against all the other houses' first-years.) Mad Dog ran third for us and had a controversial collision with a matric from Barnes, which resulted in Mad Dog finding a clear path forward and the Barnes matric missing the corner and ending up in The Guv's English classroom. When Anderson received the frying pan for the final lap, we were miles ahead. He ran with his house scarf around his neck and raised it high above his head as he broke the finishing tape.

As a reward Sparerib delayed lights-out by ten minutes, which provided Mad Dog with just enough time to cut off Potato's leg while Vern groaned and rolled around on the floor like he was having his own leg amputated.

Wednesday 27th February

Two days to the long weekend.

ADVENTURE CLUB

Mr. Hall took us off to the small forest near the dam and conducted a demonstration on setting up camp. He then told us to imagine we were lost in the bush and had to create a "rudimentary sleeping arrangement" for ourselves in just thirty minutes. Mad Dog sprinted off like a wild man and Vern must have misunderstood the instructions because he collapsed onto the ground and pretended to sleep. Mr. Hall called him a blithering cretin and told him to get up and stop farting around.

I found some vine plants and tied them together to make a hammock. I then wrapped my jersey and school shirt around the vine stems to make it comfy and used a packet of dry leaves for a pillow. The final touch was tying an orange flower to the end of the vines to give it a homey feel. There was the sound of loud banging further into the forest and I noticed Fatty was groveling around near the dam, where he was being dive-bombed by an aggressive family of wild geese.

We all gathered at 1 p.m. and Mr. Hall eyed us shiftily with his pipe in his mouth and smoke pouring out of his nose.

Mr. Hall told Vern to show us his bed. Vern collapsed onto the ground again and pretended to be asleep. Our master sucked on his pipe and considered the situation. Vern then started snoring loudly. Mr. Hall told Vern to get up, but Vern shook his head without opening his eyes and carried on pretending sleep but now whistling every time he breathed out. Mr. Hall stared at him for ages, then took a long drag on his pipe and asked us what Vern's name was. Rambo told him it was Rain Man. Mr. Hall sucked on his pipe and said, "That figures. . . ."

The group moved on and left Vern pretending to sleep. Simon had made a great bed out of sacks and straw. Rambo had stolen a canoe from the shed and said that this was his bed. Mr. Hall considered the boat, which had POPE'S CANOE CENTER in bold writing on the side. He told Rambo it was highly unlikely that he would find a canoe lying around in the bush but gave him full marks for creative ingenuity.

Everyone laughed at my flower, so I quickly took it down and stuffed it in my pocket. Mr. Hall asked me if I was a nancy and everyone laughed again. He told me to lie down on my hammock of vines. Unfortunately, the whole thing broke and I ended up on my bum with everyone laughing again. Mr. Hall shook his head and led us to the tree house Mad Dog had made. It could probably sleep six! Apparently he had found wood outside the canoe shed and nailed up an entire tree house in half an hour. Mr. Hall gritted his pipe between his teeth and told Mad Dog he was "one of a goddamn kind."

We then returned to where Vern was pretending to sleep and Mr. Hall conducted a fire-making lecture. Vern was so intrigued that he kept opening one eye to watch what was going on. Mr. Hall lit his fire and Vern eventually gave up sleeping and joined us all as we stood and stared, mesmerized by the flames.

Friday 1st March

LONG WEEKEND

After assembly we gathered in our dormitory and shook hands (and paws). I felt a little sad to be leaving the Crazy Eight. I then realized I was being ridiculous. I'm going home and I've decided to get my Mermaid back!

13:00 Dad picked me up from the bus stop in our station wagon that now sounds like a drag-racing car and has tinted windows. My father reckons he splashed out because business is booming and at last he can afford the V-8 fuel-injected diesel engine he's always wanted.

I did my best to hide my embarrassment that the Miltons are driving a supercharged hearse around town.

Mom and Dad had a fight about the car when we got home. Mom says she's the laughingstock of her book club. Dad said he blackened the windows for "security reasons." It's really weird to be home, knowing that burglars have been in my room. I double-checked that my 1990 diary was still safe. Obviously, the burglars thought it was worthless.

Blacky seems to have doubled in size since January. Dad says the dog's a maniac and in need of a jolly good thrashing. Secretly, though, he loves Blacky, and Mom and Dad now have him sleeping in bed with them so that he doesn't bark at the flying ants.

Spent the evening devising plans to get Mermaid back.

Plan 1 The romantic approach. Includes flowers, poetry, and other romantic stuff.
Plan 2 Begging, pleading, sniveling, and crying.
Plan 3 Pretend to have a casual chat and then kiss her when she least expects it.
Plan 4 Abuse and violence. Threaten her with a steak knife until she comes back to me.
Plan 5 Go and visit her, look completely disinterested, and talk about all the girls I'm kissing. (Basically, lie.)
Plan 6 Tell her I've had a breakdown and wait for her to come back. (Play mad.)
Plan 7 Commit suicide.

After careful analysis of the options, bearing in mind my tendency to be cowardly and take the easy option, I have decided on number 1. Also, Dad reckons he could score Princess Diana with his homegrown roses if he put his mind to it—I guess us Miltons should play to our strengths. This time tomorrow night I could be lying on my bed kissing the Mermaid. It's not impossible. . . .

Saturday 2nd March

Mom tried really hard to convince me that trying to win Mermaid back was a bad idea. The way I see it, there's nothing to lose except my dignity. (Which I lost anyway when I begged her to stay with me after she dumped me.)

I spent the day editing the poem I wrote last night and planning what I was going to say to her. I thought about phoning her first, but that's too scary, so I guess I'll just surprise her and see what she says.

Dad offered to drive me to Mermaid's house and then wait for me around the corner. He reckons "a man's gotta do what a man's gotta do."

16:45 Mom tried to talk me out of it just fifteen minutes before I was to embark on Mission Mermaid. She said I should "let sleeping dogs lie."

17:00 Dad roared down the street in our turbocharged hearse. In one hand I held the biggest bunch of red and yellow roses and in the other a purple envelope with the poem inside. Dad stopped the hearse around the corner from Mermaid's house and gave me a big hug. He then dabbed some of his Old Spice aftershave on my chin and said, "Secret weapon."

My heart was thumping and I felt nauseous. I found some bushes and tried to puke, but nothing came out. I crept around the outside of Mermaid's property, keeping close to the hedge and finally stopping outside the gate, from where I was able to sneak a peek at the house. The front door was open and I could see blurred movement inside.

After about twenty minutes of hiding behind the gate like a criminal, I finally psyched myself up for my big move. Just then a white Volkswagen Golf with shiny silver wheels and a yellow surfboard on the roof sped down the road and hooted impatiently. The electric gates opened immediately. I slammed the small gate shut and leapt into the hedge. The driver sped through the gates and stopped inside the Mermaid's yard. A strong-looking guy who looked like a surfer checked out his long blond hair in the rearview mirror before getting out of the car and slamming the door with his foot. He wore cutoff jeans just below the knee, a tight vest that said BILLABONG, and green flip-flops. I sank low into the shrubs as he swaggered across the front lawn whistling through his front teeth.

And then I saw her. . . . It was the Mermaid, walking out of the house and standing like a picture of beauty on the veranda. I was battling to breathe and had to steady myself against the fence. She wore a denim miniskirt and a tight red top. Is it possible that she has become even more beautiful? Then she smiled her dazzling smile. Except it wasn't for me. It was for the surfer and his white Golf. And then I had to watch them kiss!

It was like watching a horror movie. The rest was a blur, and after some time I realized that all I was staring at was a car, an empty garden, and a closed door.

I staggered down the street and must have thrown the roses away because they were gone by the time I reached Dad's car. Dad took one look at me and said, "Shit a brick." He then tried to cheer me up by saying that I would one day remember this moment and be pleased that I was freed from a neurotic girl and an even more neurotic mother-in-law. I nodded because I didn't want to cry in front of my father.

I should have listened to Mom. She probably knew anyway.

Sunday 3rd March

I didn't get out of bed until lunchtime. Mom opened my bedroom door for Blacky, who bounded in and leapt onto my bed and began licking my face and growling suspiciously at my bedside lamp. I heard the station wagon roar up the driveway and then the slam of car doors and the high-pitched screech of Wombat. I rolled over and pretended to be dead, but then Blacky started humping my leg while staring passionately at my lamp.

I walked outside and saw the usual scene: Dad blowing on the smoldering coals and muttering angrily to himself about the dropping standards in charcoal, Mom in her tanning chair holding a goblet of wine in one hand and her flyswatter in the other, and Wombat (dressed in a green velvet suit) speaking in hushed whispers from her deck chair in the shade. This time Wombat was going on about a jackpot that she was meant to have won at bingo on Tuesday. She reckons the organizers have it in for her and gave it to Beryl Edmunds instead. She then downed her glass of sherry and accused Beryl Edmunds of being an alky.

I jumped into the pool to get away from everyone, but the swimming pool made me think about the surfer in the Volkswagen Golf.

After lunch Mom made an announcement. Our flights to England have been booked for 4th July. I've never been overseas before—I'm already excited! (Despite the fact that we may emigrate and never come back home.)

18:30 Since the burglary Dad and Innocence are no longer selling booze from our house. Johnny Rogers (an old friend of Dad's) is selling the booze from his garage next to the bus shelter. Dad says he's had to put the price up to two bucks a bottle because Johnny takes fifty cents a bottle now. It turns out that Innocence's brew is so popular that she and Dad have a waiting list. The magic brew is called Innocent Moonshine.

I asked Dad if he was scared of being busted. He laughed nervously and told me that all Miltons are born winners and he'd rather take the risk than go back to dry cleaning.

On the way back from a moonshine delivery I asked Dad to drive me past Mermaid's house. I made an excuse and told him I had dropped my pen there last night.

The house was dark, and the Volkswagen Golf was still parked on the lawn.

Monday 4th March

Innocence's sister (Mbali) is doing the housework now so that Innocence can focus on the moonshine. Mom and Dad can't remember Mbali's name, so they call her Innocence as well.

Spent the day reading *1984*. It's very bleak but brilliant.

This has been the worst weekend in living memory.

WEEKEND SCORECARD

RAMBO	Shagged a barmaid in the flower bed at his cousin's wedding. He said he has proof. (Apparently his cousin busted him in the act.)

FATTY	Tried eating crocodile for the first time and said it tasted like tough chicken.
BOGGO	Worked at his stepdad's betting shop and got paid five hundred bucks a day!
VERN	Was allowed to take Roger home with him. (I think Sparerib has finally realized that his cat has dumped him.)
ROGER	Went to Vern's farm and didn't leave Vern's cupboard once.
SIMON	Admitted that his mom busted him wanking. (Blind one.)
MAD DOG	Opened up a tree house business. He reckons he has twelve orders and is charging five bucks per house. Think I might have to go into business with him!
SPUD	Found out that the Mermaid is in love with somebody else.

Tuesday 5th March

It rained all day. Everything was cold and gloomy. Every teacher gave us a mountain of homework. Feeling homesick.

Wednesday 6th March

Freezing and raining again. Boggo said there's snow on the Drakensberg Mountains.

Because of the weather, Adventure Club consisted of a rope-tying class and a safety lecture on lightning. Mr. Hall said that a total of eleven boys have died from lightning strikes since the Second World War. Fatty looked wickedly impressed with this piece of school trivia and made a note.

Sparerib called me into his office after prep and asked me if I was okay. I told him I was fine. He obviously didn't believe me because he then asked me if there was trouble at home. I told him there was nothing wrong.

Why is it that everyone can be as mad as they like, but the moment I have a bad day, I'm hauled into Sparerib's office for the Spanish Inquisition?

Thursday 7th March

Vern announced that today is Roger's birthday and dressed him up in his orange birthday jersey. We all shook his paw and congratulated the cat on his fourth birthday. Roger looked quite pleased with the attention and pranced around on Vern's locker purring loudly and head butting things.

Saw The Guv outside the dining hall and he asked me if I was all right. I nodded and told him I was late for a meeting.

18:00 Rambo and Mad Dog threw Roger into the fountain. Vern was horrified and at one stage looked like he wanted to punch Mad Dog. Rambo sat Vern down at dinner and explained that if Roger wants to be a member of the Crazy Eight, then he has to have a birthday present.

Vern eventually nodded in agreement, stuffed a lamb chop in his top pocket, and raced off to find the cat.

Friday 8th March

Still cold and wet. All sport (apart from squash) has been canceled for the weekend.

Sunday 10th March

Spent the weekend sleeping and finished reading *1984*. I can see why Dad's so scared of communists.

I don't know what's wrong with me—my nipples are so sore. If I touch my chest, I yelp in pain. It's been getting worse all week. I wonder if I'm dying? If Gecko were here, he would tell me exactly what is wrong with me.

Monday 11th March

17:00 Death Breath pushed me out of the shower. He said I was using all the hot water up. The moment he touched my chest, I screamed out in pain. Death Breath thought I was joking so he tried to shove his Colgate shampoo bottle up my bum. I galloped out of the showers, trying to cover my nipples with one hand and protecting my backside with the other.

My shower revealed two things: The first is that my nipples are getting worse. The second is that Death Breath is most probably a pervert or a poof. (Or both.)

Tried to watch *The Bold and the Beautiful* before supper, but I kept thinking about my chest. Can a boy of fourteen (nearly fifteen) get breast cancer?

I summoned up the courage and told Boggo about my nipple problem on the way to dinner. He said it sounded serious and that I should get help. Boggo then told everyone at the table that my nipples were infected. Rambo said I was going to grow big gazoombies like Dolly Parton. Mad Dog said that I might become a transvestite and grow female genitals. Then Fatty said that he had heard of a freak from Colorado whose breasts grew so big that they exploded and killed him. By now I was in a complete panic and decided that the problem was bad enough to take to Sister Collins. I pushed my sausage and mash aside and left. I could hear sniggers behind me and the sound of Fatty scraping my food onto his plate.

I rang the bell at the san. Sister Collins flung the door open with a mouth full of food. Once she had finally swallowed her mouthful of sausage, she said, "Right, young man, is this a case of grave illness or have you got a test tomorrow?" I told her I could be at death's door and that I most probably had breast cancer. She let rip with a great hacking laugh and told me to take my shirt off and sit on the examination bed. She then looked in my ears, down my throat, and told me to say, "Ahhh." She touched my left nipple and I yelped and jumped back. Then she told me to put my shirt back on and join her in her study. She sat me down and poured herself a whisky and lit a cigarette.

"Your condition is serious and I'm afraid irreversible," she said before taking a swig of whisky. "This disease is impossible to cure, and it will sentence you to a life of pain, anguish, and perversion." I felt vomit rising in my throat.

I'm going to die like Gecko!

Sister Collins sighed and looked at me with a stern face. Suddenly she broke into a huge grin and said, "I would look for a new nickname if I were you—your days of being a spud are numbered."

I felt the blood rush to my face and managed to stammer out, "W-what?" in a very high-pitched squeak.

Then Sister Collins said, "Your mysterious killer disease is called puberty. This is the first stage. The second stage is pubic hair and the third is the ball drop. Now back to prep with you before I get all emotional."

I raced back to the house skipping with glee and investigated myself thoroughly in the toilet. I couldn't really see anything and had to call off the examination because Vern kept banging on the toilet door and saying, "Oi!" Luckily I left when I did because he was already scribbling me a warning letter for bad form in the bogs and surrounds.

21:30 I called the Crazy Eight to my cubicle and announced that I was soon to be a spud no more. Everyone laughed and shook my hand. Mad Dog said he was relieved I wasn't becoming a transvestite because then he'd be forced to nail a stake through my heart. Vern shook my hand and then made me shake Roger's paw and Potato's amputated limb, which he keeps with his toiletries. Vern has hidden the rest of Potato from Mad Dog for fear of further amputations.

Tuesday 12th March

Woke up feeling the best I have in weeks. I definitely felt more rugged and manly in the showers and I'm working on a new macho swagger in my walk.

Lunch with The Guv was a ripper. We got into a long discussion about *1984* and George Orwell. The Guv said the book was an attack on power, corruption, and something called "totally terrorism," which means a dictatorship. In the book the hero is forced to confront his worst fear in a torture room called Room 101. His worst fear is rats. The Guv said I must read Orwell's *Animal Farm* next, which is all about farmyard animals rising up and taking over the farm. Sounds pretty bizarre.

He asked me why I've been so depressed lately. I told him it was because of the Mermaid. I told him about the blond surfer guy in the Volkswagen Golf. The Guv clutched his chest and cried, "The funeral baked meats did coldly furnish forth the marriage tables!" He then told me to go on. When I told him I was at last hitting puberty, he shouted, "Hurrah and huzzah!," raced to the wine rack, and cracked open a twenty-one-year-old bottle of wine.

After finishing his second bottle, The Guv started slurring badly and moaning about his wife leaving him empty and destitute. He then turned to me and said, "By God, I'll bet that Mermaid's mother has a proud pair of knockers." He then passed out in his rocking chair with a naughty grin on his face.

Wednesday 13th March

Fatty arrived at Adventure Club with a whole folder full of pictures and articles about lightning strikes that he had dug out of the library and the archives. Mr. Hall invited him to conduct a debriefing. Fatty passed around a series of grisly photographs of dead bodies that had been struck by lightning. Every single victim had been blown out of their shoes and one old man's scalp had frizzled up like bacon!

Fatty says that of the eleven schoolboys killed in the last fifty years, ten of them had died in the month of November. Even more strange was that all ten were struck between the 15th and the 26th of November, with three of them dying on the 20th. (Fatty did admit that two of the three were hit by the same lightning bolt.) Mr. Hall thanked Fatty for the lecture and sucked on his pipe. Then he nodded to us and said, "Boys, I think we've all learned an important lesson here today. Never go fishing in November."

Thursday 14th March

There was a rumor flying around the dining hall that Simon is about to be chosen for the first cricket team. I ran up to The Guv as he was heading into the staff room and asked him if the rumor was true. The Guv threw his hands into the air and slammed the staff room door in my face.

14:30 Julian came galloping up to me at choir practice looking incredibly anxious. He slammed down a pile of hymn books and said, "Oh my God, I heard you have stonies?" We both looked down toward my nipples and I told him it was true. He then thumped me on the head with a hymnbook and cried, "Don't look so smug—you have a solo to sing on this tour and if you sound like a constipated donkey, I'll castrate you and keep your nuts in a jar beside my bed!" I apologized and assured him that my balls wouldn't drop in the next few weeks.

Friday 15th March

Simon is still our cricket captain. He reckons the talk about him playing for the first team is just a rumor. Tomorrow we play St. Christopher's.

In art Mr. Lilly set us the task of painting a picture with the title *Rhapsody in Blue*. He then played a song called "Rhapsody in Blue," by George Gershwin, on his old record player. I tried to create a moody seascape with massive waves crashing against some high rocks. Unfortunately, it ended up looking like pea soup crashing into a black hat. Lilly took Vern aside for the umpteenth time this term and asked him why his *Rhapsody in Blue* looked distinctly like *Roger in Pink*. Vern looked a little alarmed and pulled out a clump of hair, making Mr. Lilly jump with fright. Our poor art teacher stared at *Roger in Pink* before giving Rain Man an emotional hug and swallowing half a jar of white pills.

Fatty had to go to the san after Boggo dared him to drink a cup of white paint.

23:30

NIGHT SWIMMING

Rambo told us the Crazy Eight were becoming lame and needed to do something illegal to get our street cred back. He said our severe lack of night swims this term was unacceptable and that we were setting a bad example to the first-years.

Rambo and Mad Dog woke up the Normal Seven and told them to pad up for the mother of all night swims. One of the Darryls started crying, and Thinny pretended that he'd died in his sleep. Fatty was outraged that Thinny was being so cowardly, so he farted on his head. Thinny was instantly revived from the dead but then threw up in the bin. He then tried to get out of the night swim by claiming he was ill. Rambo told Thinny to "raise his game" and made him take the bin with him so that he could wash it in the dam.

Runt started sobbing and begged Boggo to let him stay in bed. Boggo considered his request while holding poor Runt out of the window by his feet. Runt screamed in terror, and suddenly there was the sound of doors opening and slamming. Emberton and Anderson marched into the dormitory brandishing hockey sticks and sugarcane and demanded to know what was going on. Half the first-years were hysterical, and once again we were caught red-handed. Anderson took one look at the dormitory and told the Crazy Eight to line up for a thrashing. Rambo refused and said that the first-years had food poisoning and were vomiting everywhere. Emberton scoffed and thrashed a locker with his sugarcane, which immediately started two of the Darryls sniffing again. J. R. Ewing stepped forward and said, "It's true, Mr. Anderson, I gave them dried fruit that must have been off." Rambo showed Anderson Thinny's vomit in the bin, looked Anderson straight in the eye, and swore on his mother's life that we had done nothing wrong. We got away with it. (Not sure about Rambo's mom, though.)

I must admit the night swim was one of our worst ever.

The night was so cold that our teeth were chattering and my feet were completely numb by the time we reached The Glock's lemon tree. Then Roger chased after a lizard and disappeared. Rambo said we had to find him now that Roger's a full Crazy Eight member. Eventually, we discovered the crazy animal in a tree looking wild and hunted. Vern tried to coax him down with his stupid cat language, but Roger ignored him and climbed higher into the tree. Fatty tried to lure him down with some stale bread, but Roger seemed hell-bent on staying up the tree and stuffing up our night swim. In the end Mad Dog hurled a rock at Roger that knocked him clean off his branch and sent him screeching down to earth. Vern dived on Roger to protect him from further cruelty, but Roger hissed and lashed out at his master for the first time ever before tearing off into the night. Rambo eventually let us move on without Roger, but the atmosphere was gone and the dam was freezing.

About the only good thing I can say about last night was that we didn't get busted or thrashed.

Saturday 16th March

16:00 I put my name down for the St. Joan's second-year social next Saturday. Boggo has opened sex betting and the Crazy Eight are all going. (Except for Roger.)

Monday 18th March

Wombat called and accused me of stealing a case of her White Horse whisky. I told her I'd been at boarding school for two months and don't drink whisky. She then called me a vermin, said she was phoning my headmaster, and hung up.

I called Mom immediately to tell her Wombat was harassing me at school. Mom told me not to worry about it. There was a terrible howl in the background, and then Mom said, "Oh for God's sakes, not again!" Turns out Dad's erecting an electric fence around our property and had just electrocuted himself for the fourth time in ten minutes. Mom said she refuses to be sympathetic because the fencing people offered to put up the fence free of charge. Apparently, Dad gave them an "over my dead body." Which, according to Mom, may just be an accurate prediction.

I returned from lunch to find the prefects turning my cubicle upside down. Anderson was rifling through the drawers under my bed, Emberton was pulling things out of my footlocker, and Julian was inspecting my underpants. The Crazy Eight had all gathered around like curious onlookers at a car accident. Death Breath wouldn't let me near my bed and said they were investigating a report of theft.

My heart sank. So my wonderful grandmother had really called The Glock!

I called Mom and gave her the number for the Town Hill Mental Asylum in case she needed it.

Tuesday 19th March

Looks like Vern has made friends with Runt and two of the Darryls. They all followed Vern around on his afternoon bog inspections. Apparently the third Darryl is too homesick to leave the dormitory.

Julian told me that he is directing the house play next term and that he wants me to "study up" in the holidays for a leading role. I asked him what play we were doing.

He didn't say but said it would most probably be a classic.

Wednesday 20th March

Mr. Hall casually mentioned that our three-day hike next term involves carrying a thirty-three-pound backpack over thirty-six miles in three days! Even worse is that we have to set up camp in pairs and will have no staff guidance or help. Judging by my lack of camping ability, there's a good chance I'll die of frostbite or get my face eaten off by a pack of jackals!

Viking gave me a list of classic plays. I spent the afternoon hunting them down in the library. I plan to spend the holiday reading classic plays and preparing for my next great stage performance.

Thursday 21st March

Mom called to say that she had taken Wombat to see a psychiatrist. Unfortunately, the wily Wombat was completely sane as soon as they got there and never once even repeated herself. The shrink told Mom there was nothing wrong with Wombat and that Mom was overreacting. Mom said she then went back to Wombat's flat and found twelve bottles of White Horse whisky in the fridge. She also found a plate of kippers and moldy mashed potato under Wombat's bed. Wombat was outraged, blamed the yogurt thief, and tried to phone the police.

Sunday 24th March

The social at St. Joan's on Saturday didn't go very well.

FATTY	Was warned for stealing food—the school matron caught him loading up sausage rolls into his kit bag.
SIMON	Spent the entire night romping in a matric girl's room.
RAMBO	Got embarrassingly rejected by a blond girl and spent the night trying to cause a fight with boys from Blacksmith College.
MAD DOG	Was locked in the school bus within five minutes of arriving after pretending to wank in front of a group of girls. He then caused quite a bit of damage to the bus.

BOGGO	Reckons he has met the love of his life. Her name is Ali and she's an eight out of ten. He says they nearly kissed.
VERN	Spent the night dancing by himself. His dancing was so spasmodic that it was too embarrassing to let on that we knew him.
ROGER	Missed the social and spent the night in Vern's locker snuggled in his underpants. (Roger refuses to sleep on anything except underpants. When Vern has run out of jocks, he moves onto Vern's shorts cupboard. Boggo reckons it's a very controversial sign even by cat standards.)
SPUD	Spent the whole night unsuccessfully trying to make eye contact with a beautiful girl with long blond hair.

The sex auction was a bit disappointing. Simon offered up a 32B black bra, which Boggo bought for twenty bucks. Vern offered up a pink bag with a girl's schoolbooks and dirty hockey clothes. Boggo accused him of theft and paid him five bucks for the whole lot.

Mom phoned the telephone company from a call box to report that the home phone isn't working. Mom blames Dad, who erected the electric fence without once looking at the instruction manual. I could hear muffled banging and shouting from outside the call box. Clearly Dad doesn't agree. Mom also reckons she's taking Wombat to a friend who's a spiritual healer. I think Mom's terrified she will have to send Wombat to the nuthouse and Dad's petrified that Wombat will come and live with us.

Monday 25th March

Emberton whacked my locker with his sugarcane and told me I had a phone call. I rushed down the stairs, picked up the phone, and heard some frantic groveling for coins and angry muttering about the phone company being infiltrated by left-wing radicals. Then there was loud tapping and scuffling followed by a huge bang, and then the line went dead. I think it's safe to say the call box is now out of order as well.

Spent the entire afternoon at choir practice. Julian is behaving like a man possessed. We leave for Johannesburg on Friday, and clearly perfection isn't good enough for him!

Tuesday 26th March

Mom called from Mermaid's house, where she was visiting Marge. I kept listening for background voices, but there were none. I could exactly picture Mom sitting in the dining room talking to me on Mermaid's phone. She reckons the home phone is still broken and that Dad is considering a violent protest march on the nearest phone company office. Yesterday she took Wombat to the spiritual healer, who said Wombat has cabin fever. According to the spiritual guru, cabin fever is when you stay in the same place for too long and your cheese starts slipping off your cracker. Unfortunately, the next sentence gave me the worst news since February 15th.

Mom and Wombat are coming to Joburg to follow the choir tour!

I felt a sharp pain in my head followed by a tidal wave of nausea.

SHIT!

Wednesday 27th March

14:15 I HAVE THREE BALL HAIRS!!!

(In truth only one is a ball hair proper; the other two are further north.)

I sprinted up the stairs and told the dormitory I was no longer a spud. They all rushed into my cubicle and Simon, predictably, brought his toy magnifying glass, which never fails to crack everyone up. (It was quite funny the first time.) After a thorough inspection Rambo announced that I was still a spud. I tried to argue, but then Boggo cleared his throat and said we might be "splitting hairs here." Everyone roared with laughter and suddenly Vern grabbed hold of my willy. There was instant silence. Everybody was watching Vern sniggering like a cretin and holding my willy between his thumb and forefinger. I was too shocked to move, so I joined everyone else in staring at Vern.

Vern's sniggering died away and his moronic face reddened. He let go of my willy and his hand shot up to his head and ripped out a knot of hair. He looked at us like a maniac, said, "Spud," and then ran out of the dormitory. Roger didn't follow.

Rambo called a meeting on the spot. He reckoned that Vern is getting worse and should be in a mental institution, and then everybody got all excited and aggressive and the meeting dissolved into a pillow fight. I slipped out of the dormitory and headed toward the bogs to check on developments.

Thursday 28th March

Had a chat with The Guv after assembly. He said he's going to see his brother in England over the holidays. He wished me luck for the choir tour, shouted something in Latin, and sent me on my way.

Practiced my solo on "Jesu, Joy of Man's Desiring." Julian called it "a triumph." I didn't tell him about my ball hairs. He's so stressed out he may well have had a breakdown.

Bags are packed. I can't wait to finish the choir tour and get home to my own bed for the holidays.

Friday 29th March

10:00 After saying goodbye to the Crazy Eight, I boarded the choir bus to Johannesburg. Julian ordered me to sit with him at the back and he draped me in a blanket to keep out the autumn chill. Actually it was sweltering hot on the bus, but I didn't dare argue.

The entire choir struck up the school hymn as we passed through the school gates. We turned the bend onto the main road and I stopped singing. Parked on the shoulder of the road under a tree was a lime green station wagon with darkened windows. Through the windscreen I could just see a great shock of purple hair. I felt the blood rushing to my face as the school hymn continued around me. I can't believe Mom and Wombat are following the choir bus. Even worse, Mom seems hell-bent on following as close behind the bus as humanly possible without actually touching it.

I asked Julian if I could sit at the front, but he refused. I sank low into my seat and prayed nobody would notice them.

But being my life, it didn't take long for word to spread around the bus that two old ladies were stalking us. Ntoko (a third-year who sings a mean baritone) waved at the station wagon. Mom waved back nervously and Wombat picked up her handbag and hid it behind the back seat. Wombat then pointed at Ntoko and said something to Mom, who thankfully dropped back to a more reasonable following distance.

We're staying in a community center in Parktown in Johannesburg.

Saturday 30th March

11:00 The entire choir assembled in our naffy robes and marched down the aisle of the St. Martin's in the Veld Anglican Church singing:

> And did those feet in ancient time
> Walk upon England's mountains green . . .

I sang with all my heart. The choir sounded beautiful. Poor Julian was dripping with sweat and looked like a lamb being led to the slaughter. Wombat and Mom were sitting in the front row and waved at me as I walked past. I kept singing and didn't look up from my hymnbook. We performed ten songs and two solos. (My solo's tomorrow at the Johannesburg Cathedral.) After the final number (a fiery rendition of the school hymn), two old ladies in the second row started to applaud. Wombat looked horrified that somebody should clap in a church. She turned around to face the illegal clappers and let rip with a loud "Sssssssssh!" The two old ladies stopped clapping immediately and sat down looking embarrassed. Wombat shook her head and looked appalled.

Our evening concert was at a special home for disabled children. Julian told us to sing like nightingales and not to laugh at them.

I felt so sorry for the disabled children, most of whom were in wheelchairs. They loved our singing, and afterward we gave them chocolates and posed for photographs. I couldn't help noticing that the mentally handicapped kids share a similar demented expression to that of my cubicle mate.

Thankfully, Mom and Wombat didn't come along to the concert because Wombat says she finds retarded people very disturbing.

Sunday 31st March

EASTER SUNDAY

Johannesburg Cathedral is huge and magnificent. I was really nervous during the warm-up and I could hear my voice shaking on my solo. Mom and Wombat arrived an hour early and watched the entire warm-up from their spots in the front row. Wombat applauded loudly after my trial run.

08:45 We were ordered to the vestry to get into our party clothes. People were piling into the cathedral, and outside, the traffic had come to a standstill because of all the cars waiting to park. The old bongo drum in my chest was banging away and I could taste that dry salty taste in my mouth that I always get before singing or acting.

Suddenly a powerful arm yanked me out the door of the vestry into a little rose garden outside. I was face-to-face with a wild-looking Julian. "Listen to me, Spud," he said, looking intensely into my eyes. "Today is probably the last time I will perform publicly in this choir. This cathedral is as good as it gets." He breathed deeply and looked to be fighting off tears. "Spud, I want you to know that yours is the finest schoolboy soprano voice I have ever heard. In a month it will be gone—forever. This is your last chance." He looked at me sadly and placed his hands on my shoulders. "You've done this before. It's just a bigger cathedral. But have you heard those acoustics?" Julian gripped my shoulders tightly and said, "I want you to sing like you have never sung before. This is your last five minutes of glory, so go out there and be glorious!"

I marched down the aisle feeling like I was ready to chew metal. Thank God my solo was the last song of the service, so I had time to calm myself and make sure my voice was well warmed up. The cathedral was packed and the choir sounded brilliant. Julian was right. The acoustics were the best I've ever heard. The dean of the cathedral gave a long sermon about the Ten Commandments and then made us pray in silence for ages. I don't feel that confident about praying anymore because I'm not sure God has much time for me and my little life. Anyway, because I was feeling terrified and had nothing to lose, I asked God to keep me calm and make my last solo as a spud absolutely perfect. The prayers ended and then Julian sang "I'll Walk with God" while the congregation received communion. He sang with such passion that his voice was cracking with emotion on the high notes.

The end of the service approached. The dean of the cathedral blessed the congregation and said, "Our final hymn is 'Jesu, Joy of Man's Desiring' and will be sung solo by John Milton." I stepped forward as the organ began quietly. I took a deep breath, opened my mouth, and my high-pitched girl's voice poured out. There was no shaking this time. It sounded better than ever. Halfway through the solo the choir started processing out around me. Julian had planned the final procession out to the exact moment. His plan was to leave me alone at the altar as the choir disappeared out through the back of the cathedral. It worked brilliantly because the atmosphere as I sang the final lines alone at the altar was magnificent. And then it was finished. There was dead silence in the cathedral. Hundreds of pairs of eyes stared at me. I closed my hymnbook and walked slowly down the aisle. The congregation remained standing in utter silence. It felt weird and wonderful at the same time. I walked into the vestry, and there was a loud cheer from the choir and a huge hug from a tearful Julian.

Monday 1st April

THE HIP HIGHVELD CHOIR COMPETITION (HHCC)

Julian was outraged when we only came second out of a total of twenty school choirs and called it a hometown decision. (Clearly our head of choir didn't study geography, because the winning school was from Upington.) The choir sang the school song on the pavement next to the bus, and then the great choir tour of 1991 was over and the boys scattered in different directions to begin their Easter holidays.

Wombat slept the entire way home. Mom wouldn't say if she had drugged her mother or not, but Wombat passed out exactly ten minutes after finishing a bottle of soda water. It was a relief to be able to sit in silence and watch the flat, golden scenery as it shot by.

Tuesday 2nd April

Returned home to find a list of kitchen regulations stuck to the fridge, which Mom had obviously left for Dad while she was on the choir tour.

MOM'S KITCHEN REGULATIONS

- Switch off stove after making toasted cheese.
- The tins in the cupboard above the kettle are Blacky's food. (NOT TUNA!)
- The food in the fridge is your food. (NOT BLACKY'S!)
- Cooked meals in Tupperware inside fridge. (One per day.)
- Make sure water in kettle before boiling.
- No more than three cups of coffee a day.
- Blacky's dish must be kept outside. (Flies.)

- Blacky must be kept outside. (Fleas.)
- If my mother calls, please don't try and confuse her with funny voices.
- Frank not allowed on the property. (Even in an emergency.)

By the looks of things, Dad hadn't obeyed many of the kitchen regulations. Mom found dog hair on her side of the bed and Frank's jacket hanging over a rosebush in the garden. Mom said we all needed a nourishing meal and cooked up some chicken breasts and vegetables that came out of the oven looking gray and tasting revolting.

Dad stuck the cooking course envelope on the fridge before setting off with Blacky to find a pizza takeaway.

Saturday 6th April

It's been great to relax and do nothing for almost a whole week. I still wake up every day at 06:15. It takes my brain at least ten minutes before it registers that a rising siren hasn't gone off and that I'm not sleeping next to a lunatic. I then drift back into a deep sleep and usually dream about the Mermaid until ten o'clock. Then it's breakfast, shower, and play with Blacky. After lunch I read a play, although I usually start having fantasies about playing the leading role and end up acting out monologues to Blacky, who whimpers and looks guilty. Mom brings sweet milky tea in the afternoon and we chat about school and my dreams about being a famous actor and writer. She loves the school stuff but doesn't seem too happy about my chosen career. Every day she finishes her tea, takes my cup, and tells me that I'll make a great lawyer before heading to the kitchen to try and cook supper. It's about this time that a dark and heavy cloud enters my head and marinates my brain with uncontrollable thoughts.

I have to concentrate on my breathing to stop myself from gasping or sobbing. It's a completely weird feeling, much worse than homesickness.

And then I find myself on my bike, thundering down the road.

Durban North is beautiful in the afternoon light. The trees are evergreen and shine golden green-yellow. Kids play on the streets. Some of them wave as I go by, while others just scowl or ignore me altogether. It's almost as if my bike knows the way to Mermaid's house. I get the feeling it might go there every afternoon whether I ride it or not. The bike stops next to the coral tree in the park around the corner from her house. There is so much bush and tree cover on the verges that it's easy to stay hidden, although I dread Marge spotting me one day and telling my mom. Most days I don't see Mermaid. Some days I see the Volkswagen Golf parked in the front yard. It doesn't really matter either way. Even on the odd occasion that she does slip out into the garden, I have to duck away like a criminal. She can never know that I'm there. Seeing her still gives me a sharp pang in the ribs, although I'm not sure if that's love or adrenaline. Around 17:30 Marge switches on the lights inside the house. That's my cue to leave. I return to the park, unchain my bike, and cycle as fast as I can back home. When I arrive home, I always make out that I'm totally exhausted. Dad thumps me on the back and goes on about me winning the Tour de France cycle race one day. Mom runs me a bath and fusses about me catching a chill. Then it's supper, an old *Matlock* rerun on TV, the news, weather, and then one by one the Miltons begin yawning and drifting off to bed. I try and read at night, but my mind swirls with a million thoughts and I find myself staring at the ceiling. I dunno why, but most nights I fall asleep with the light on.

Sunday 7th April

Because we missed Easter Sunday, Mom insisted on us going to church today. There was a guest preacher at the service. He had silver hair and a bright red face and his name is Archdeacon Simons. Our local priest seemed hugely excited that the archdeacon had chosen our church to deliver his sermon.

The archdeacon bowed rather nobly at the altar and stepped up to the lectern. He then stared at us for a few seconds and said: "Easter time is about reflection. It's a time when we Christians have to take a good look at ourselves and ask, are we living the sort of life that Jesus wants us to live?"

Dad shuffled uneasily next to me. The archdeacon paused again and said: "I don't think we are. Because inside each and every one of us there is a cancer that eats away at every little fiber of our spiritual souls. We can turn our heads away in denial, but every single one of us is guilty. Every single one of us is afflicted with the cancer of racism!"

Dad's body jerked like a puppet on a string. A bizarre whine squeaked out of his throat. His hands fumbled awkwardly in his pockets, and I could see his eyes darting from side to side like a crazy man. Mom scowled at him. Dad looked angrily back at Mom, and then both of them looked at the archdeacon again. There was uncomfortable wriggling all around us and quite a few nervous coughs and urgent whispers.

The archdeacon continued. "But in every moment of darkness God gives us a trail of light to follow. He offers us the path of redemption that his son Jesus Christ left us while nailed to the cross. In every age there are leaders of light that follow in God's path. In this benighted land we are led by a powerful and courageous torch. That man is our very own Archbishop Desmond Tutu."

I gritted my teeth and waited for an explosion. Dad thinks Tutu's the devil because he told the world to give us sanctions and made sure we didn't play international sport. To quote my father, "He put our boys out of business!" Dad also says Tutu looks exactly how Satan looks in his brain, so therefore the Anglican archbishop is most certainly Satan and possibly worse.

Dad stormed out of the church and slammed the door with a bang. Mom went white and refused to look up from her prayer book. I pretended the man who had just left wasn't my father, so I shrugged and shook my head in disgust.

After communion Mom pushed me out of the back door of the church and we found Dad sitting in the car talking to himself. Mom didn't say a word. I couldn't tell if she was angry with Dad or with the archdeacon, but either way she was as mad as a snake. In fact, from my position in the middle of the back seat, it looked like her lips had disappeared completely. We reached the big turning circle at the bottom of the road. Still not a word had been spoken. We sped around the circle and completely missed our turnoff. Dad sped around the circle again and again . . . and again. I was starting to feel terribly carsick.

I wonder if my father's madness is inheritable—Fatty reckons it can skip a generation. In that case I may have a psychotic son one day!

After countless laps of the turning circle with Dad making his crazy whining sound and Mom with her head buried in her hands, Dad suddenly hit the anchors and headed the station wagon back in the direction of the church.

Back at the church, Dad jumped out of the car, slammed the door, and disappeared into God's house. Mom let out a long sigh and then ran after him. I briefly considered taking the car and never coming back—Holden Caulfield with wheels. . . . Unfortunately, I can't drive, so I sprinted after my parents into the church as well.

The action was all going down in the vestry.

There was the archdeacon still dressed in his black shirt and dog collar but with his pants off. Dad had his fists raised and was hurling abuse at the poor preacher. Mom was shouting at Dad and trying to hand the archdeacon his black pants. The archdeacon looked perfectly calm and stood facing Dad in his starched white underpants with his palms outstretched. Dad accused the archdeacon of ruining his holidays and said if he ever mentioned Tutu's name in the pulpit again, he'd thrash him within an inch of his life. The archdeacon told Dad he wasn't scared of dying and that at the end of the day, we all have to answer before God.

Dad didn't know quite what to make of the archdeacon's reply, but he still kept his fists raised and let out a scary whimper. The archdeacon said, "Perhaps one day when we lay down our fists and stop fearing, we'll discover that the people we call terrorists just want to live each day like we do, raise their children and live in peace."

Dad now looked terribly confused, and his eyes darted around like a wild animal's (possibly with rabies). He dropped his fists but still looked crazy. The archdeacon took a step toward my father and said, "We don't deserve to live in fear, and neither does your boy."

At that moment fear walked through the door.

Standing before us was Mrs. Shingle. The largest woman in the world. (Wider than Fatty.) Mrs. Shingle was my standard-four Sunday school teacher, and she still terrifies me to this day. Barry van Rensburg, who used to be in my standard-four Sunday school class, reckons she put on over a hundred pounds in the year after her husband died. A coincidence? I think not.

Mrs. Shingle didn't ask questions. She grabbed Dad by the shirt and hurled him out the side door and into the graveyard. She told him he wasn't welcome at the church anymore and accused him of having airs and graces because he had sent his son to a snobby school. Dad tried to say something, but Mrs. Shingle wouldn't let him even so much as utter a word. Dad then called Mrs. Shingle a dyke and sprinted toward the station wagon like his life depended on it.

Mom got in the car and told Dad that she wanted to talk in a civilized manner without fighting.

They fought all the way to Wombat's flat.

YACHT CLUB LUNCH (with Wombat)

HIGHLIGHTS

- My steak and garlic butter was delicious.
- Dad drank Coke throughout the entire meal. (Although his last three were laced with double brandies.)
- Mom was in a far better mood and seemed to have forgiven Dad for his earlier madness.
- The weather was perfect and there was a yacht race in the harbor, which gave me something to watch while Wombat crapped on about the standard of television in the country.

LOWLIGHTS

- Wombat choked on a fish bone and then coughed it back onto her plate.
- Mom drank more than usual and knocked over the salad dressing.
- Wombat kept asking whose birthday we were celebrating.
- Dad and Wombat accused the Indian waiter of cheating us on the bill. The bill turned out to be correct. Dad apologized; Wombat didn't.

Friday 12th April

Dad hasn't been himself since his fight with the archdeacon. He's only tried to thrash Blacky once this week and that was because he (Blacky) dug up the same rosebush twice in one day.

I saw Mermaid with her boyfriend in the garden. Marge wasn't there and they both lit up cigarettes. It felt weird to watch the Mermaid smoking. It didn't look right—a bit like a power line running through a perfect field of beautiful trees.

The Miltons are going on a caravanning weekend tomorrow to Park Rynie on the Natal South Coast. Dad is borrowing the caravan from Frank, who has in turn borrowed it from Les Wright. Frank reckons he's had it for so long that Les Wright seems to have forgotten that he ever had a caravan in the first place. Mom's not happy about the caravan and called Frank a criminal. Dad said it doesn't count as theft if you steal from your friends.

My father has been preparing his fishing tackle since Tuesday, and we spent the whole night preparing fishing traces, telling stories, and giving each other pulls on the fishing rod. Dad is extra excited because Wombat isn't coming. She refused to come along because she says caravanning is beneath her.

More good news is that I will be celebrating my fifteenth birthday at home this year, which means no bogwashing, fountain dunking, or ball polishing this time around.

I now have twelve ball hairs, although still waiting for the big ball drop.

Saturday 13th April

MILTON CARAVANNING TRIP TO PARK RYNIE

My father nearly killed us three times before we made it to Park Rynie. The first near-death experience happened near the airport when Dad got a bit carried away with watching a plane coming in to land. He was so busy trying to keep up with the SAA Boeing 737 that he nearly ran over three hitchhikers standing in the emergency lane. Mom told Dad he was a "bloody fool."

The second near-death experience occurred under the Umgababa bridge. Dad reckons that the Umgababa bridge is a death trap because "the bastards" throw bricks off the top and try and kill you. By the time we reached the dreaded bridge, Dad had scared the clappers out of himself and was as highly strung as Wombat in a bank line. In a high-pitched voice he ordered me to lie flat on the back seat and place the fishing tackle box on my head. As we approached the bridge, Dad swung the car wildly from the left to the right to try and outfool any possible brick throwers. Unfortunately, Dad was so worried about the trouble from above that he didn't notice the gigantic sugar truck bearing down on us from the fast lane of oncoming traffic. As Dad turned around to give me a high five, Mom screamed and pulled wildly on the steering wheel. The station wagon slid back across to the left. The caravan tried its best to jackknife, but Dad was too quick and he straightened us up again. Dad shook his head and told us the country was becoming more dangerous by the day. Mom stared out at the passing banana plantations without saying a word.

The third blunder happened right near Park Rynie. Dad was so eager to see the surf conditions and check which direction the wind was blowing that he didn't stop at a railway crossing and nearly had us written off by a train. After Dad had finished swearing at the train driver, he winked at me and said, "Light northeaster . . . Johnny, let's go catch ourselves a hundred pounder!"

I took a stroll around the campsite. In site 18 across the road there was a bunch of surfers and their girlfriends sitting in deck chairs drinking Lion Lager. One of the girls was rather delicious. She smiled at me as I walked by. I tried to smile back, but my mouth wouldn't open, so instead I ignored her and slipped into the communal toilets. I sat down on a closed toilet seat and thought about my possible options. Then I realized that if I took too long, the girl would think I was releasing a prisoner. Simon says beautiful girls never fart or release prisoners, so just in case she was wondering what I was up to in the toilets, I scuttled out and strolled back past campsite 18 looking as cool as a cat. This time the girl was facing away from the road and a surfer with long blond hair had his arms around her and was kissing her neck. I'm beginning to develop a deep hatred for blond surfers!

When I got back to our caravan, Dad was waiting for me in his fishing kit. He clapped his hands like a loon and shouted, "Come come come come . . ." as if I had been wasting his time. He then announced that the bluefish were running amok in the bay, thrust a fishing rod into my hands, and marched off toward the beach.

We staggered across rocks and jumped over rock pools for about a mile before Dad pointed at a gully and said, "X marks the spot." We set about rigging up our tackle. Suddenly Dad gave a loud agonized scream and hurled down his pyramid sinker. He had left the bait in the caravan freezer. He then sat down on a rock and stared out at the sea like a psychopath considering murder. Then he said, "I bloody give up, I just bloody give up! Everything a Milton does is a bloody disaster. I mean, what's the bloody point?" I wasn't sure if Dad was becoming suicidal, so I told him I'd just seen a huge fish jump out of the water in the gully in front of us. I turned back to my father, but he was already halfway back to the caravan park, jumping from boulder to boulder like a rock rabbit.

To say the bluefish were running amok in the bay wasn't quite true. By five o'clock we hadn't had a bite. Dad was looking edgy and kept trying different baits but without any luck. He then told me that Sappi, the nearby paper factory, was to blame for the poor fishing. He took a sip of seawater and told me it tasted oily. Suddenly my line went completely slack. Dad's eyes lit up and he started shouting, "It's a bluefish! It's a bluefish! Reel! Reel! REEL!" I reeled like a maniac and then the line went tight. Dad shouted, "Hit the guts out of it!" I jerked the rod back violently and the fight was on.

17:04 I landed my biggest bluefish ever! Dad reckoned it was two and a half pounds. I took the hook out of its mouth as Dad sprinted back to our bags to get his camera. I took some time to get a good grip on my slippery fish and then I held it up with a big grin. But my father didn't take a photograph. Instead he stuck a hook through the top of the bluefish's head and another just below the dorsal fin and said, "Live bait, Johnny!"

Dad lobbed my beautiful fish into the bay, handed me his rod with a wink, and said, "Now we catch its great-grandfather!" After my initial disappointment at my record fish being relegated to bait status, I began imagining a tussle with the finest sport fish in Natal. Dad cracked a beer and burped loudly before kicking into a raucous version of "Top of the World." Thankfully, there weren't any bystanders.

After about twenty minutes of holding Dad's huge rod and staring out at the horizon and feeling manly, I felt a sharp knock on the line. Dad stood behind me and whispered in a weird voice, "Stay calm, boy. He's just checking it out. Give him time to swallow. Nice and easy . . ."

Unfortunately, the knock was all I got and when I reeled up, I discovered that all that was left of my beautiful bluefish was its head and a few bloody tendrils of guts and gore. Dad studied the bluefish head, took a swig of his beer, and said, "Shark."

My blood ran cold—I had just been messing with Jaws! We got fishing again and soon Dad pulled in two bluefish which he said were both just less than two and a half pounds. He rigged up our rods with wire trace and cast out the bluefish for us. There we stood like two warriors waiting for a deadly battle against the most feared beast on earth. Dad gave me a few swigs of beer, saying it would put hair on my chest. I'm not greedy. Personally, I'd settle for a couple more ball hairs. (Total ball hair count sixteen as of lunchtime.)

Then suddenly Dad's rod tip shook violently from side to side. He passed me his beer and crouched into a striking pose. His eyes bulged with anticipation and he started talking to himself. The shark screamed off like a wounded Ferrari. Dad whooped loudly and began staggering across the rocks toward the bay so that he could fight the shark from the beach. I reeled up my live bait and left the fish in a rock pool before running across to catch up with Dad on the beach. He reckoned the shark had already stripped off more than half his line and was nearing Madagascar. Since it was getting dark, I ran back to where our bags were on the rocks and brought them back to the beach. I gave the live bait its freedom because I felt sorry for it gulping away in its green and slimy rock pool.

Back at the beach, Dad was starting to lose hope. His back was causing him trouble and the nylon had cut through the skin on his left palm. It was like the Old Man and the Sea, although Dad didn't seem too impressed when I told him so. Unfortunately, the shark pulled a sneaky move and began moving parallel to the beach toward the left. Dad tried his best to stop him, but his line was burned off around the reef. My father didn't seem too upset, perhaps because the shark had already worn him out or maybe, like his son, he was secretly terrified of what he might just pull out of the water.

Back at camp, I had to make the fire because Dad was too busy marching around from campsite to campsite telling stories of the big one that got away. He told the guy next door that it was well over five hundred pounds and probably a ragged tooth. Our neighbor looked a little worried and said that he would advise his family to keep out of the water. After striking fear into the entire Park Rynie caravan park, Dad happily settled into his deck chair and ordered me to write a full account of his shark fight in my diary.

22:00 Dad just went and shat on the surfers for playing their music too loudly. They were quite rude to him and called him a "ballie" once his back was turned.

Sunday 14th April

Great day suntanning. No fish or sharks.

Monday 15th April

Five days until my birthday! Fifteen definitely sounds a lot older than fourteen. The Miltons took a drive down the coast and had lunch at a pub called The Orange Octopus. They were playing fishing videos on a TV in the corner and Mom had to keep telling Dad to stop watching and listen to her stories. But Dad already had that wild fisherman glint in his eye and ate his burger so quickly that we had to stop at a pharmacy on the way home for a bottle of antacid.

I caught two more bluefish in the afternoon, but this time there were no sharks around. Dad filleted one of my fish and we cooked it over the fire along with sausages, lamb chops, chicken kebabs, and last night's reheated rump steak. After dinner everyone was so stuffed that we all went to bed before eight o'clock.

21:00 I lay awake listening to Dad snoring and Mom grinding her teeth. After a while I slipped out of the caravan, trailing my sleeping bag behind me. I closed the door, tiptoed up to the fire, and threw some more wood on the coals. The smaller pieces caught fire and I settled down for a night beside the campfire. By the looks of things, the surfers were setting up for an evening's party, and soon music was booming from the blond surfer's car stereo. They were playing *Out of Time*, REM's latest album. I've heard it coming out of Death Breath's room every afternoon since half term. I lay down next to the flames and looked up at the stars and listened to the sound of the waves breaking and sliding up the beach. I thought how magical it would be if Mermaid was lying here with me. She also loves perfect moments like these. I closed my eyes and gritted my teeth because I could feel a lump in my throat.

That's me in the corner
That's me in the spotlight
Losing my religion

Tuesday 16th April

Four days until D-day!

The moment we were home, I told the folks that I was off for a cycle. I tore down the street and made it to Mermaid's house. Everything was locked up. They must be away on holiday.

Saturday 20th April

HAPPY BIRTHDAY, SPUD MILTON!

I got a Sony Walkman from Mom and Dad. For once my presents weren't complete rubbish. (Apart from Wombat's, who gave me three British stamps to the value of forty-eight cents.) Even better news was that with my music voucher from Uncle Aubrey and Aunt Peggy, I bought REM's *Out of Time* and spent the afternoon playing it over and over while walking around and singing. Blacky gave me a box of chocolates, though he growled at me when I opened it. The Guv called me and sang the entire "Happy Birthday" song and then abruptly hung up.

11:30 Mom dropped a pink envelope onto my bed and casually sauntered out of my room without saying a word. Just one look at the writing and I knew who it was from. I ripped the envelope open. Inside was a card with a picture of a big red tomcat licking his lips.

Dear Johnny,
Happy birthday.
Love,
Mermaid

PS I miss u.

I jumped off my bed, forgetting that I was wearing my headphones, and ripped them clean out of my Sony Walkman. I then had to piece the ripped envelope together to see where it was posted from. Turns out it came from Jeffrey's Bay, the big surf spot near Port Elizabeth. Mermaid must be on holiday there with her boyfriend. Did she send me the card because she's feeling guilty or because she still loves me? I read the card a few more times and hid it under my pillow. I played "Losing My Religion" and pressed repeat.

18:45 Mom shook me awake and told me to get dressed for dinner at Mike's Kitchen. We waited on the road for Dad to arrive with Wombat.

Eventually headlights came into view and the old station wagon screeched to a stop.

It was clear from the outset that my father and Wombat had been fighting on their way to our house. Wombat accused Dad of trying to cut her head off in the window. Dad said he was trying to close his own window and had hit the wrong window button. Mom tried her best to cheer everybody up, but Wombat was so angry that she didn't even wish me happy birthday.

Dad told our waiter that we were having a family emergency and that he should bring a double round of drinks at once. Dad winked at me and then ordered me a Castle Lager. Clearly Mom and Dad have decided that fifteen years old is a perfectly reasonable drinking age. What with my balls about to drop and now legally having a beer on my birthday, I doubt I'll be called Spud for much longer. Mom spotted a woman from her book club sitting at the next table and urgently ordered me to hide my two beers under the table, but before I could move, the woman's large face was looming over us like a cold front. Mom looked down in embarrassment. The book club lady tried her best not to stare at all the booze in front of me but couldn't help her eyes darting from the beer to my face and back to the beer again. Dad then pointed at me and said it was my birthday. The book club woman said, "Happy birthday," and then asked me how old I was. I said fifteen, but if you were going by the high-pitched tone of my voice, she'd probably have thought twelve. The book club woman left us, and Mom and Wombat spent the next half hour gossiping about the cold front's sex life. (She basically sounds like a female Boggo.)

Sometime after dessert Mom, Dad, Wombat, and the waiter sang me a raucous version of "For He's a Jolly Good Fellow." Everybody in the steak house turned to stare although nobody sang along. After the cringy hip-hips and hoorahs, Wombat stood up to make a speech to the restaurant. She raised her champagne glass and thanked everyone for attending her birthday party and said that she was feeling younger by the day. She then sat down and wolfed down a plate of melba toast.

Sunday 21st April

I arrived home after my afternoon bike ride to another rendition of "For He's a Jolly Good Fellow." My report card had arrived.

- 3 A's (English, history, and drama)
- 3 B's (science, biology, and geography)
- 2 C's (Afrikaans and maths)

On the back side of the card was a comment from Spareribs. (Obviously a new ruling from The Glock.) I have stuck it into my diary:

John needs to apply himself more to achieve what I believe to be his full potential. He is a well-liked member of the house but is sometimes prone to moments of introspection and solitude. While finding him to be a well-adjusted boy, I feel he needs to maintain higher levels of scholastic endeavor to realize the faith this school has put in him. A suggestion would be less focus on writing in his diary and more on the coming examinations. John has impressed me with his courage and despite his late physical development has bravely borne the trials of recent months and continues to exude warmth amidst a troubled year of boys. I continue to follow his development with great interest.

Underneath Spareerib had signed his crablike signature.

I couldn't resist writing Sparerib's report card.

Sparerib is a solid enough housemaster who needs to do more should he want to achieve the post of headmaster. Besides looking like a gnome and having to shoulder a serious defect (pardon the pun), he is also beset with squint eyes, bad breath, and a slutty wife. He allows boys to bully, tease, mock, raise cats, and show signs of extreme madness while thinking that his weekly thrashing of some boy is a good example of keeping discipline. Despite all these problems he continues to be an unliked housemaster and a compulsive skulker. I continue to follow his lack of development with little interest.

I considered posting Sparerib's report card back to school, but by then my anger was gone, so I stuck it in my diary instead.

Sunday 28th April

Tomorrow it's back to school. For once I'm actually looking forward to getting back to the old asylum. (Although I know I'll be regretting it the moment I set foot into the quad.) I'm also determined to be brilliant in the house plays. I have taken Julian's hint and have read quite a few classic plays over the holidays in preparation.

MY EASTER PLAY READING LIST

(With comment and rating out of ten)

- *Pygmalion*, by George Bernard Shaw. Not bad but not as good as the musical version, *My Fair Lady*. Spud rating, 6/10
- *Death of a Salesman*, by Arthur Miller. A bit boring but still very good. Spud rating, 7/10
- *Endgame*, by Samuel Beckett. Very disappointing and nowhere near as good as *Waiting for Godot*. Most of the time I didn't know what was cracking. Spud rating, 2/10
- *Saturday Night at the Palace*, by Paul Slabolepszy. Despite his weird name I reckon this is the play of the holiday. Hoping Julian chooses this one and I can play the character of Forsie. Spud rating, 9/10

Monday 29th April

HOLIDAY SCORECARD

RAMBO	Has taken up smoking. He reckons he can smoke twenty a day if he really wants to.
FATTY	His mom put him on strong medication and he says he's lost ten pounds, although it's impossible to tell if this is true. On the downside he seems to have brought a trailer-load of snacks back to school.

SIMON	His parents got divorced. He says he doesn't give a stuff.
BOGGO	Spent the entire holiday with his new girlfriend, Ali. He says that on Sunday night, he got her top off but it was too dark to see anything and Ali wouldn't let him switch on the light. To prove he wasn't pulling a fast one, he hauled out a whole series of photographs of himself and Ali at a party. I must admit she's a lot prettier than I expected.
VERN	Hard to tell, but it sounded like Rain Man killed a sewer rat with his hat. When I asked him how big the cane rat was, Vern indicated that it was up to his waist. (?)
MAD DOG	Was arrested for driving a car on a provincial road. His father (Dad Dog) was fined two hundred bucks and was told to keep his son under control. Dad Dog then thrashed Mad Dog with a leather belt.
ROGER	Spent the holidays in a cupboard sleeping on Sparerib's underpants.
SPUD	Got a Sony CD Walkman. (I kept the caravanning at Park Rynie to myself.)

Mad Dog told us he had arrived before everyone else this morning and had spent the day booby-trapping the first-year dorm. After congratulations and high fives we crept into our old dormitory. The Normal Seven were still awake and chatting, but when they heard us coming, they dived into their beds and played dead. Rambo stepped forward and said, “We know you’re awake.” There was complete silence. True to form, the cowardly first-years were obviously under the impression that if they didn’t make a sound, then we would all give up and go to bed.

Mad Dog moved to the nearest bed, pulled out his deodorant, and sprayed his candle flame. A huge blue and orange flame lit up the room. There was a terrified squeal and then one of the Darryls jumped up and fell back against his locker clutching his face. Rambo spoke again. “Anybody else still asleep?” There was a chorus of groans and whimpers and gradually the Normal Seven moved out of their beds and sat on their lockers.

Rambo welcomed them back to school and told them that they would be seeing far more of us this term. Spike then stupidly told Rambo that he would report us to his brother if we so much as touched any of them. While Rambo twisted Spike’s arm behind his back, Boggo informed him that his mother was rubbish in bed and has serious body odor problems. In the ensuing chaos, one of the Darryls tried to make a dart for the door but was caught by Vern, who shouted, “Stop, thief!”and wrestled him to the floor. Simon and Boggo told the fleeing Darryl to take his pajamas off and sing the school hymn. The poor Darryl slowly took off his shirt and then his pants. Vern immediately grabbed hold of Darryl’s willy and shouted, “Spud!” He then cackled with laughter.

Maybe he realized he was behaving like a psycho because he then let go of the Darryl's penis like it was burning hot, and his hand shot up to his head. Runt looked horrified and held on to his own crotch, probably without realizing it.

There was a flick of a knife up in the rafters, Mad Dog shouted, "Bombs away!" and Thinny and his bed were instantly drenched by a bucket load of water.

Mad Dog instructed Rambo to make the entire Normal Seven sit on J. R. Ewing's bed. The Normal Seven may be short on spine, but they are crafty and sneaky when it comes to getting out of trouble. They realized that Mad Dog must have rigged something nasty above J. R.'s bed and they all moved toward us instead to get away from certain disaster. I decided to flex my muscles and ordered the Normal Seven to J. R. Ewing's bed immediately. Maybe it was the spudly voice or the fact that half of them are bigger than me, but nobody moved. Rambo and Boggo sniggered and suddenly everyone was watching me. I should have just shut up, but now I was in a catch-22. If I backed down, then I would never be respected again in either dormitory, but if I didn't back down, then that meant I had to do something to someone!

I viciously swung a hockey stick into the back of Thinny's thighs. He screamed, stumbled a few feet, and fell over. I felt awful. The Normal Seven panicked, sprinted to J. R. Ewing's cubicle, and squashed onto his bed. Above us there was a wicked cackle, then a snip, followed by a cascade of eggs raining down on the first-years. They groaned and whimpered as the eggs splattered all over their heads. Mad Dog jumped out of the rafters and onto the floor with a loud baboon bark. He then put away his hunting and filleting knife and led the Crazy Eight back to our dormitory.

As we lay in bed giggling and mocking, I could hear J. R. Ewing sobbing in our old dorm while he changed his bedding, and suddenly I felt ashamed and couldn't sleep.

Tuesday 30th April

Saw The Guv outside the vestry. He was reading a notice about God and spiritualism that Reverend Bishop had obviously stuck up in a moment of religious excitement. I stood behind The Guv, but he continued to read with absolute focus. When he'd reached the end, he sniffed and then banged on the vestry door, shouting, "The truth will out, Vicar! You may rob me of my pride, but the truth will out!" He banged again and shouted, "Frailty, thy name is Bishop. Priest by day, yellow belly by night!" I wasn't sure what was going on, but it looked like The Guv was picking a fight with Reverend Bishop. A few boys gathered around, eager to see a lunatic English teacher beat the hell out of a crazy priest. The Guv gave up and swung around, looking wildly into my eyes. He then jumped back in fright and said, "Madness, Milton! Madness! He butchers me at a game of tennis and now spurns my moral masculine outrage!" The Guv looked wildly at the door again and shouted, "Injustice, Vicar! Agony piled upon shame!" Then he turned to me and said, "Monday lunch, Milton—for you sure as bloody hell won't get a decent education around here!" With that he turned on his heel and strode off.

Thinny's got a huge bruise on his left thigh. He's also behaving weirdly to me. He doesn't say a word but keeps staring at me at mealtimes.

22:30 The bastards did it again! Like something out of last year's birthday nightmare, I was carried down to the bogs by a mob of marauding Spud attackers. This time I kicked and bit and scratched and shouted until I had no more strength left. I managed to injure about three people before Fatty sat on my chest and nearly crushed me to death. I looked around the mob and saw the triumphant face of Thinny, who was watching with glee as Rambo shaved my ball hairs off with an electric razor.

I have stubble for the first time—unfortunately, it's in the wrong place.

Wednesday 1st May

The Crazy Eight (minus cat) are going on the Adventure Club three-day hike next week. The other five hikers are from Larson House. One of them is Geoff Lawson, who used to be my big buddy but still hasn't forgiven me for running off with Amanda last year. Mad Dog is beside himself with excitement. The moment Mr. Hall left the class, he jumped up and whooped loudly. He then tied Simon to his chair and teased him about being a tennis player. Simon lost his sense of humor, so the class left him tied to the chair in Mr. Hall's classroom. I snuck around the corner and waited until everybody had gone to lunch and then slipped back into the classroom and untied our cricket captain. Once he was released, he said, "Bastards!" and stormed out without even looking at me or saying thank you.

Thursday 2nd May

Boggo has invited us to his girlfriend's house for a party. He didn't say when it was going to happen. All he said was that it's going to be "wild, sick, and porno." I'm very excited.

RUGBY PRACTICE HORROR

Mongrel is the under-15C rugby coach! The man is a sadistic, brainless, heartless monster. I wish I had taken tennis instead. We spent the first hour of practice running and the second half leopard crawling. A former veteran of the Rhodesian bush war should not be coaching under-15C rugby or any rugby, for that matter. Just about everybody collapsed or puked at some stage and poor Vern ran into one of the posts by mistake and had to go to the san because he was seeing double. Mongrel said we were the worst rugby side in the school last year and we have to pay for the shame we have brought on our comrades. With his thick mustache (he looks like a traffic cop) and thick accent, he keeps saying, "You guys is a bunch of girls!" or, "Rugby are not a game for poofters!"

Last year's under-14D captain, Pig, said he was seeing triple and staggered off to the san to see if he could convince Sister Collins that he had a serious and possibly life-threatening injury.

Friday 3rd May

We visited the first-year dorm in another Crazy Eight show of strength. Boggo forced Spike to shag his pillow and make orgasm noises. Spike was very realistic, and after a few minutes it started to look like he was enjoying himself and everyone felt a bit embarrassed. Thankfully, Fatty farted and we all scattered back to our beds. I lay down and shouted out, "Good night," to the Crazy Eight. Unfortunately, it came out as a terrible squawk that sounded like a cross between a donkey bray and the shriek of a six-year-old girl. I drew my hand up to my mouth, but it was too late. Within seconds I was surrounded by a crowd of cackling mouths. I didn't know whether to feel embarrassed or proud, so I laughed and blushed and shook seven hands and a paw. I was then told that I had just had my first knack jump. Once the laughter died down and everyone had taken their turn making a joke with Simon's toy magnifying glass, I settled on the window ledge and looked out at Pissing Pete. I heard the sound of a distant train clattering along through the Midlands and tried to work out whether it was coming or going. I felt a surge of excitement—in fact, I felt more relieved and proud. At last, my balls are dropping!

Saturday 4th May

Extra rugby practice. We carried huge logs up and down the rugby field until our backs were too sore to carry on. Mongrel called us a bunch of mommy's boys and ordered us to run the cross-country course. Even worse was that he ran along with us, blowing his whistle and calling us girls. This is worse than Mordor!

Sunday 5th May

MY VOICE IS BREAKING!

I could hardly get through a verse of the school hymn without knack-jumping. In the end I mimed singing. The first-year sitting next to me in the choir stalls thought I was insane and kept looking at me out the corner of his eye. I hope this terrible donkey squawk doesn't hang around for long or this could get really embarrassing.

Monday 6th May

House plays auditions are taking place next Monday. Last year house plays were canceled because of *Oliver*—so this will be my debut in a nonmusical. I was the first person to write my name on the board. The play is *The Glass Menagerie*, by Tennessee Williams, and according to the director (Julian), it's a classic. Apparently it's all about a woman with a deformed foot who falls in love with a good-looking friend of her brother. Julian said he was planning on playing the girl with the deformed foot.

13:00 I knocked three times on The Guv's back door as usual. There wasn't a sound from inside the house and all the curtains were closed. I tried the handle and the door opened. I called out, "Sir?"

From a pitch-black lounge came a low voice. "Milton, damn and blast your punctuality." I said, "Afternoon, sir." Then the voice from the dark replied, "Do not set forth upon this room." He then went on a long rampage about technology and how it was the great evil of the earth. I hung around in his hallway. I noticed his answering machine had thirty-two unheard messages. The red lights flashed urgently on the machine like it was begging me to do something. "Right, you miserable little whining stickleback, that will teach you." There was the snapping of plugs and then came a loud shout—"Enter!"

I found The Guv in the middle of his lounge, standing beside a slide projector with his walking stick.

"Pull up a pew, Milton. I guarantee a religious experience."

I felt for the armchair while my cricket coach snapped on the first slide. It looked like an ancient old house somewhere in England. The Guv tapped the slide projector with his walking stick and said, "This, Milton, is where the greatest writer of all time laid his seed." I wasn't sure what he was on about, so I just grinned back at him like a loon. "And in case your corrupt adolescent mind thought I was talking about barbaric sex, I refer of course to Shakespeare's house!"

I told him it looked very nice. The Guv barked in uproar and thoroughly abused me for calling the "Mecca of literature" nice. He then opened the curtains and collapsed into his rocking chair, looking exhausted. "God, living is such an awful waste of one's energy." He uncorked his wine and said, "Good holiday, Milton?" Before I could answer, he said, "As you can see, I went off to the Isle of Pom. Gray and dismal, old man. There's no two bones about it. You're abroad in July?" It sounded so grand the way The Guv said it that I shrugged nonchalantly like going abroad was a standard Milton holiday.

And so the wine disappeared and The Guv continued his descriptive abuse of everything from the weather to the lack of basic hygiene on your average Brit. After a lunch of chicken and salad he handed me Alan Paton's *Cry, the Beloved Country* and told me it was a belter. The Guv poured more wine and began telling stories about people from his university days before falling asleep in his chair.

Tuesday 7th May

12:30 We have been given our hiking instructions by Mr. Hall. We have to walk over twenty miles a day and we are carrying thirty-five-pound backpacks. (That's almost a third of my weight!) We leave school tomorrow morning and set up camp on an old boy's farm near Fort Nottingham. The second day we go cross-country and camp at the foot of Inhlazane and then on the final day we make the eighteen-mile trek back to school. Surprisingly, Fatty looked really excited about three days of trekking through the bushveld. Mad Dog was so excited that he asked Mr. Hall if we could leave tonight. Mr. Hall took a long drag on his pipe and told us to be patient and prepare ourselves for the mission. We have each been given:

Backpack
A wafer-thin mattress
Tent
Bottom sheet
Bowl, mug, spoon, fork, and knife
Small gas cooker
Tin pot
Miniature torch
A length of rope
Raincoat
Mini first aid kit
Compass
Map
Two drumsticks (not sure how they got into the ration)
A packet of food rations

After lights-out everyone packed up their backpacks. Mine was so heavy that Vern had to help me sling it over my back and steady me when I was upright. Mad Dog threw his backpack into the corner of his cubicle and then dug around under his bed. He then pulled out his own heavy-duty rucksack that was already packed with everything a hiker could possibly need. Mad Dog reckons his own backpack is forty-two pounds but said it was like carrying a feather. He told us that he once carried a dead goat for eight miles. He didn't say why.

Meanwhile Fatty announced that he would rather be well fed than comfortable, so he left everything behind except for food and cooking equipment. He then added about ten pounds of nosh from his own snack reserve.

Vern packed all his toiletries, including a razor and shaving foam. He tried to pack Potato the teddy bear into his backpack but then couldn't fit in his cooking pot. Eventually he gave up and told Potato that the mission was too dangerous and that he should stay behind to protect the dormitory.

I think Roger knew that Vern was going away because he slept the night in his backpack.

Wednesday 8th May

THE GREAT THREE-DAY HIKE BEGINS. . . .

07:00 We all gathered in the main quad for a prayer with Reverend Bishop and a lecture from Mr. Hall. The weather was clear and bright although there was a nasty backstabbing wind that snuck around the cloisters and made my teeth chatter.

Mad Dog reached the fence to cross the railway line before the rest of us were even out of the school rose gardens. The Larson boys stuck to themselves as a group and so did we, although Geoff Lawson did come across and say, "Howzit." Unbelievably, Fatty was full of cheer and even got us singing an old marching song as we made our way toward Fort Nottingham.

After a few minutes Mad Dog had disappeared completely—obviously he's not doing the group thing. Then there was a crunch of tires and a small white truck came into view. Smiling behind the wheel was Geoff Lawson's farm housekeeper, Joseph. We all followed Geoff and sprinted to the truck. We leapt on the back but then had to jump off again and help load Fatty on. Joseph pulled a tarpaulin over our heads and soon we were bouncing along the road listening to the roar of the diesel engine. Underneath the tarpaulin Fatty and Geoff shared a high five. Fatty winked at me and said, "Spud, I love it when a plan comes together!"

I'm not sure this is quite what Mr. Hall had in mind for our adventure hike, but a relaxing day at Lawson's stud farm sure beats lugging thirty-five pounds up and down hills all day.

Mad Dog missed a day of fine food, fishing in the dam, and a Crazy Eight versus Larson House touch rugby match. Fatty said he would be the ref but sat under a tree eating sandwiches and shouting, "Forward pass!" whenever he felt like it.

16:00 Joseph dropped us a few hundred yards from Eaglederry farm. It would have been splendid to sleep at Geoff's farm instead of the old boy's farm, but it was decided that it could be risky because the farmer old boy could rat on us if we didn't pitch up. On arrival we all tried to look as exhausted as possible in case the farmer was watching us through binoculars. Mad Dog was there already and had set up a huge green army tent with a veranda attached in the pine plantations. Fatty took one look at Mad Dog's mansion and announced that he was sharing with him. He settled himself down on Mad Dog's veranda and started unloading twenty-five pounds of food.

Simon suggested to Rambo that the two of them set up their tents next to Mad Dog's. Rambo looked at Simon like he was mad and said he didn't want to sleep next to a tennis player. Simon tried his best to laugh it off but then moved away and started erecting his tent by himself. Rambo and Boggo moved off together and started setting up some distance from the rest of us.

Unfortunately, that left me with Vern. My cubicle mate put his arm around my shoulders and said, "It's you and me, Spudeee." The thought was horrible, so I said, "Sorry, Vern. Actually I'm setting up with Simon." Vern looked confused and a little crazy like he couldn't comprehend me not sleeping alongside him every night. Then there was a voice from the bushes. "If you so much as set up within ten feet of me, I'll shit in your tent, Milton!"

18:00 It was nearly dark, and Vern and I were still nowhere near getting our tent up. Twice it looked like I had worked out the tent riddle, but twice Vern got caught inside the tent, freaked out, and pulled everything to pieces. Simon, Fatty, Rambo, and Boggo shouted nasty comments at us from Mad Dog's veranda.

While I was brushing my teeth at the tap near the dam, I heard loud shouting from the direction of Mad Dog's palace. I sprinted back to camp to find Fatty in a foul mood and Mad Dog holding out his hunting and filleting knife. Mad Dog told Fatty he wasn't sleeping in his tent and called him a slob.

Later I slipped into Mad Dog's tent to find him sharpening his hunting and filleting knife in the light of his gas lamp. His tent was huge and looked extremely warm and comfortable. He looked at me as if he was about to tell me to get lost, so I jumped in quickly and asked him if I could join him on the hike tomorrow. I told him I wanted to get the real adventure experience and not hang around at Lawson's farm. Mad Dog shrugged and said, "Cool." I thanked him and returned to my backpack, pulled out my sleeping bag, and used my raincoat as a pillow. I added some logs to the fire and settled down for a night under the African stars.

Thursday 9th May

Mad Dog and I left Eaglederry farm at first light and made our way down the dust road and then scrambled through a fence and into some open grassland. We marched along at a good pace with the rising sun warming our backs and with the crunch of fresh stalks of grass beneath our walking boots.

Later in the morning Mad Dog showed me a brown bird called a honeyguide that he said would lead us to a beehive. He pointed at the bird that was calling madly at us and said, "Spuddy, I bet you ten bucks he's gonna take us to honey." Mad Dog explained that honeyguides lead honey badgers to a beehive and then pick up the scraps once the animal has eaten himself to a standstill. This is quite a cunning hunting ploy for a bird who isn't brave enough to rob the hive himself.

After trailing this crazy bird for what seemed like half a century, we approached a small patch of wild forest. Mad Dog pointed toward the trees and said, "I bet you a hundred bucks the honey is somewhere in that forest." Mad Dog's bet had just jumped tenfold, so I figured the chance of actually finding honey was improving. We stored our backpacks behind a big rock and then started running after the honeyguide, which was looking more and more desperate as it flew from tree to tree. I knew we were getting close to the hive because there were bees buzzing everywhere and the bird was becoming more and more hysterical. Mad Dog told me to hang back and disappeared into the thick bushes ahead. I retreated to a rocky outcrop and waited for something to happen.

Mad Dog returned with a huge honeycomb brick and about thirty nasty bee stings. We sat down on the warm rock and tucked into a delicious breakfast of stale bread and fresh honey. The honeyguide was chirping loudly and hopping closer and closer to our rock, begging for his share of the loot. Mad Dog slid his hand into his backpack and pulled out his catapult. Before I could even try and stop him, there was a loud THWACK and the honeyguide lay stone dead and bleeding on the rock in front of us. I felt terrible for the poor bird. The surprise of being betrayed was still frozen onto his death expression. Fatty would say Mad Dog has now completely screwed up his karma and will be in for some misfortune.

Mad Dog roasted the honeyguide corpse over his gas burner, feathers and all. After his breakfast of honey and honeyguide, he started pegging his hunting and filleting knife into the ground rather close to my foot. I soon realized that the point of the game was to peg the knife as close to my foot as possible. I charged off and hid behind a tree. Unfortunately, Mad Dog then started pegging the knife into the tree very close to my head. I decided to surrender before Mad Dog became even more dangerous and I was murdered with a hunting and filleting knife to the brain and accepted his offer of a blindfold while he spent the next ten minutes throwing his knife at the space next to my foot.

An important lesson has been learned.

Mental note: Never hike with a madman.

14:30 Arrival at the foot of Inhlazane. The local farmer didn't seem overly thrilled to see us and told us to set up camp as far away from his farmhouse as possible. Mad Dog chose a flat patch under some trees near the farmer's dam. I collapsed in exhaustion and put off trying to set up my tent until I was rested. Of course Mad Dog had his mansion up in minutes. He then said, "You're in with me tonight, Spuddy. You can set up your sleeping bag on the far side." I was terrified. I told him I wanted to sleep alone, but then he pulled out his hunting and filleting knife and started sharpening it on the tent pole. I lost my confidence and carried my backpack meekly into the Mad Dog mansion.

17:00 There was a huge commotion when the others joined us at the camp. Boggo and Rambo accused Simon of trying to spade Geoff Lawson's maid. Simon told them to f-off and set up his tent away from the group again. He seems to be having a miserable hike and is now being called Billie Jean King by everyone.

Then Rambo pulled out two bottles of vodka and four liters of Sprite. Fatty pulled out two loaves of bread, cheese, tomatoes, and a whole roast chicken. The feast was on! Unfortunately, Rambo said that we could only eat dinner after drinking five shots of vodka and smoking a cigarette. Simon told everyone to get stuffed and sulked in his tent. The rest of us shot back the vodka. It was like setting fire to your throat. Why would anyone drink it unless they were forced to?

Vern downed a cup of neat vodka, lit his cigarette at the wrong end, and then vomited on the fire. The smell of burning Vern vomit was awful and everyone ran for cover. In the commotion I made a break for the bushes and threw up in peace against the trunk of a tree. Only Mad Dog, Fatty, and Rambo were able to reach dinner without throwing up.

I was hoping that the release of the booze might mean that it wouldn't affect me. However, I found it very difficult to stand up and everyone kept laughing at my voice, which was not only slurring but knack-jumping badly as well. Vern passed out on Mad Dog's veranda while Rambo led us on a raid on the Larson Losers, who had set up camp near the dam. Fatty launched himself like a jumbo jet and managed to completely flatten two Larson tents in one fell swoop. The others sprinted away into the bush, so Boggo pissed all over some poor guy's sleeping bag and Fatty stole their food rations.

19:00 A drunken debate broke out about how everyone was planning on getting back to school tomorrow. Fatty said he would rather commit suicide than walk the eighteen miles back. It seems that Joseph has to drive to Pietermaritzburg tomorrow, so he won't be able to drive us around. Mad Dog told us that if we walked for an hour in a northwesterly direction, we would find a tar road from where we should get a lift to school. Mad Dog then announced that we (he and I) would be walking back over the Seven Sisters (also known as the Seven Bitches). I didn't argue in case Mad Dog slit my throat while I was sleeping.

Friday 10th May

05:10 Mad Dog shook me awake. I felt awful. My head was throbbing and I still felt groggy. I tried to puke again, but nothing came out. I sat on the grass trying to convince my body to wake up while Mad Dog flattened the tent. It was still dark, and the early morning mountain breeze made my teeth chatter. I desperately wanted to sleep some more and then get a lift back to school with a kindhearted farmer or a hot farmer's wife. I was also terrified that Mad Dog would torture me again and murder more wildlife. I approached Mad Dog while he was cleaning his cooking equipment and told him I was feeling ill and that my left leg had gone lame. He pretended not to hear me and carried on with his cleaning. I repeated my speech again, but Mad Dog walked away without even listening. I tried a third time and this time he just handed me my backpack and said, "Let's hit the road."

In my sorry state I followed Mad Dog up a steep slope that never seemed to end. I couldn't see where I was going, but it felt like torture and I kept stopping to vomit but nothing came out. In that moment I made a solemn vow to myself:

I WILL NEVER DRINK AGAIN!

Thankfully, Mad Dog didn't torture me today because he was too busy killing wildlife.

MAD DOG'S MIDLANDS MASSACRE

- A purple-crested loerie
- Ten doves (which he had baited with bread)
- Two guinea fowl
- Three blue-headed lizards
- One stray cat (Mad Dog said it was a stray cat, but he did shoot it in close proximity to a farmer's yard. It also had a blue collar and a bell.)
- If Fatty's theory about karma is true, then Mad Dog is in serious trouble with the man upstairs.
- We staggered into the school grounds (I was staggering, Mad Dog was still marching along) just in time for war cry practice.

22:45 The rest of the Crazy Eight came stumbling into the dormitory like they'd spent a year in the desert. In actual fact, they had been on an eighty-mile round trip thanks to a deranged chicken farmer who drove them all the way to Mooi River. Fatty was so exhausted he collapsed onto his bed and asked Mad Dog to put him out of his misery. Mad Dog pulled out his knife and looked quite keen to oblige until Rambo had to explain that Fatty wasn't being serious. Mad Dog looked a little disappointed and sheathed his knife before returning to sticking the loerie's wings to the side of his footlocker.

Saturday 11th May

True to his word, Mongrel has dropped me from the under-15C rugby team. At first I was feeling hurt and embarrassed, but after watching the team lose 36–0 to Blacksmith, the sideline looked like a good place to be. Mongrel was so angry that he kicked over a rubbish bin and slapped Pig on the back of the head.

Mental note: Check into the san on Monday night.

The first team won 12-5 but still didn't look like the mean machine of last year.

Tonight I couldn't sleep. I kept thinking about the Mermaid and am still wondering whether I should write to her after her birthday card. Simon reckons that if I write back to her, she'll cheat on me again one day. Rambo agrees and says that if I want to dominate a woman, I need to learn to smack the dog.

I thanked them for their help and made a mental note never to ask them for advice about girls again.

Sunday 12th May

I've been dumped by the choir!

As I arrived in the vestry to get on my choir robes, Julian said he wanted to have a little chat. He walked me out into the rose garden and said that he wanted me to step down from the choir until my voice had settled. He said my voice had gone from "nightingale to toucan in just eleven days." He then started getting weepy, so I said it was fine and went back to bed.

17:00 Feeling depressed about being kicked out of the choir. I decided it was time to focus on my acting career and tomorrow's house play auditions. I read *The Glass Menagerie* under the pine trees and spent the afternoon practicing my American deep South accent. I'm auditioning for the role of Tom.

19:00 Wedged in between Vern and Mad Dog, I experienced chapel from the top of the gallery. Every time I mimed a hymn, the Crazy Eight would snigger or poke me in the back and call me Milli Vanilli.

Monday 13th May

Runt is behaving weirdly. He keeps staring at me in a mesmerized kind of way. I caught him staring at my balls in the showers, so I accused him of being a sicko and told him to get lost. Was very relieved to see that he obeyed me, although he didn't at any stage look particularly frightened.

There has been a house play mutiny! Julian is no longer directing and the play is now *Noah's Ark*. I didn't know the Bible story had been turned into a play. It was Pike who led the rebellion. He said there were only two roles for men in *The Glass Menagerie* and the play was three hours long. In the end Pike won the matric vote and Julian was kicked out. I asked Pike where I could get hold of a script for *Noah's Ark*. Pike dropped his pants and showed me his backside. He then kicked the door of the common room open and disappeared inside.

HOUSE PLAY AUDITIONS

Seated in the prefects' room (cop shop) were Anderson, Emberton, Death Breath, Pike, and another matric from Barnes House whose nickname is Ricketts. (I recognized Ricketts—he's big and strong and ugly and the first-team rugby player.) Ricketts munched on a piece of toast and asked me if I was retarded. Pike then whispered to Ricketts, "This one's the fag. The retard's coming in next." Ricketts looked disappointed and shoved the rest of the toast in his mouth. Emberton, sensing a pause in conversation, thrashed his sugarcane into one of the seats and told me to start. I asked him what he wanted me to perform. Pike looked at me like I was an idiot and said, "I don't care, turd hole, just do something and then get out of my fucking face!"

By the looks of things, my stumbled Bible reading from Genesis didn't impress the matrics one bit. After just three verses of my dramatized reading of *Noah's Ark*, Pike told me to stop. Anderson then asked me if I did any animal impressions, so I did my dove call and they all laughed. Emberton thrashed his stick onto the chair and said, "Jeez, you'd think with a scholarship he could tell the difference between a bird and an animal!"

Eventually Pike told me to moo like a cow. Unfortunately, my voice knack-jumped, making me sound like a donkey instead. The seniors all fell about laughing and Ricketts told me to get lost before he vomited up his toast. I opened the cop shop door and then heard Pike calling, "Oh, Spud, before you leave . . ." I darted back inside, hoping for some good news. Pike grinned at the others and then said, "Don't call us, we'll call you." I closed the door on loud guffaws and mocking shouts. Standing outside was Vern, dressed in a very tight zebra outfit. He gave me a thumbs-up and strode confidently into the cop shop.

The laughter was deafening.

Tuesday 14th May

Boggo's long-awaited party is happening on Saturday. His girlfriend is going to pick us up from the old gates at 8 p.m. and take us to the party, which is at her parents' cottage. We are all bunking out and hoping for the best.

I caught Runt watching me during dinner. I tried to ignore him, but I lost my appetite and gave my pork chops to Fatty.

Thursday 16th May

The cast for *Noah's Ark* was pinned to the house notice board.

NOAH .... Anderson
GOD ALMIGHTY .... Devries
NOAH'S MATES ..... Emberton, Boggo, Death Breath
BABOON .... Rambo
THE FLOOD .... J. R. Ewing, Spike
ARK ANCHOR .... Fatty
GAY AUSTRALIAN SHEEP .... Simon
DOVE OF PEACE .... Spud Milton
THE THREE DARRYLS .... as themselves

Underneath it said:

WRITTEN BY .... Pike
DIRECTED BY .... Anderson
PROMPT .... Rain Man

Please report to the cop shop Sunday 19th May @ 20:30.

From Oliver to the Dove of Peace! Worried I might be getting stereotyped as pure and innocent characters. Once my balls have dropped completely, I'll have to play a villain or a psychopath.

Friday 17th May

Fatty has been making a lot of noise all week about Friday the 13th, in spite of everyone telling him that it's actually Friday the 17th. Still, he reckons there's a good chance of calling up Gecko's ghost. Rambo ordered Fatty to prepare for a séance and called the gathering for 22:00.

22:00 The séance was delayed because Roger pissed on Simon's duvet while Fatty was trying to summon up spirits of the underworld. Mad Dog tried to catch Roger, but the wily animal jumped out Vern's window and escaped down the drainpipe. Once Simon had changed his bedding, Fatty began murmuring and humming to himself and shaking what sounded like a bag of marbles. Then Pike and Devries came in and made ghost noises and said we were childish. Pike let off a stink bomb that led to a mad scramble into the first-years' dorm. Fatty kicked J. R. Ewing out of his bed and set up for his séance once again. (Fatty still regards his old bed as rightfully his and frequently inspects his former headquarters.) Unfortunately, one of the Darryls freaked out and thought we were devil worshipping. He burst into tears and kept repeating the Ten Commandments to himself. Fatty canceled the séance and instead we followed Mad Dog out of the window and out onto the vestry roof.

Mad Dog led us through the thick mist toward the dam. I ran up alongside him and asked him where he was leading us. He said, "This is going to blow your mind." He then stopped abruptly and held up his hand for complete silence. We all stopped in our tracks. In the fog it was difficult to make out the trees looming over us. Everything was creepy and lurking, like the dark spirits were following us along on our journey. Suddenly Mad Dog dived into the bushes beside the road. "Somebody's coming," he hissed. We all followed him into the bushes sounding like a herd of stampeding buffalo running into a hedge. We crouched down, panting and shivering, and waited for something to appear.

And then there was a very disturbing clinking sound coming from the direction of the dam. Out of the mist came a deformed creature that looked half human, half beast. It was hard to make out in the gloom, but it looked suspiciously like a character of cloven hoof, limping his way to wreak havoc on the school. Then a long moaning howl rose out of nowhere and made my hair stand on end. Turned out the howl was coming from Roger, who had just discovered the Crazy Eight and was announcing himself to Vern. Rain Man started calling to his cat, but Mad Dog clamped his hand over Vern's mouth and half his face. The cloven hoof figure stopped and slowly turned toward us. You could hear his heavy breathing like Darth Vader. Fatty lifted his huge silver crucifix high into the air in case the Satan creature attacked. But then the creature seemed to lose interest and limped on up the path toward the sanatorium before disappearing into the misty gloom.

Once the creature was gone, there was a breathing-out moment. Fatty turned to us and whispered, "I dare anyone to say to my face right now that we have not just seen the face of Satan himself. You see—what did I tell you? Friday the thirteenth . . . bad shit always goes down on Friday the thirteenth!" Vern started muttering the Lord's Prayer to himself but forgot the words halfway through. Boggo stood up and said, "Fatty, as always, you've cocked it up. Not only is it not Friday the thirteenth, but that wasn't Satan, you toss box. That was Morgan McMurtry from the laundry. He has a deformed leg and nasal problems."

Soon we all accepted that we had in fact just had a standoff with a cripple from the laundry and that we'd never mention this again.

After thoroughly abusing Fatty, we followed Mad Dog on through the mist, and after some serious bushwhacking we landed up at the foot of a big tree. It was the tree house Mad Dog had made during Adventure Club. Mad Dog disappeared up into its branches, and soon there was a pale yellow light leading the way up the trunk. We held on to the ladder of nails that had been hammered into the tree trunk, and one by one we made our way up to find the most amazing tree house I've ever seen! Mad Dog has done some serious work on it since last term's Adventure Club lesson. The entire floor was covered with black rubber car mats. Under a canopy of leaves was a room big enough for all of us to sit in. Then there was a small veranda for two people that overlooked the forest. Mad Dog had bags of straw to use as seats, and the walls and the frames were all slabs of wood tied together with rope and dry grass. Once we were all seated, he said, "Welcome to the Mad House." He then looked embarrassed and kicked Vern for no reason. Mad Dog confessed that he had been working on the Mad House just about every day since the Adventure Club lesson and that all the wood, rope, building tools, and car mats had been stolen from the school workshop and bus yard.

Rambo reckons we should turn the Mad House into our own personal den—for use only by the Crazy Eight and to be kept in complete secrecy from every other living human being. Everyone was getting so excited about having our own private hideaway. It was like something out of *Dead Poets Society* except cooler and better disguised. Mad Dog said that the tree house was invisible from the ground and the only way we could ever be discovered was if we were followed or if somebody blabbed. Rambo made us shake on a vow of silence and then ordered us each to bring back a single item for the Mad House after the half-term weekend. He then offered cigarettes around (nobody was allowed to refuse) and we all officially christened the Mad House.

And then Fatty started up with his ghost stories and we sat there smoking with the pale gloom of the moon about us and the pitch-black forest below.

Saturday 18th May

THE PARTY

20:00 Boggo's girlfriend was waiting for us at the old gates. She was much hotter than I expected. In fact, it's a complete miracle, but she seems to really like Boggo.

More good news is that the prefects and matrics have all gone to a big party in Pietermaritzburg. (In third-year and matric you are allowed two weekends leave per term.) This means that the chances of getting busted are minimal. Boggo has already bribed the third-years to cover for us at lights-out by saying we are at a social at St. Joan's.

When normal people say "cottage," they mean two rooms, a kitchen, and maybe a toilet outside. When rich people say "cottage," they mean a mansion with a thatched roof.

(Mental note: I must stop jumping out of the car and saying, "Wow," when I arrive at rich people's houses. I always get laughed at and then people keep coming up to tell me that their dad's holiday house makes this mansion look like a chicken run.)

There were at least eighty teenagers drinking up a storm with not a single adult in sight. More people were arriving all the time, and the front lawn was covered with bodies dancing to Springsteen. The Crazy

Eight made their way to the main lounge. Everyone stopped talking and all eyes fell on Vern, who seemed to be having some angry words with himself at the entrance to the lounge. Rambo looked at the crowd and said, "Don't worry about him, he's deranged." Vern grinned and gave a thumbs-up and everybody laughed.

I wandered down to the bottom of the garden and sat on a swing bench. I didn't feel like having a down-down competition with Fatty and Rambo. I didn't feel like drinking beer or smoking cigarettes either. I was thinking about Mermaid. Should I write back? Use the excuse of thanking her for the birthday card? Then I tried to forget about her and focused on the sound of screams and wild splashing coming from the dam.

I looked up at the sky and thought about her again. I was about to stand up when I heard footsteps approaching. I sank into the bench hoping Vern hadn't discovered my whereabouts, but I was too late. I felt the lurch on the bench as somebody sat beside me. I smelled the scent of vanilla. I remember turning my face and locking onto a pair of dark brown eyes.

It was Amanda.

Before I could say a thing, she was kissing me. I got such a fright my left leg started shuddering like it had a life of its own. I felt like I was slipping off the swing. After the kiss she smiled at me and said, "Hello, Oliver." I tried to speak, but my voice sounded like a donkey. She laughed her husky laugh and said, "So at last the spud becomes a man. . . ." I smiled but didn't say anything. And then she kissed me again. I mean, like she just grabbed the back of my head and pulled me toward her. After some vigorous kissing Amanda pulled back, looked me in the eyes, and—

AMANDA	How's your girlfriend?
SPUD	What girlfriend?
AMANDA	You know—big boobs, all bright-eyed and bushy-tailed . . .
SPUD	Um . . . she . . . I mean, we broke up.
AMANDA	Good. Do you want to be my toy boy?
SPUD	[*Not sure what to say, finally manages*] Ummmmm.
AMANDA	Then you're going to have to keep a secret.
SPUD	Why?
AMANDA	So that my boyfriend doesn't find out, you dork!
SPUD	You have a boyfriend?
AMANDA	Second-year varsity. Studying politics. He calls these parties examples of infantile masculinity.
SPUD	What do you think?
AMANDA	I like infantile sexuality.

More kissing on the bench at the bottom of the garden.

We didn't talk much after that. We just looked out over the

moonlit dam and watched the stars, and my fingers were entwined through hers.

Sunday 19th May

It feels like last night was just a strange dream. Everyone was teasing me about spending the entire party with my tongue down Amanda's throat. I tried my best to pretend I was embarrassed.

After chapel and breakfast Mad Dog made me go on a lynx hunt with him. After hours of hunting we hadn't seen so much as a francolin, so we returned to the Mad House, where I spent the afternoon trying to read *Cry, the Beloved Country* while Mad Dog and Rambo made noisy squawks from the branch below. I hardly read a word and kept thinking about Amanda.

I have to say that sharing her with an older man isn't ideal. Simon reckoned the relationship is doomed because there's no trust and everything is only physical. Boggo said it sounded like his dream relationship.

20:00 There was a long debate at play rehearsal about how Fatty would appear as the ark's anchor. It was decided by Pike that Fatty would be lowered down from the roof by means of a fly bar. The rope from the fly bar would also look like the anchor rope and the blue light would look like the sea/flood. Pike bravely phoned Viking at home to find out if this was allowed. Unfortunately, Viking refused and said Fatty's weight would pull the fly bar out of the roof and could bring the entire theater down with him.

The three Darryls were all fired for being untalented and over-emotional.

Monday 20th May

Sparerib called me in to his office for a chat. He looked at me with his wonky eye and said, "John, I'm really looking for an improvement on your results this term." I told him I would do my best. He sniffed snootily and gave me a dodgy look that indicated that he didn't think my best would be good enough. He scratched his chin for a while and asked me if I had given any thought to my choice of subjects for matric. I informed my housemaster that I wasn't taking science or biology and instead I'll do drama, history, and geography. Sparerib went red in the face and his eyes bulged with surprise. He said, "Are you sure you're making the correct decision?" I told him I planned to become a famous actor. Sparerib looked horrified and began fidgeting with his fountain pen. He clearly didn't know what to say next, but he told me to give the matter some serious consideration.

Spud: 1
Sparerib: 0

Flushed with my success over Sparerib, I called Amanda. She wasn't in, but her dad gave me a number where I could reach her. I called the number and a man answered. I asked for Amanda. He said, "Hold on." There was some whispering and scuffling and then Amanda came to the phone. I was shaking with excitement and looked down at the little piece of paper I held in my left hand. On it I had written:

CONVERSATION DEFINITES

1. How are you?
2. Thanks for Saturday night
3. How is school?
4. When can I see you again?
5. Defeat of Sparerib

POSSIBLES

1. African Affairs and general struggle talk
2. A date on the long weekend (depending on her answer to no. 4 above)
3. Wombat stories
4. Overseas trip

Unfortunately, I had barely got through point one of the conversation definites when Amanda told me never to call her at that number again and hung up.

I sat staring at the phone for the next five minutes, praying it would ring. It did, but it was Vern's mom.

20:00 Our first real rehearsal of *Noah's Ark* was a complete shambles. The script still isn't ready. Pike said he was working on the fourth draft, but obviously nobody believed him. Not sure what kind of part the Dove of Peace will get when the script is finally complete. Vern had nothing to do as the prompt, so he spent an hour doing a very dodgy impersonation of a goat. Rambo asked if his Baboon could have a huge set of blue balls.

Julian (who has been brought in as set designer) said it was a thrilling idea and promised to make them himself.

After lights-out I sat on the window ledge and thought about Amanda. I know in my heart that I should write her off. She has never taken me seriously, and quite obviously her boyfriend will always be more important than me. Unfortunately, she's just too beautiful to ignore, so I plan to lie low and wait for her to come to me. I then thought about Mermaid but then started struggling to breathe, so I thought about cricket instead.

Tuesday 21st May

I went up to the dorm during break and found Runt in my cubicle rifling through my locker. He blushed and said he was looking for a pen. I accused him of being a thief and told him to get lost or I'd thrash him within an inch of his life. He smiled at me but left in a hurry. I then felt myself blushing, not because of Runt, but because I sounded exactly like my father. Think I'll have to report Runt to the Crazy Eight for dodgy and possibly very dodgy behavior.

Thursday 23rd May

Call from home. Mom sounded happy and excited and said that Wombat was making great strides. Also more good news is that all the booze is now being brewed at Johnny Rogers's depot. Innocence works the mornings on housework and the afternoons at the moonshine depot. Dad is now branching out into selling insurance and has been having discussions with a man called Dennis who sells life and death policies.

She then reminded me it was just forty-two days until we leave for London.

Dad came to the phone and asked me how the rugby was going. I told him I was fly half for the under-15Cs. He warned me that rugby was a dangerous game and asked me if I had a comprehensive life cover. I didn't know what he was talking about, so I told him I needed to get to class and hung up. Eight days until the long weekend!

Friday 24th May

I told my dorm mates about how strangely Runt has been behaving. I explained the constant staring and how I'd caught him on Tuesday going through my locker. Almost before I had finished, Mad Dog stormed into the first-year dorm; there was a loud squeal and then Mad Dog returned carrying Runt under his arm. He plonked Runt down on the floor and asked him if he was a bum rusher. Runt went bloodred and then burst into tears. By now the Crazy Eight had all gathered around to inspect the situation. Poor Runt looked pitiful sitting on the floor of my cubicle sobbing his heart out. Rambo pulled him up with one hand and said, "Right, you little piss drop, why are you staring at Spud like he's Cindy Crawford?" Runt burst into tears again. Mad Dog then lost his patience and threw Runt over the wooden partition and onto Simon's bed.

I have to admit it was quite a sight seeing Runt flying through the air like a paper plane. There was a loud snap and a cry of agony. Rambo howled with laughter and said, "Hey, Runt! If you're looking for a bum rushing, you're lying in the right bed. Simon's a raging poof. . . ."

Boggo laughed so much he fell back over Vern, who was busy pulling at a large clump of hair. Vern giggled and stashed the clump of hair in his laundry bag.

By now everybody was doubled over with laughter, except for Simon, who pushed Rambo and told him to piss off. The next second there was a sickening thud and Simon was on the deck holding his left eye. Everyone was shocked into silence. Then Rambo called Simon a fag once again before leaving the dormitory with a slam of the door. Runt seized the moment and galloped back to his own dormitory. The rest of us stood around just staring at poor Simon, who was sniveling and sobbing and holding a pair of underpants over his eye to stop the bleeding. Mad Dog and I helped him to his bed while Boggo snuck down to the prefects' kitchen for some ice and a dishcloth. Mad Dog said he was going to find Rambo, flung on his khaki hunting jacket, and disappeared through the chapel window.

We spent the next few hours trying to cheer Simon up as he held the dishcloth over his eye. His mood improved as time went by and he even giggled when Boggo told him he looked like Yasser Arafat.

Mad Dog didn't return, and neither did Rambo.

Saturday 25th May

Sparerib hauled Simon into his office and demanded to know why his face was disfigured. Simon told him he was hit by a hockey ball in the dormitory. Sparerib then asked him who had hit the hockey ball and Simon said he'd hit it himself. Sparerib said that considering Simon's ball skills, this was unlikely and then tried unsuccessfully to get Simon to rat on Rambo. Rambo apologized to Simon at breakfast and said he wouldn't call him a poof anymore. Simon nodded but didn't say anything.

21:00 The school is like a morgue. Usually at this time of night there would be voices from the cloisters below and the sound of somebody sprinting across the quad. Tonight all I could hear was the far-off rumble of the train and the never-ending trickle of Pissing Pete.

Sunday 26th May

The atmosphere in the dorm was weird, so I set off for the pine trees with *Cry, the Beloved Country*. It's a beautiful story of a black priest who travels from the Midlands to Johannesburg to find his son. He discovers his son is in prison for the murder of the son of his white neighbor back home. (It sounds more complicated than it is.) I got halfway through and then had to stop because I was feeling so sorry for Reverend Khumalo. I then started thinking about the African Affairs meeting tonight, and then I thought of Amanda and how much I want to kiss her again. But then my thoughts turned toward the long weekend, and riding my bike to the Mermaid house, and hopefully getting a glimpse of her blond hair like a waterfall. I felt a stabbing pain in my chest and had to think of cricket for about ten minutes before it disappeared.

House play rehearsals were canceled because Pike hasn't finished the script yet. Why does it feel like I'm the only person worried by this?

I got into shit at the African Affairs meeting because I lost the minutes of the last meeting. I hate being secretary—it feels like I'm doing an exam on a Sunday night instead of sitting around drinking coffee and being a freedom fighter. Linton Austin was livid with my mistake and put a motion forward that I should be suspended from AA for two meetings and be replaced as secretary of the society. Nobody seconded his motion, so he ended up looking like a turd. After Linton had finished his tirade, I took a deep breath before asking if I could retire as secretary. Everyone laughed at me. (This may have been due to a spectacular knack jump rather than my attempt at resignation.)

Monday 27th May

Boggo rushed into lunch and told us that Fatty had been invited to the Natal Inland hot-dog-eating competition and he will be representing Nottingham Road. The event takes place at the Royal Show in Pietermaritzburg in June. Fatty was so excited that he lost his appetite. (Not a great start.)

Back in the dorm, the excitement had spread. Boggo stuck Fatty's invitation letter up on the wall with an old piece of chewing gum. (Since becoming Fatty's eating agent, Boggo opens all Fatty's mail.) Boggo flicked over the invitation and showed us where the prizes were listed. The winner gets a thousand bucks; second, five hundred; and third, two-fifty. Fatty said if he won anything, he would use the money for upgrades to the Mad House. Boggo (who gets a thirty percent manager's fee) didn't say what he would do with his money.

Fatty sat on his bed like a Buddha and said, "If you think nine giant sausages was something, wait for the hot dogs. . . ." He then informed Boggo that he would need to practice. Boggo took a collection from everyone. (Vern had to pay double for Roger.) Mad Dog offered to pay in for me because my pocket money ran out last week. I felt a bit embarrassed but promised I would pay him back. Boggo snatched up the money, borrowed Thinny's bike after threatening him with a razor blade, and cycled off to the trading store at the railway station. He returned with four packets of Estcourt Vienna sausages, fifty-four rolls, and a *Scope* magazine. Anderson has miraculously allowed Boggo to keep the sausages in the cop shop fridge, and the rolls were stashed under Fatty's bed.

Anderson must be pretty excited about Fatty's eating competition because he put a sign on the fridge saying:

TOUCH FATTY'S SAUSAGE AND DIE!!!

Rambo accused Boggo of defrauding the Crazy Eight because he bought the *Scope* magazine with our money. Boggo denied this and swore on his mother's life that he had used his own money. It was then pointed out that Boggo hates his mother and stands to inherit millions if she dies. After a long argument Rambo threatened to shit on Boggo's pillowcase, and it was quickly agreed that the magazine would be circulated weekly. Rambo threw it into his locker and said he was taking the first week. I get my hands on it after five weeks, which means I will only get it next term, by which time Boggo will have cut it to pieces. (Poor Roger has to wait seven!)

Wednesday 29th May

I got a bizarre letter from Amanda.

Spud no more
Wait for my call
Out of the blue
I will come to you
A

QUESTIONS ABOUT WOMEN

1. Are they all mad or are they just acting mad to get their own way? (How does one tell?)
2. If they say they love you, does that mean just today or forever?
3. If I squeeze a woman's boob, will she hit me?
4. Will she like it?
5. What do they think about when they are not talking?

I asked Boggo and Rambo about how one goes about squeezing girls' breasts. Rambo reckoned there were two methods.

1. The Easy-Easy Catchy Mammary Approach

This is when you are kissing her and you allow your hand to run down her side and then onto her breasts.

2. Rape and Escape Method

Boggo says this is when you grab her tits and run like hell.

Thursday 30th May

One day until long weekend.

There was a notice on the house notice board that read:

WITNESS FATTY'S FIRST HOT DOG TIME TRIAL ABSOLUTELY LIVE.
WHERE: 2ND-YEARS' PREP CLASSROOM
WHEN: 20:30
COVER CHARGE: $2 (CRAZY EIGHT & PREFECTS FREE)

20:30 Mad Dog's gas cooker kept the sausages warm and Boggo had spent the entire prep buttering rolls and working out how much profit he would make. Mad Dog had stolen a bottle of ketchup from the dining hall and a jar of mustard from the staff room. Fatty sat behind a desk in the middle of the classroom, and around him chairs had been set up in circular rows. The turnout was excellent and about forty of us crowded around and cheered Fatty on as he wolfed down twelve hot dogs before Boggo told him to stop. Everyone booed because we wanted to see how many Fatty could eat before he exploded or vomited.

Boggo shook his head and shouted, "We're not trying to break any records yet, guys! This was just a test run. But I'm sure you'll agree that our eating champ is looking in ravenous form." Everyone clapped and whistled. Fatty let rip with a loud and foul-smelling burp, and everyone cheered and then charged for the door. And to think other schools call us snobs?

Friday 31st May

LONG WEEKEND

I haven't seen the folks for over a month. It was great to see them both waiting for me at the bus stop. Unfortunately, Dad had parked in the middle of the bus parking lot, so there was a lot of hooting and reversing and maneuvering before the school bus finally came to a halt. My parents started sniffing and wiping away tears when I walked up to them. Mom told me I'd grown, and Dad said I was looking like a real man. I quickly got in the car in case they started asking me personal questions. Mom jumped in the back seat with me, which was a bit embarrassing, and explained for the tenth time that she finds it too emotional to come up for rugby matches and then leave me again and she won't let Dad come by himself in case he gets out of hand.

MILTON NEWS

- Our house is on the market. Dad said nothing but gave me an "over my dead body" look. We are having a Show Day on Sunday, which means that people can legally walk around my room and look in my cupboards.
- Wombat has booked us into the Kensington Palace Hotel for just about our entire stay in London. According to Wombat, Princess Diana lives next door and the queen visits regularly. (Not sure why the princess is living next door to a hotel?)

- Innocence has bought a car, which she's parked under the acacia tree. Unfortunately, she doesn't know how to drive, so it hasn't left the Milton yard in three weeks. Dad has been grumbling that his servant has a better car than he does.
- Blacky has been threatened with a fate worse than death after releasing a series of prisoners on the concrete around the pool. Mom reckons the poor animal gets stressed by the Kreepy Krauly (which cleans our pool). Dad reckons shock treatment is the only way to sort Blacky out, but Mom has thus far refused to let Dad throw Blacky headfirst into the electric fence.

Mom went off to make lunch, and Dad pulled out a huge pile of papers from a shabby old briefcase. He laid them carefully out in front of me before leaning back in his chair, saying, "Johnny, I think it's time you thought about death."

I told my father that seeing as though I only had a few days' holiday, I would rather think about life instead. Dad snapped his fingers and pulled out another pile of yellow papers. He dropped them in front of me and prodded them with a greeny fingernail. "Life!" he said, and sat back triumphantly in his seat. Then he leaned forward, picked up his pen, and asked me how much money I had in my savings account. "About three hundred and fifty bucks," I replied. Dad looked grim and his pen hovered shakily above a pale green form. He then shook his head like I had just betrayed him and told me I was practically broke and that we'd discuss life and death again when I left school. He stuffed all his forms and papers back in his bag, spent the next ten minutes looking at his car keys, and then left without saying where he was going.

I asked Mom why Dad was selling life and death policies if he was still making money out of the moonshine. She said Dad was only getting a fraction of what he was making when Innocence was selling booze and brewing from home.

Dad returned about an hour later smelling of booze. He said he'd been taking stock and that he's already sold death policies to Wombat and Frank and that his business is on the up. He apologized for being angry earlier, poured himself a whisky, and then showed me something called a spreadsheet that proved that he could be a millionaire in five years. Mom then arrived with egg sandwiches that still had half their shells on. I told Mom I wasn't hungry and went to my room.

I waited until the folks had settled down for their afternoon nap and then slipped out of the house and unchained my bike in the garage. I freewheeled quietly down the driveway, hoping for a quick getaway. Unfortunately, a black shape tore around the side of the house, barking and snarling at my wheels. I tried to shush Blacky, but he kept barking at my front wheel and running around in circles in a state of great agitation.

There was a loud shout of "Bugger off!" from my parents' bedroom. Blacky was now barking even louder, so I jumped off my bike and laid it down on the grass, hoping it would calm Blacky down. It didn't help. There was another shout from the bedroom window. "Stop teasing the bloody thing! It's Friday afternoon, for God's sakes!" I shouted back that

I was just trying to go for a ride and that Blacky was behaving strangely. There was a pause and then Mom called, "Just kick him in the balls!" I managed to sneak out of the gate and then steam off down the road, leaving Blacky and Dad to sort it out between them.

Mermaid was home. At one stage I heard her speaking, but I never got to see her. There was no sign of the white Golf. After spending an hour crouched in her garden hedge, my leg started cramping, so I gave up and headed for home.

Saturday 1st June

Fatty called at 7 a.m. to say that he had tickets for the Currie Cup rugby match at Kings Park. Natal vs. Western Province. Dad was so thrilled that Fatty was coming to pick me up that he charged off to the café for charcoal and lighter fluid. I tried to tell him that Fatty was just picking me up and not coming for lunch, but he was already reversing the station wagon down the driveway with Blacky's head hanging out the passenger door window. When Dad got back half an hour later, Mom tried to explain to him that Fatty wasn't coming to eat. Dad shot her a nasty look and cried, "He's practically the bloody finest sausage eater in Natal! And besides, he told me my grilling was the best he'd tasted—and that was cooking with gas!" I didn't think this was the time to tell Dad that Fatty tells everybody that they're the best cook in the world. Fatty calls this form of lying "good karma."

Dad made me stand at the gate and shout as soon as I saw Fatty's mom's car coming down the road so that he could throw a pile of steaks on the fire. In my half hour of waiting around at the gate, I came to realize that Blacky is a complete racist. He barks savagely at any black person who walks past and then wags his tail and yaps like a Maltese when white people stroll by. Clearly he's been spending too much time with Dad. I had a terrible image of Blacky attacking Luthuli in front of me. Like a master of psychology, I turned Blacky's brain upside down by shouting at him when he barked at black people and surreptitiously whispering, "Get him! Bite him!" when a white person approached. Unfortunately, Blacky didn't make much progress in his first session.

12:30 Fatty's mom is very large. She smokes all the time and judging by the amount of wool on the back seat does a fair amount of knitting too. I shouted to Dad that Fatty had arrived. I heard some wild shouting and then a call for "Water!" I told Fatty that my dad was cooking him lunch. A huge smile spread across his face. He then turned to his mom and said, "Back in a sec, Ma." Fatty's mom nodded and lit a cigarette.

Dad was thrilled to see Fatty, although he was very disappointed that Fatty's mom wanted to stay outside in her car on the road and not join in with the great cook-up. Dad shook Fatty's hand twice and offered him a beer. Fatty blushed and opted for a Coke. Dad ordered Mom to get the drink and then congratulated Fatty on making it to the Royal Show before shaking his hand a third time. Fatty sat on a sturdy chair and said, "Mr. Milton, I have never tasted grilled meat as fine as that day at the cricket." Dad waved his hand and blushed before saying, "Ag, I'm not one of those guys who get all finicky about it." (Dad has been marinating his steaks in a secret sauce concoction since 07:30 this morning.)

After twenty minutes of nonstop talk about steak and sausages, lunch was served. Dad seemed a bit disappointed that Fatty only ate two large pieces of meat but cheered up when Fatty called his mystery basting sauce "classic." Dad then sprinted down the driveway with two steak rolls and said he was going to give them to Mrs. Fatty.

13:20 Fatty's mom's car was parked under a tree across the road. We found her reclining in the driver's seat listening to Radio Port Natal and knitting what looked to be an enormous blanket but turned out to be a school jersey for Fatty. The weird thing was that Mrs. Fatty seemed quite happy waiting for an hour under the tree across the road from my house. Once we had driven off, Fatty burped loudly and said that Dad's steak rolls tasted weird. Fatty's mom glanced across at her son and said, "Sidney, how many times do I have to tell you to open the window when you do that. This car smells like a frigging butchery!" Fatty apologized, opened his window, and started noshing another steak roll.

We drove to Kings Park in complete silence apart from the sound of loud chewing and the tinny music being played on RPN.

I thanked Fatty's mom for the lift, but she didn't appear to have heard me. Instead she fished out some money from the cubbyhole, handed it to Fatty, and said, "Don't be a pig." Fatty laughed, gave his mom a kiss on the cheek, and slammed the door.

The game was really exciting although Natal lost quite badly in the end. There was a man sitting in the seat behind me who reckoned the ref was cheating. He stood up after the game and said that Vleis Visagie (who plays for Natal) could marry his daughter, but he's not letting Hugh Reece-Edwards (Natal fullback) anywhere near his son. Some other guy in a yellow windcheater joined in the debate and shouted out in a very la-di-da accent, "Bring back Penrose, I say!" The drunken man behind me shouted, "Stuff Penrose!" before lurching down the stairs and disappearing into the crowd.

After the game Fatty said we had to go to Rovers for the party. We walked across fields of parked cars and then found ourselves at the Rovers clubhouse. The adults all hung around the bar while the field was covered with teenagers. Even better news was that there were by far more girls than boys. Fatty bought us a ginger beer each and we sat on the bank eyeing out the passing trade. We spoke about girls and then rugby and then girls again. . . .

Eventually we ran out of conversation altogether and sat silently on the bank watching the pretty girls walking past. I was just starting to get really irritated with the sound of Fatty chewing on his straw when he removed the straw from his mouth, pointed across the field, and said, "Check, Spud, it's your ex-squeeze." I followed his podgy finger across the field of people and my eyes came to rest on a girl with red hair facing away from us. It wasn't Amanda—she'd never be caught dead at Rovers. Fatty shook his head and pointed again. "No, man, over there. Long blond hair . . . the Mermaid."

My heart was pounding, but my eyes couldn't focus. All I could see was blond girls everywhere. Then BANG! There she was, standing near the hockey goalposts with three other girls. I realized I was creeping backward up the bank in fear. Fatty sniggered at me and told me to go and talk to her. I told him I needed the toilet. What I really needed was time to think and make a plan. After pretending to pee behind a bush, I told Fatty that I needed a way in. It would be way too embarrassing to just walk up to her and start a conversation. Besides, she's the one who dumped me, so she should be making all the moves.

Fatty then had a brain wave. He would walk past Mermaid and say hello and then tell her that I was across the field. By that stage I would have joined a group of hot girls to make Mermaid think that I'm a real stud and scoring a whole group of girls at once. This would hopefully make her jealous and try and kiss me. Fatty set off at a loping run, and soon he was chatting to the Mermaid and pointing toward me across the field. I sidled up to a group of girls, who didn't seem to notice that I was there. After a while they began to start looking at me and whispering to themselves. I looked down and pretended to be thinking deeply. Then I heard one girl say, "Weirdo," and another say, "What a loser." Then they were gone, and I realized that I was an island in a sea of empty space. I looked around frantically for a group I could attach myself to. And there she was, standing there. The Mermaid was smiling at me.

I stammered out a "Hi." She said hi back. At that moment I realized that Fatty was also standing next to me. His mouth was open and he was staring at Mermaid's breasts with his eyes all glazed over. The idiot got everything right except for the part about leaving me alone with the Mermaid. My brain felt frozen and my tongue as thick as a pork sausage. Mermaid looked so beautiful. I looked at her and realized why we could never be together. She's a beauty queen and I'm just plain old Spud Milton, the laughingstock of my dormitory. I must be raving mad to think that I have a shot with her.

"Good game, hey?" That was Fatty, breaking the ice with a real cracker. Mermaid smiled and said she'd missed it. Fatty grunted and returned his attention to her breasts. Mermaid looked at me and said, "How are you?" Obviously Fatty thought she was talking to him because he replied, "Not bad, but I could do with a chow. Do they serve burgers around here after hours?" Mermaid didn't know what to say, so she giggled. Then a group of girls appeared out of nowhere and told Mermaid that their lift had arrived. My heart sank. Mermaid looked at me with a desperate look in her eyes. I tried to smile but probably just looked terrified. She waved goodbye and left. Fatty and I watched the girls move across the field like butterflies. At one stage they all stopped, turned, and looked at us, then they giggled and disappeared into the crowds.

Sunday 2nd June

When I woke up, I realized there were seven people standing in my room. Like any animal surprised in his bed, I decided to play dead. The estate agents didn't seem to care that it was Sunday morning on my long weekend. In fact, they all spoke at the tops of their voices and ripped open the curtains. One of the ladies called my room "poky" and another said it would make for a fair-sized office. Then they left without closing the curtains. I got up and made some coffee. Dad was sitting on a stool in the kitchen staring at the oven with Blacky sleeping at his feet. I said good morning, but all he said was, "Bastards . . ." It turned out that Dad wasn't cooking anything at all—apparently Mom had sent him and Blacky in here and had told Dad to look busy. Dad said he never thought he'd see the day when he'd have to pretend to be busy in his own house. I told Dad his disguise would probably be a bit more effective if he turned the oven on. Dad said he didn't want to waste electricity.

Over a cup of coffee Dad started getting emotional about how much he loved the house and how much work he'd done on the garden. He reckoned he would commit suicide if he had to live in England and drink warm beer every day. I nodded and looked sympathetic, but I was thinking about Rovers last night. I was running over every single moment in my mind and replaying it like a movie.

The door swung open and the crowd of people came in. They took one look at Dad sitting in front of the oven and muttering to himself and left. I heard the front door slam, and then Mom came into the kitchen in a foul mood. She glared at Dad and said, "You look like a hobo, and please don't mutter to yourself in public—I don't want half of Durban North thinking I've a madman for a husband." Dad shook his head like a martyr, and then Mom turned her fury on me and told me my room was a disgrace. (She's getting worse than Anderson. . . .)

Dad and I have been instructed to show the next group of people around the house. Mom left, still in a bad mood, and drove off to Wombat's flat. The next group that arrived didn't even look at the house. Dad told them that the reason we're moving is because of the horrific crime wave in the area. The estate agent's lip hit the floor and she looked at Dad like he was crazy. Dad said, "Look, I'll be honest with you. The old guy on the corner was murdered a few nights ago." The potential buyers looked shocked and whispered something to each other. The agent folded her arms and said, "Now who might that have been, Mr. Milton?" Dad said the guy's name was Alfred Nobel.

When they'd gone, Dad gave me a high five and said, "Johnny, together we'll fight the bastards off! Now go get a pad and paper."

Dad and I made a long list of things that could possibly be wrong with the house.

- Rats
- Snakes
- Termites
- Leaky pipes
- Used to be a brothel
- Was the scene of a murder many years ago
- Haunted

After three more groups the estate agent didn't come back. Dad cracked open his whisky, and I went back to bed and read *Cry, the Beloved Country*.

Monday 3rd June

Helped Mom load up a pile of junk into her car and take it to the dump. I found a green and white gnome with an orange hat in a carton of weird odds and ends. Mom said his name was Gilbert and that Dad packed him away in the garage because he was bad luck. I have decided not to be superstitious and that Gilbert is moving to the Mad House.

Had to visit Wombat on the way to the bus. She loves seeing me in my school uniform and told me I was immensely handsome. I thanked her and then (as instructed by Mom) asked her about the London trip. She then prattled on about the White Cliffs of Dover and the palaces of the queen. After twenty minutes Mom stopped her midway through a pre–Second World War foxhunt to tell her we were leaving. Wombat became very anxious and started accusing us of coming around to steal her money. (Basically a Gollum moment.) Mom tried to reason with her, but Wombat told us to clear off or else she'd call the police.

We scuttled into the station wagon looking like a small band of thieves who prey on the elderly and then raced down the driveway. (Mom reckons when they fought last Thursday, Wombat threw a dinner plate at Mom's car as she was driving out of the driveway.) I scanned the windows for danger, but all I could see was a pale, frightened face at the study window. I didn't tell Mom, but I think Wombat was crying.

WEEKEND SCORECARD

FATTY	Went to rugby with Spud and has a new woollen jersey.
MAD DOG	Says he had the worst weekend ever. He had to go to Johannesburg to visit his granny. He complained that there was nothing to shoot except Indian mynahs, go-away birds, and old people walking down the street.
RAMBO	Went to Cape Town with his dad and stepmother. He reckons he nearly got involved in a threesome, but then one of the girls chickened out. (Rambo didn't mention if the near threesome nearly involved

	his stepmother or if she was the one that chickened out.)
BOGGO	Traveled to the Drakensberg with Ali and her family. He says it all went downhill after he beat Ali's dad at a game of checkers. Then Ali accused him of being "gross" after Boggo stupidly showed her some of his porn collection. By the end of the weekend the only person talking to Boggo was Ali's granny, who has no teeth and thinks Winston Churchill is still prime minister of England.
ROGER	The usual weekend in the underpants drawer.
VERN	Jabbered away about his birthday party and how he has now turned sixteen years old. According to the school list, Vern's birthday is on December 18th. Just in case, we threw him in the fountain.
SPUD	Saw the Mermaid, stopped his house being sold, and had a fight with Wombat.
SIMON	(Whose wounded eye now looks bloodred and demonic.) Spent the whole weekend with his inbred cousins from the Eastern Cape.

In the middle of our post-lights-out discussions we heard the sound of soft padding feet through our dormitory. Mad Dog pulled out his knife and apprehended the late night lurker as he reached the door. It was Runt.

Vern shone his torch in Runt's eyes and shouted, "Stop, thief!" Poor Runt looked like a frightened rabbit caught in headlights and stammered out an apology and said he was on his way to the bogs. Vern shone his torch on Runt's balls and accused him of bad form in the bogs and surrounds. Then Rambo accused Runt of trying to bum-rush me under the cover of darkness. Runt looked at me for help, but there was no way I was getting involved. Boggo then told the first-year that he had made passionate love to Runt's mother on Saturday night and that she smelled even worse than she looked. Runt looked Boggo straight in the eyes and said, "My mother's dead." He then walked out of the dormitory and closed the door. Rambo turned to a shocked-looking Boggo and said, "Nice one, Boggo. You shagged Runt's old lady to death."

Tuesday 4th June

Rambo had a costume fitting in Julian's room to try out the bright blue baboon balls. Rambo said the baboon gonads are gigantic and look suspiciously like two beach balls sewn into a blue velvet sack. The fitting lasted over an hour.

Wednesday 5th June

Work is piling up. Exams are two and a half weeks away, and I also have to enter an essay for the Alan Paton creative-writing competition.

It's no coincidence that I've just finished *Cry, the Beloved Country*—I sense this is my moment to shine. Only problem is that I'm competing with thousands of kids from all over the province.

We had a bass-fishing lecture at the dam during Adventure Club. Nobody caught anything, but Vern had to be taken to town because a treble hook went through his finger and he needed a tetanus shot. Vern seemed quite thrilled about going to the doctor and saluted us before getting into Sparerib's car, but the heavily bandaged middle finger on his left hand made it look like he was pulling a rude sign at us instead.

Friday 7th June

MAD HOUSE GOODIES

MAD DOG	A camouflage tarpaulin (for the roof—also waterproof)
BOGGO	A gigantic poster of Madonna with gold stars on her nipples
FATTY	A Bob Marley flag that says, NONE BUT OURSELVES CAN FREE OUR MINDS
VERN	A pink toilet roll
ROGER	A mug with Hello Kitty written on it
SIMON	A small Persian carpet
SPUD	Gilbert the Gnome
RAMBO	Three bottles of Mellowwood brandy

Boggo was furious with Rambo for bringing booze to school. Rambo told him to keep his panties on and said he had already stashed it at the Mad House. Mad Dog and Rambo offered to take the rest of the goodies along to the Mad House after their rugby match tomorrow while all the prefects and teachers would be watching the second fifteen play Waterfall.

21:00 Phoned home to wish Dad a happy birthday, but the phone just rang.

Sunday 9th June

Still no sign of the *Noah's Ark* script. Still no sign of any rehearsal notices. Still no sign of panic from anyone else with just over three weeks to go.

The Mad House is looking brilliant. The proud owner has done more improvements on it this week. The main section of the tree house is smaller than it used to be, but Mad Dog said the smaller size made it more hidden from the ground. It was a bit of a squeeze when we were all up there, so Rambo told Vern and me to piss off. We joined Fatty at the foot of the tree. (He said he couldn't make it up there today.) The three of us headed toward the dam feeling embarrassed, leaving the clink of brandy bottle on glass behind us.

Monday 10th June

Phoned Dad again to wish him happy birthday. He thanked me for the new pair of slacks. I tried my best to make out that I'd bought them myself. He said nobody had made an offer on the house, but Mom's keeping it on the market until we go overseas. Dad said he pruned the roses three months early so that the place looked as ugly as sin. He reckons he'd rather live in New Zealand than England and said at least New Zealand has a rugby team worth supporting. I nearly told Dad about the Mad House but was able to control myself and told him I was entering the Alan Paton writing competition instead. Dad said Paton was a commie and then handed the phone over to Mom.

Pike's script is ridiculous!

Noah has a vision after drinking too much Coke one night and starts building a boat. He has an argument with his family and then rounds up some random animals and waits until the rain starts falling. It seems like most of the dialogue is written to piss off the teachers. At one stage the narrator says, "Noah shot a Viking with a Glock and then cooked some crispo spareribs with the bishop, who was actually a mongrel." Anderson thought it was hilarious and fell about with laughter, calling the play a classic. I don't have a single line. In fact, the Dove of Peace isn't even mentioned in the script! After rehearsals I plucked up the courage and asked Pike why I didn't have any lines. Pike looked at me smugly and replied, "Because you're an awful actor and doves don't speak, you fucking retard!" I could feel myself going red and there was a lump in my throat, but I stood my ground and asked him why he had cast me in the play if I was such a crap actor. Pike spread his arms out and said, "So that I can show the world how bad you are." He told me not to quit my day job before trying to stab me with the sharp end of a coat hanger. Why did I ever audition for this in the first place? My entire acting career could be destroyed by Pike.

Mental note: Never get on the wrong side of playwrights.

Tuesday 11th June

Julian congratulated me in the showers because he said my willy had doubled in size in just over a week. I had to leave the showers quite speedily because everyone started staring at my penis and arguing with Julian about whether it had grown or if it was actually getting smaller.

Wednesday 12th June

Kings College rugby fever has already kicked in and Boggo's opened up a betting shop. He's offering 15 to 1 on our first team winning. Nobody was interested in a bet except for the Normal Seven, who were forced to bet five bucks each as a show of school spirit. One of the Darryls gave me a note at lunchtime. It said:

Milton the Poet
Literary Lunch
Friday 21st June
Bring your wits and first-draft Alan Paton essay.

Underneath it said:

The Governor

Thursday 13th June

I've been called up to the under-15B side for a practice match against the under-15As.

Spud Milton
1976–1991
Killed on active duty
RIP

Mental note: Next winter take up tennis.

Saturday 15th June

KINGS COLLEGE (away game)

Bad news—the under-15Cs lost 22-16

Good news—we came closest to beating Kings College out of any team in the entire school. (The first team got pounded 36-3.)

Mongrel gave us our first compliment of the season when he said: "You mommy's boys did not at least embarrass me today." I admit it wasn't much of a compliment, nor was his use of grammar up to scratch, but it's better than being called traitors.

Most of the matrics headed off for weekend leave. For once I wasn't jealous because the Saturday night movie was a cracker. In fact, seven of the Crazy Eight (Roger fell asleep during the opening credits) voted it the greatest movie ever. Not only that, Boggo, Simon, Fatty, and myself voted it the most disturbing film ever seen. It was called *Silence of the Lambs*. Anthony Hopkins is brilliant as the genius cannibal, Hannibal Lecter. It was so disturbing that one of the Darryls asked Julian if he could go to bed early because he was so terrified. Vern plucked a massive hole in the side of one of the common room couches and kept muttering and shaking his head. There was also a nasty scene when the serial killer (Buffalo Bill) starts dancing in the nude in his dungeon hideaway. Buffalo Bill turns around to face the camera and between his legs is nothing. He has no lunch box! There was a massive uproar in the common room. Devries stood up and called Buffalo Bill a transvestite because he had no balls. A third-year called Marco told Devries he was a dickhead and that no balls means the guy's a transsexual. Julian then shut them all up by saying that he wasn't a transvestite or a transsexual because all Buffalo Bill had done was squeeze his lunch box between his thighs. Pike said that was impossible, so Julian pulled down his pants and proved it. Thankfully it was immediately agreed that Julian was right and we were able to get back to the movie.

Silence of the Lambs movie rating, 9 (excellent)

After lights-out Pike crept into the first-years' dorm and started tormenting two of the Darryls. He was doing a bad Hannibal Lecter impersonation and trying to get at least one of them to start crying. Rambo snuck up to the door and said in a deep voice, "Is Anthony Hopkins here tonight?" There was dead silence from the first-years' dorm. Rambo sniggered and then said, "I thought not."

I howled with laughter! It was splendid to see Pike getting some of his own medicine after abusing my acting ability at rehearsals. But Pike, as always, was not amused. He charged into our dorm and crashed into Vern, who must have been creeping around in the dark near the door. Vern flew into a locker and then collapsed on the floor groaning in agony. Pike then leapt onto Boggo's bed and started laying into Boggo. Mad Dog tore past me and launched himself at Pike, who seemed to be jumping on Boggo's stomach. Eventually we all piled on and Pike took a serious hammering.

Then Spike dived into the scrum of bodies to try and help his brother. Unfortunately for Spike, Fatty thumped him on the head with one of his size-twelve rugby boots and then hurled him back through the door and into the first-year dorm. While we all held Pike down, Mad Dog pulled off his pants and jocks. Rambo rubbed Deep Heat all over Vern's towel and then spread it all over Pike's balls. Pike left screaming.

Sunday 16th June

Tried to sleep in but failed dismally. I decided to have a nice long shower before all the matrics woke up and used up the hot water. Unfortunately, Runt followed me down and the two of us showered in silence. I knew he was looking at me, but I kept my eyes closed and pretended to be very involved with my shower. Then out of the blue he said, "I saw you in *Oliver* last year." I nodded and he nodded. He didn't say anything else, which probably means he thinks I was crap.

Vern switched on the shower next to me and stared at Runt's balls. After about ten seconds of staring he looked at the roof and blew his nose loudly on his hand. Runt stared at Vern in complete amazement. Then they both started staring at me. I decided that things were getting a bit freaky, so I switched off my shower. Runt switched his off immediately and followed me. Vern, who was covered in soap, also switched off his shower and marched toward the second-year drying area. I could see Runt watching me drying myself out of the corner of his eye. Vern followed me up the stairs making unhealthy breathing noises with his back and shoulders still covered in soap.

Mental note: Whenever possible, try and avoid showering with weirdos.

Monday 17th June

Boggo was in a foul mood at breakfast. Sparerib has banned us from watching Fatty's hot-dog-eating competition at the Royal Show this weekend. He doesn't seem to be very happy about Fatty stuffing his face in front of hundreds of people. Sparerib's popularity is at an all-time low.

Sparerib called me into his office and asked me how things were going. I told him I was working like a slave. He looked at me for ages with his wonky eye and then asked me if there was anything I should tell him. I shook my head. There was another horrible pause before he asked, "You still keep a diary?" I nodded and he nodded back. I sat staring at his desk with my toes cringing in my shoes. Eventually he said, "My better half would like a chat. She's in her office." Great. From Sparerib to Eve.

REASONS WHY EVE SHOULD NOT BE THE SCHOOL COUNSELOR

1. She shagged Rambo last year.
2. She's mad (due to the above).

3. She married Spareribb.
4. She's a hippie.
5. She's a communist (according to Dad).

In fact, I think she's the one who needs a counselor!

Eve sat me down in her office and asked me questions. She kept trying to talk about Gecko, and clearly I wasn't saying the right things back because she told me I was repressing my grief. I told her I didn't want to talk about it anymore, so she gave me a fake smile and said her door was always open. (Rambo told us that last year!)

I get the feeling Sparerib and Eve both think I'm weird. Nobody else has been taken in for a psychological examination.

Wednesday 19th June

Boggo posted this notice on all the house notice boards:

Watch Fatty eat 15 hot dogs in one sitting! Final dress rehearsal before the Royal Show finals on Sunday.

CRAZY 8 Classroom

Donation Required

Thursday 20th June

21:00 *NOAH'S ARK* IS SINKING!!!

I'm feeling a little grim that my second appearance on the stage (after last year's triumph in *Oliver*) is going to be as a nonspeaking peace pigeon in a very bad house play.

As the prompt you are meant to read the actor his line, but Vern seems convinced that he has to perform the line as well. Eventually Anderson, Emberton, and Pike were deliberately fluffing their lines just so they could watch Vern perform their own lines back at them. Julian has quit as the designer. He called *Noah's Ark* a "fiasco" and said he was washing his hands of it.

Rambo reckons all the Crazy Eights should pull out of the play as a protest. Boggo jumped up hopefully and asked, "A protest of what?" Rambo looked sour and said, "A protest about looking like morons in front of the whole school in two weeks' time!" Everyone nodded, but no protest happened.

Friday 21st June

The Guv fed me roast beef and Yorkshire pudding. He banged his plate with his spoon and shouted, "Silence!" This was a bit unnecessary because I wasn't speaking at the time. He then folded his left arm behind his back and led with the spoon. "This British initiation literary luncheon, Mr. Milton, is in your honor before your travels abroad to the green and pleasant land. May God help you!" He then sat down and poured wine into his glass. With a mouth full of food he shouted, "God, yes, Milton! Christ's College Cambridge. It's where the less illustrious Milton studied. And don't forget the mulberry tree!" I didn't know what he was going on about, so I nodded and said it was already on the list. He peered at me over his spectacles and asked, "You're not taking your grandmother, are you?" I nodded and said she had to come because she's paying for the trip. Then The Guv said, "Christ almighty!" and shook his head in amazement before returning to his nosh. At the end of the meal we sang a raucous version of "For She's a Jolly Good Fellow" to Gloria as she was packing up the plates. Gloria smiled and curtsied. The Guv told Gloria her meal was so good it could be deemed counterrevolutionary. It was clear that Gloria didn't have a clue what The Guv had just said and replied to him in Zulu and then exited to the kitchen. The Guv asked what Gloria had said. I shrugged. He leaned back in his chair and stared at me. "Milton," he said after about thirty seconds, "how the blinkers do we form a bond with these people if we can't speak their language?" I didn't know the answer, so I did my African Affairs trick where I shrug sadly and then look forlornly out the window.

I then read out my Alan Paton essay, which The Guv called "a triumph." I should point out that by this stage he was onto his second bottle of wine. He did say that my repeated mentions of Alan Paton in my essay, titled "Changing Colors," smacked of butt kissing.

Then The Guv made my week.

I charged back to the dormitory to tell the others that The Guv was taking us on a school outing on Sunday. And that outing is to the Royal Show in Pietermaritzburg!

The Guv said he would book a minibus and sign off the day as a cultural and learning tour. Not only are we going to watch Fatty live in action, we're also not breaking any school rules, which makes for a change.

Thanks to my English teacher, I am the most popular boy in the dorm.

21:00 Fatty's final dress rehearsal was broken up by Spareribs, who ordered the huge crowd of boys back to their houses and confiscated all of Fatty's hot dogs. Boggo was so outraged that he hurled six eggs onto Sparerib's roof after lights-out. Poor Fatty hadn't gone to dinner and had to be content with a quarter loaf of bread and a packet of Big Korn Bites.

Saturday 22nd June

Another day of rugby carnage. We were the only under-fifteen side to win against Rustrek. We took it 22-18. My body felt like it had been pulverized. Mom and Dad came up and remarked on how much I had grown and how I was really becoming a man. I felt pretty rugged in my boots and rugby jersey. Soon the word *spud* will be a distant memory. Thank God!

Sunday 23rd June

Nasty day of studying. I'm feeling the pressure what with Sparerib slinking around and breathing down my neck.

House play rehearsals were canceled because Anderson wasn't feeling well. Think this might have been a ruse to avoid rehearsing because

Fatty said he saw Anderson in the line for seconds at lunchtime and Boggo spotted him playing touch rugby in the afternoon.

Friday 28th June

Exam Predictions

ENGLISH	A
AFRIKAANS	B
MATHS	B
HISTORY	A

My grades spell out ABBA. Fatty said this would only be counted as a supernatural sign if I was studying Swedish.

GEOGRAPHY	A
SPEECH & DRAMA	A
BIOLOGY	C
SCIENCE	D
ART	C

Half the school turned out for touch rugby in the Friday afternoon rain. Then there was the final war cry practice of the year, followed by aggressive horseplay down at the bog stream.

I decided my handwriting was illegible, so I spent prep rewriting my Alan Paton essay and made the writing bigger and clearer just in case my marker is old or nearsighted. Unfortunately, it now looks like the essay was written by a twelve-year-old. I handed "Changing Colors" in to Spareribjust seconds before the lights-out siren. Spareribdidn't bother to wish me luck or even congratulate me on finishing my masterpiece. All he could do was tap his watch with his finger and glare at me with his wonky eye.

I suspect my housemaster has no imagination and no creative-writing ability. Why Eve agreed to marry him remains a mystery.

Saturday 29th June

Pig gave us a stirring speech behind the rubbish bins before we charged onto the field for our final game of the year against St. Luke's. At halftime Mongrel shat all over us for being a bunch of idiots and told us to keep our discipline. He also told Vern to stop holding his crotch when he's waiting for the ball because it offends the ladies. I was busy sucking hard on an orange quarter when I saw a beautiful redheaded girl striding along the touchline. It was Amanda. I turned to run off in a rugged fashion, but Vern was standing right behind me muttering away to himself and pulling savagely at his laces. I fell over, clashing heads with Rain Man in the process. Any chance of nobody witnessing the disaster was gone when Vern got up and tore across the field like a headless chicken, screaming at the top of his voice.

There was wild jeering and laughter and unfortunately Amanda, too, was doubled over and ended up having a coughing fit.

After the game, Amanda followed me back toward the house. She says Vern is the most extraordinary human being that she's ever seen.

When we got to the house door, I told Amanda to wait outside for me, but she didn't listen and followed me up the stairs and into the dormitory. The next minute she was lying on top of me on my bed and we were kissing full-on. I knew that I could get into some serious poo if Sparerib found me, so I ended the passionate kiss and headed for the showers.

Back in the dormitory, I found Amanda standing in Boggo's cubicle with a huge grin on her face. She pointed at his locker and said, "Whoever sleeps here has porn. And a lot of it." I wanted to kiss her again, but then I noticed that her eyes were watching something over my shoulder. Vern was standing at the door blushing bright pink. Amanda tried her best not to laugh and said, "Hello, Vern." Vern looked at the floor and didn't answer.

Amanda said, "Do you know who I am?" Vern giggled and blushed and looked around in a shady manner. He then said, "Mermaid," and ran out of the dormitory. Amanda asked me why he'd called her a mermaid. I told her that's what he calls all girls.

Amanda kissed me again in the main quad in the full view of Boggo and Rambo. Then she strode across the grass and disappeared through the archway. Mad Dog gave me a vicious high five and celebrated by humping the gutter pipe and making loud orgasm noises. Rambo didn't say a word and stalked into the house.

I am definitely in love with Amanda.

Sunday 30th June

THE ROYAL SHOW

The less said about The Guv's driving, the better. In fact, I'm not even sure he should have a driving license. By the time we got to the show grounds, Fatty said he was feeling carsick. We all followed Fatty into the toilet while The Guv said he would catch up to us later because he wanted to attend a pig auction.

Wild screaming welcomed our man onto the stage. Fatty waved at the crowd and blushed a deep purple. He took his seat at the end of a long table with ten chairs. Bad news was that Fatty wasn't the biggest; he wasn't even the third biggest. One of the contestants was a lady. Her name was Sonja, but Boggo said she could be a man in disguise. The hugest man was Heinz from Wartburg. He had ginger hair and enormous curly sideburns. Turns out Heinz won last year. In fact, he hasn't lost an eating competition since 1987, when he was in jail and couldn't take part. According to one of the organizers, Heinz then became a born-again Christian and started eating for charity and making speeches at churches. The announcer said the Royal Show and the city of Pietermaritzburg were honored to welcome Heinz back for another year and hopefully yet another victory. He didn't say anything about the others except to wish them luck and announce their names.

When Fatty's name was called out, The Guv stood up and shouted, "That's our man Falstaff!" (The Guv calls Fatty Falstaff for some unknown reason.) Pretty girls in pink bikinis brought out trays of hot dogs. The crowd whistled and cheered while Mad Dog barked loudly and shouted, "Hubba! Hubba!"

RULES

- Each contestant has twenty minutes to eat as many hot dogs as possible.
- No hooching (vomiting). This is an instant disqualification.
- No leaving of your contestant's chair until the twenty minutes is up. (Also disqualification.)

A starter pistol was fired and Fatty launched into his hot dogs like a demon. The crowd roared and clapped as ten gluttons piled into their trays like they hadn't eaten in weeks. Five gluttons dropped out before reaching ten hot dogs, and Fatty was the first to call for a second tray. Sonja the transvestite also called for a reload, but the corners of her mouth were turned down like she'd had enough. She also placed her hooch bucket right next to her, and Rambo said this was a definite sign that she was a psychological mess.

Boggo also noticed this because he pointed it out to Fatty and then repeatedly thumped him on the back like a jockey hitting a horse. The next tray arrived, and while Fatty doctored half of his hot dogs with ketchup, Boggo kept shouting, "Come on, big boy, you can do it!" Rambo didn't like the way Fatty only sauced half his rolls—he reckoned it was sending a negative sign to the opposition. Another huge man with GLENCOE written on his shirt ordered another tray of hot dogs and downed a big glass of water. (Boggo has banned Fatty from drinking water—he claims a glass of water takes the space of one-and–a-quarter hot dogs and may only be used in case of choking or fire.)

From across the table Heinz stood and waved to the crowd. He called for his second tray and then lit up a cigar. The crowd seemed thrilled with this and everyone chanted, "HEINZ! HEINZ! HEINZ!"

Unbelievably, the skinniest person in the competition (Boris from Howick) raised his hand and called for another tray. The tension was now heating up: Fatty was leading with twelve hot dogs, with the others still eating their eleventh. There was a long discussion between our man and his manager before Fatty began on his thirteenth hot dog. In fact, it wasn't really a discussion, but more like a lecture from Boggo, who kept prodding the hot dog with his finger and shouting in poor Fatty's ear. I couldn't hear what was going on, but Fatty had his head bowed and seemed to have had enough. Sonja stopped eating after her eleventh, but unfortunately she didn't need her hooch bucket. She sat back in her seat and kept her eyes pinned on Fatty.

Heinz stubbed out his cigar on the table and then began preparing himself for more hot dogs. Glencoe finished his eleventh but then stuck his head into his hooch bucket. The crowd went mad as Glencoe staggered off the stage and disappeared behind it. Fatty finished hot dog number thirteen and Boggo massaged his shoulders and kept whispering in his ear like a boxing trainer in between rounds.

Boris from Howick is the Ivan Lendl of hot dog eating. He showed no emotion, chewed at exactly the same speed every single time, and was also the only contestant who ate his hot dogs without ketchup.

With six minutes to go, nobody was eating and all three contenders (plus Sonja, who was obviously hoping someone would hooch her into third place) were sitting back in their chairs looking down at their trays. Fatty picked up number fourteen and the crowd cheered. He ate it quickly, took a few deep breaths, and then sat back in his chair again. Heinz unfortunately proceeded to his number fourteen and nailed number fifteen straight after. The huge giant sat back in his chair and smiled at Fatty. Ivan Lendl didn't move. He just kept watching the big clock countdown. Obviously he was happy with third place.

Fatty then ate number fifteen, and we could all tell he was finished. Boggo was obviously thinking the same thing because he was pushing the hot dog tray away from Fatty. The worst thing that could happen would be for Fatty to throw up because that meant instant disqualification. But Fatty had other ideas. He was holding the ketchup bottle in his left hand and pulling the tray toward him with his right. I heard Boggo shout, "Stop, Fatty, stop! It's still five hundred bucks for second!"

Heinz nailed number sixteen in three bites!

Rambo elbowed me in the ribs and said, "Check Heinz. He's psyching Fatty out." Heinz was daring Fatty to eat another hot dog. The crowd were chanting, "GO! GO! GO!" We were shouting, "NO! NO! NO!" Fatty picked up number sixteen and took a bite. But then the dam wall broke. There were groans from the crowd as Fatty disappeared under the table with his hooch bucket. The starter pistol was fired. Heinz was champion again, followed by Ivan Lendl, and Sonja, the man/woman, took third. While Heinz was mobbed by his fans, Boggo kept passing glasses of water under the table to Fatty. The Guv, who had been drinking out of a hip flask, stood up and shouted, "Don't kick the bucket, Falstaff!" The Guv then pointed in the general direction of school and said, "Onward, Christian soldiers! I have a bird in the oven!"

We all thanked The Guv for taking us to the Royal Show. He replied, "Nonsense, boys, the pleasure was all mine. It recalled to my mind two eras of extravagant excess: wild Elizabethan gluttony and the vomitoria of ancient Rome." He then told us all to f-off because it was lunchtime and he had an important meeting with a man called Sir Cabernay.

13:30 Fatty got off the bus and charged straight into lunch because he was starving again. He said he would eat anything except a hot dog. He got roast pork and went back for thirds. Boggo has called Fatty unprofessional and is refusing to talk to him.

The Crazy Eight spent free bounds at the Mad House. Everyone kept picking up Gilbert the Gnome and talking to him like he was real. Vern was the only one who really did think he was real. Rambo and Boggo finished a bottle of brandy and got completely sozzled. They skulked back into the house just before roll call and then passed out.

One of the Darryls told me that my mom had phoned three times and my dad twice. He then asked me if my dad was deranged like Vern. I told him to drop for twenty for insulting my father, but the Darryl just giggled and ran away. My respect in this place is at an all-time low!

Monday 1st July

Starting to get really excited about going to England. I'm also relieved that I'm leaving early on Thursday morning so I won't have to skulk around the school in embarrassment after the house plays debacle, which is on Wednesday.

Julian watched our house play rehearsal and told us it was "an infantile disgrace." He said the jokes were so last year and that whoever made the decision to use third-year Norman Whiteside's canoe as *Noah's Ark* was a halfwit. Pike's cunning plan is that Vern as the prompt will hide in the canoe and give people their lines when they get stuck. Emberton suggested as backup that Runt should be stationed in a dustbin near the back of the stage. Anybody who forgot their lines could then either examine the ark or throw something in the bin and get a line reading.

My Dove of Peace part is completely embarrassing. After the flood (two blue blankets tied together and waved by Spike and J. R. Ewing) Noah ties a message to my leg and I have to run across the stage flapping my hands and cooing like a dove. Noah then opens a cool box and cracks open a six-pack of Castle Lager with his friends and celebrates the end of the world. They all haul up the anchor (Fatty hiding in the orchestra pit with a long rope attached to his foot) and then hold up their beers (beer bottles with Coke inside) and shout, "Cheers!" as REM's "It's the End of the World as We Know It" ends the play.

Julian suggested that we should call it off and cancel our house play entry. Anderson told him to get stuffed, and Emberton spent the rest of the rehearsal kicking the bin and terrifying Runt.

Tuesday 2nd July

Vern and Runt spent the afternoon watching me pack my trunk. Once I'd banged it shut, they both left the dormitory without saying a word.

Mom called to say that Dad would pick me up at 7 a.m. on Thursday morning. My whole body shivered with excitement at the thought of London, England!

Wednesday 3rd July

HOUSE PLAYS HUMILIATION

As predicted, we came in stone last in the house plays. There was almost constant laughter from beginning to end, although this was aimed at us rather than with us. It all started badly when Vern forgot to get into the canoe before the play began and then tried to creep onstage after the curtain had already gone up. Unfortunately, Vern's attempt at getting headfirst into the canoe without being seen caused so much laughter that the first five minutes of the play wasn't heard.

Then Devries forgot his lines and pretended to rummage around in the garbage bin for food like a tramp while Runt was giving him his line. (Devries was playing the part of God Almighty.) Anderson got a bit thrown by the sight of God Almighty rifling through a rubbish bin and forgot his next lines. There was a long pause as all of us ark animals stood around waiting for Anderson/Noah to say something. Simon (the gay Australian sheep) let off a timid bleat to fill the silence. The bleat started off some loud guffaws among the cast but didn't manage to jog Anderson's memory. Eventually Anderson/Noah announced he was going to check on the ark, marched over to the canoe, bent over, and stuck his head into the hole. There was a lot of loud whispering until Vern became frustrated and started shouting Anderson's lines loudly from inside. Emberton stepped forward, pointed at the canoe, and said,

"Hear the word of the Lord!" Everyone packed up laughing (including all the actors and animals), but then Vern got out of the canoe to a loud chorus of laughter and applause by the school. He bowed to the audience before turning to Anderson and showing him his lines in the script. Anderson tried his best to cover up for the fact that the prompt had just become a part of the play and accused Vern of being a tramp who had been illegally sleeping on the ark. Vern looked terribly confused and furiously paged through the script looking for a line about tramps. Anderson didn't know what to do, so he turned to the other actors and carried on with the scene. Vern, realizing that he had made a blunder, crouched down and then crept offstage in a very sneaky and disturbing manner.

But it got even worse when Roger came strolling onto the stage and started meowing at the canoe and calling for Vern. Pike jumped forward and said, "Look, Noah, a pussy!" and the whole school erupted again. Poor Roger scuttled off the stage in terror. Then Rambo stepped forward with his hands around his massive blue baboon gonads and shouted, "Behold!"

My Dove of Peace was completely humiliating. To make matters worse, one of my wings fell off before I reached the other end of the stage. Rambo stepped forward as the talking baboon and said to Noah, "My Lord, your dove of peace is now a dove in pieces." I sat in the wings waiting for the nightmare to end and felt my cheeks burning with shame.

It also turned out that Noah and his mates weren't strong enough to pull the anchor (Fatty) out of the orchestra pit. When it became obvious that the ark anchor wasn't budging, Vern (closely followed by

Roger) streaked on from stage left and joined in the rope tussle. Then God Almighty entered the fray and with the others started heaving away at the rope and managed to lift Fatty to the very edge of the stage. Unfortunately, they couldn't pull him over the lip and poor Fatty fell headfirst into the orchestra pit with a shriek and loud crashing of cymbals. Thankfully Pike (hiding in the lighting box) decided that enough was enough and plunged us into darkness before playing out with "It's the End of the World as We Know It."

The adjudicator was an old woman who used to be a big cheese on Springbok Radio. She called our play "an aberration." On the plus side she said that the performance of the brain-damaged tramp/prompt character was extremely realistic and incredibly disturbing.

Barnes House took the whole thing far too seriously and did a serious play called *My Footprints on Water*, which won the trophy. It was completely boring, although the adjudicator called it "mature and measured."

After lights-out I said my goodbyes to the Crazy Eight and then lay awake for hours thinking about London and how weird it is that tomorrow night, I'll be on a Boeing 747. I then thought of beautiful Amanda and how we kissed like lovers on my bed. But then I thought of Mermaid in her bikini and was forced to think about cricket instead.

Thursday 4th July

MILTON OVERSEAS ADVENTURE BEGINS

12:00 The folks, Wombat, and I traveled to the airport in a big yellow

Eagle taxi. Mom and Wombat spent the entire trip discussing the hottest neighborhood gossip. Dad's big buddy Frank (who is house-sitting our house and feeding Blacky) has a new girlfriend who is only nineteen years old. (Frank is forty-nine!) Mom said it was sickening. Wombat said it was grotesque. Dad said, "Lucky bugger." Mom and Wombat pretended they didn't hear him and demanded my opinion on Frank. I didn't know what to say, so I did my AA trick (shaking my head and looking forlornly out the window). It obviously worked because Mom said, "You see, Mom, it's sickening. Even Johnny's upset." Wombat commented that Frank was old enough to be the girl's father. Dad piped up and said, "But if the cap fits . . ." He forgot the rest and said, "Then Bob's your uncle?" By the end of the journey even Alvin Naidoo the taxi driver was shaking his head at Frank and his nineteen-year-old girlfriend.

Mom has finally persuaded Wombat to visit her sister in Brighton so that she can bury the hatchet. Dad looked at me and said, "The only place she knows to bury a hatchet is in somebody's head." I asked Mom about Wombat's sister, but she said she had to concentrate on not losing the passports and said she didn't have time for questions.

12:45 Wombat had a fight with our taxi driver over the fare. She said forty bucks was highway robbery and reminded Alvin that he was an Indian and that she was on to his shenanigans. Alvin tapped the taxi meter and said there was nothing he could do. Wombat then accused Alvin of having a faulty meter and demanded a complete refund plus damages. The next minute there was a really loud burst of church music from the speakers of the yellow taxi. (Wombat had obviously switched on the radio instead of the meter.) Wombat eventually got out of the taxi and said, "I got him down to thirty-five. Really, it's a scandal! This wouldn't happen back home." She then tapped me on the shoulder and said, "Remember, Roy, take care of the pennies and the pounds take care of themselves. . . ."

13:06 Wombat drank three gin and tonics on the flight to Johannesburg. When the plane touched down, she thought we had landed in London and applauded the pilot.

We had four hours to wait at the airport, so I took my Walkman and my *Sports Illustrated* magazine and settled at a safe distance from the Miltons. The woman next to me was sobbing to her husband. He kept saying, "Think forward, Cheryl. Remember, we said we were going to think forward. We're doing it for the kids!" This didn't seem to work because Cheryl started howling and digging in her bags for tissues.

I returned to find the Miltons all reading different sections of the *Citizen* newspaper. Dad, who had the sports section, said, "If Tony Watson doesn't make the bloody Springboks again, I'll eat my head off." Wombat was shaking her head about an elderly couple who were murdered on their farm and Mom was cursing because she had forgotten to set the tape for the final episode of *Twin Peaks*. I turned up the volume on my Walkman and stared at the list of cities on the departures board.

London
Paris
Geneva
Frankfurt
New York

One day I'll see them all.

Our Olympic Airlines jumbo touched down in Athens in the middle of the night. Wombat applauded again and welcomed us all to London. Mom told her we were in Greece. Wombat looked horrified and asked if the plane had been hijacked. Dad sneakily gathered up a huge pile of empty mini brandy bottles, dumped them in his sick bag, and then slid the bag under Wombat's seat.

We had an eight-hour wait for our flight to London, so we decided to take a taxi into Athens and see the Acropolis. It was pitch black outside and Wombat hailed seven taxis before she found an honest driver. (She reckons you can tell by the shifty look in their eyes.) The only word we all understood was *Acropolis*. This didn't stop Mom and Wombat from giving the poor man half an hour of recent Milton history. Dad asked the taxi driver what time the sun rose. The taxi driver rattled off a long reply in Greek. When he had finished speaking, there was a pause before Wombat turned to Dad and said, "What did this gentleman say, Roy?" Dad shrugged and said it was all Greek to him. He then roared with laughter and thumped his hand on the dashboard. The taxi driver must have seen the funny side because he laughed along with Dad.

The climb to the top of the Acropolis was a real test for Wombat, who at times seemed to be walking horizontal to the ground. Dad reached the top, took a look around, and said the place was falling to pieces. I told Dad it was thousands of years old, but he still wasn't impressed. I then showed my father the ancient theater of Dionysus, where theater first began. Dad said the place could do with a face-lift.

The sun rose over Athens, revealing a dusty, dirty but beautiful city. I feel like a real traveler in a far-off land.

Heathrow Airport is gigantic! It's like a whole city with planes instead of cars. It also makes the last one look like a chicken shed. Wombat was thrilled to be "home" and shook hands with every security person she came across. She proudly showed off her British passport and gave me a pound and told me not to spend it all at once.

Dad was stopped and searched at customs. He blamed it on Tutu, who he says has given white South Africans a bad name abroad.

15:10 (Greenwich mean time) Wombat had yet another argument with a taxi driver, who wanted forty quid to take us to our hotel. Wombat called him a shyster and shouted, "This doesn't happen back home, you know!" before slamming the door of the cab and pointing us to the tube station.

Mental note: Keep Wombat away from taxi drivers wherever possible.

The tube thundered into the station, and around us people swarmed onto the train. There was a desperate rush to lug all the suitcases on board before the doors closed. Poor Dad was lugging huge cases backward and forward while Wombat stood in the middle of the coach shouting, "Don't close the doors! He's one of us!"

We found ourselves packed into the tube like scared little sardines, clutching our suitcases. The people on the train all read newspapers and listened to Walkmans. It amazed me that nobody spoke—it was like a traveling morgue. Wombat lectured one Londoner on his ripe body odor and asked him when he had last taken a bath. The man didn't answer. In fact, he didn't even look up once from his magazine. Dad looked at me grimly and said, "Welcome to London."

The Kensington Palace Hotel isn't quite what Wombat was expecting. It's a massive hotel with tiny rooms and the longest corridors I've ever seen. All the maids and cleaners are Filipino and don't speak much English. (Actually most of them don't speak any English.) I doubt Princess Diana has ever set foot in the place.

Saturday 6th July

MADAME TUSSAUDS AND PUB LUNCH

After a greasy breakfast of egg and kippers the Miltons hit the streets of London. Wombat and Mom decided that our mission was to see the Madame Tussauds wax museum. London is a mad hustle and bustle of people from all over the world. Dad was shocked to see a beautiful blond girl walking down the street hand in hand with a black guy. I must admit it did look strange. We all stopped in the middle of the pavement and watched the young couple walk by. Wombat told us that it would never have been allowed in Thatcher's day.

Madame Tussauds is truly amazing. Dad made me take pictures of him standing next to Roger Moore and the Beatles, although he told me to chop John Lennon off the side because he was a commie. Wombat curtsied before having her picture taken with the queen. Mom, Dad, and Wombat posed with Margaret Thatcher. After the photographs Wombat said she was exhausted and was off to find a chair. I posed with Anthony Hopkins and Michael Jackson. Unfortunately, there was no replica of John Milton (the poet).

Then Dad and I went down to the Chamber of Horrors, where we saw the Jack the Ripper murder scene. Further down the chamber a huge crowd of Japanese tourists were jabbering away and taking pictures. We pushed through the crowd with Dad saying, "Saki saki," to everyone as if he was greeting them. There was another crowd of Japanese photographers snapping away in the far corner of Murderers Row. As we got closer Dad and I stopped dead in our tracks. A large sign read DOCTOR CRIPPEN. Next to the sign was a bench. On the bench was Wombat, fast asleep with her mouth open and her yellow tongue exposed. The Japanese were pointing at her, shouting, "Kippen! Kippen!" and snapping away with their fancy cameras. Dad took out his camera and snapped a picture too! Then a second crowd of Japanese tourists came over and photographed Wombat. I told Dad that half of Japan would think Wombat was a savage serial killer. Dad shrugged and said, "Who am I to argue with half of Japan?"

11:30 After spending the morning impersonating Dr. Crippen the serial killer, Wombat peered up at the overcast sky and announced that the sun was over the yardarm. The Miltons piled into a local pub. Dad seemed thrilled with the place and said, "You can say a lot about the English but when it comes to pubs . . ." He gazed around looking impressed and whistled softly to himself. Wombat handed Dad a twenty-pound note and told him to get a round of drinks. Dad looked around to see if anybody had seen him taking money from his mother-in-law and then shot off to the bar. We found a table and settled down to a lunch of pork pies and chips with gravy. Dad drank three pints of Guinness and got completely smashed. He blamed the Irish, who he says make crazy beer. Our lunch cost us sixty-eight quid. Mom and Dad were astonished. Wombat didn't seem too concerned about the cost although she had drunk five gin and tonics and had repeatedly piped up with morbid old war songs whenever there was a pause in conversation.

Sunday 7th July

OXFORD STREET

Mom and Dad said they were jet-lagged. They sent me down to the Pakistani corner shop, where I bought them bread rolls, cheese, and pickles. They reckoned they were going to spend the day watching TV in bed. Wombat shouted, "When you're tired of London, you're tired of life!" and then turned to me and said, "Come along, young man, we're going to Oxford Street."

Wombat is brilliant in London. She's also not shy to abuse people where necessary. We hopped onto one of the red double-decker tourist buses and sat on the open top roof. She showed me so many landmarks and interesting historical buildings that I was starting to think that perhaps Wombat isn't losing her marbles at all until she pointed at a Barclays Bank building and told me it was Buckingham Palace.

We jumped off the bus and made our way up Oxford Street. There were so many CD shops—looks like tapes are soon to be a thing of the past. We stopped at a fancy coffee shop called Lace & Syrup for what

Wombat called "elevenses." (Basically a pit stop between breakfast and lunch.) Wombat ordered a pot of tea and a round of egg sandwiches. I had a huge stack of crumpets and a chocolate milk shake and then felt too full to carry on living. After elevenses Wombat gave me twenty pounds and said she was off to buy shoes. We agreed to meet back at the Lace & Syrup in half an hour.

I figured that with twenty pounds, I had enough money to buy a new release and a cheap old CD. I found a small music store under the level of the street where you could listen to music on headphones for free.

I decided Elton John, Phil Collins, Erasure, Fleetwood Mac, and Lionel Richie were too naff. I thought about impressing everyone at school by buying Metallica or Iron Maiden, but I hate heavy metal. I settled for U2's *The Joshua Tree* and Bob Dylan's *Greatest Hits*.

I arrived back at the Lace & Syrup to find no sign of Wombat. By one o'clock I realized Wombat was missing. I suddenly felt scared. There I was, stuck and disoriented in the middle of London with hundreds of people around talking in different languages. I walked up and down Oxford Street looking in each shop for my grandmother. She was gone. I was too scared to take different roads because I had the feeling that I'd never make it back to Oxford Street again. I took a few deep breaths and counted the money in my pocket. Three pounds fifty!

I tried to retrace my steps to where Wombat and I had got off the bus. But then I noticed buildings that I was sure I hadn't seen before, so I turned around and walked in the opposite direction. Around me were London traffic and shops and strange faces. It felt like I was striding along in a great army of ants. (Except all the other ants knew where they were going.) I stopped to get my bearings once again. A blond lady about Mom's age walked up to me and said, "All right, son?" I must have looked in a bit of a state of panic because she put her arm around me and asked, "Where you going?" I don't think I answered her because I was a little caught up with her strong Cockney accent. I eventually told the woman I was staying at the Kensington Palace Hotel. She said, "Oooh, bless." I then told her I was South African. She said, "Oooh, dear." My final killer blow was when I mentioned that I had been deserted by my grandmother. She shook her head sadly and said, "Well, lovey, you stand here until a big red bus comes and then you stay on that selfsame bus until you find South Kensington." I repeated the words "South Kensington" like a moron. She nodded and said, "From the station it's down the road and you can't miss it." I thanked her for her help and stood behind a line of wombats waiting for the big red double-decker bus.

I bought my ticket and climbed up to the top deck. The sun was shining and the city of London was flashing by. I flipped open my Walkman and loaded *The Joshua Tree*. I wasn't scared anymore. Now I felt like a real traveler surrounded by complete strangers in one of the greatest cities in the world with the perfect greens of the park on one side and three-hundred-year-old buildings on the other. My left foot was tapping to the bass and my head was nodding along with the jangling guitars:

> I want to run
> I want to hide

I want to break down the walls that hold me inside
I want to reach out and touch the flame
Where the streets have no name

There was mass celebration when I returned alive to the hotel. Mom and Dad (who claimed to have been worried sick about me) were still in bed surrounded by food and a couple of empty wine bottles. Wombat had arrived back ages ago with ten pairs of K Shoes and half a dozen petticoats. The K Shoes are all exactly the same color (white) and look like very embarrassing tennis shoes. Wombat refused to apologize for deserting me in London and said she wasn't here to babysit. I informed everyone that I wasn't a child anymore anyway, marched out of my parents' room, and slammed the door, nearly bashing into the Filipino waiter who was bringing up more wine.

I returned to my tiny room and watched the BBC news.

Monday 8th July

BUCKINGHAM PALACE AND VARIOUS PARKS OF LONDON

It was another early start for the Miltons. For the third morning in a row the Filipino waiter brought me yogurt and nuts when I ordered a cheese and mushroom omelet. Wombat told the waiter he was a disgrace to England and then told him to buck himself up and clean up his act. The waiter grinned and nodded and then took away our orange juice. Mom and Wombat agreed that England had become a godless place.

Today was a walking day. We made it through the massive Hyde Park and then St. James Park and Green Park and finally to Buckingham Palace. Wombat was beside herself with excitement and pointed out the queen's bedroom. Soon a small group of tourists were standing next to us listening to Wombat's descriptions of the palace and what the queen would be doing at this very moment. Unfortunately, Wombat then pointed at the window next to the queen's window and told us all that it was her own bedroom. The tourists laughed and then quickly moved on, although a Japanese tourist took Wombat's picture and bowed to her.

HYDE (HIDE) PARK

At Hyde Park Corner there's something called Speakers' Corner. On a stage with a microphone members of the public are allowed to stand up and make a speech about whatever is on their minds. A crowd gathers below and either heckles or cheers on the speaker depending on what he is saying.

When we got there, a punk with orange hair was shouting on about foxhunting. I hardly heard a word he was saying because his accent was so bad. Most of the crowd looked bored and chatted among themselves.

Next up was an old Welshman who went on about getting compensation for the closure of the coal mines. He told the crowd that Margaret Thatcher should be tried for crimes against humanity.

Then there was a whiny woman who went on about rates and taxes. The crowd ignored her completely and a few people told her to get lost.

Tuesday 9th July

Dad said he was exhausted after all the walking yesterday and decided to spend the day having a pub lunch. Wombat said ten-thirty in the morning was an obscene time to start drinking and stayed behind in the hotel for elevenses and forty winks. Dad gave me three pounds and told me to buy another CD. I told him that CDs were twelve pounds, so he told me to buy a record instead. I nipped into the corner shop and headed straight to the magazine racks. There on the top shelf was the magazine I had seen on Saturday.

Racked and Stacked UK

My heart was pounding. I was terrified the Pakistani shopkeeper would think I was a pervert and call a policeman. My hands were shaking as I reached up and grabbed hold of the shiny magazine covered in plastic. (No doubt this is a cunning plan to keep perverts from getting horny and performing dodgy deeds in the shop.) Then there was an enormous crash as about ten magazines and five tins of baked beans fell to the floor. I felt myself blushing and there was a weird humming noise in my ear. I quickly started picking everything up, but I had obviously caught the storekeeper's eye because suddenly he was looming over me asking if he could help me with anything. I said, "No, I'm fine," but had a terrible knack jump in the process. I felt myself blushing and quickly packed up the magazines and left the store trying not to make eye contact with anyone in the shop. Strange things are happening to my mind and body. Let's hope I'm not turning into a Boggo.

Wednesday 10th July

WIMBLEDON

The journey to Wimbledon took up most of the morning. In the end we had to take four trains and a taxi. It should only have been two trains and a long walk, but Wombat made us get off the second train because there were too many blacks in our carriage. We then boarded the third train, which turned out to be on the Circle Line, and we ended up back where we had started in the first place. We finally arrived at Wimbledon and discovered the longest line in the history of mankind. Dad tried to push to the front but was forced out by an angry woman with a yellow umbrella. Dad skulked back to us and said the Brits were a "miserable race of people."

Then Wombat became disoriented and seemed to think that we were lining up for war rations.

After a few minutes of us trying to reassure my grandmother that the war had ended nearly half a century ago, a tall man in a gray suit approached us and offered us black market tickets. Wombat asked him for a case of tinned sardines and a gallon of drinking water. The man in the suit ignored her completely and asked for a hundred and twenty pounds for three tickets. Mom haggled him down to eighty quid and took the money out of Wombat's handbag. Dad graciously said he would miss the tennis and said he would rather check out the town of Wimbledon instead. Mom gave him a big kiss and Wombat gave him his thirty-five quid pocket money. We arranged to meet again at five o'clock in a pub down the street and Dad set off in high spirits singing the "Wombles of Wimbledon Common" song.

Unfortunately, things went downhill after that. Turned out our black market tickets for the men's final were fake and that Wimbledon had finished last weekend. The line we were standing in was for a Ladbrokes betting shop, and a light rain was starting to fall.

We wandered off to take shelter in the pub, where we discovered Dad at the bar with three very loud South Africans from Pretoria. They were all dressed in Northern Transvaal rugby jerseys and kept chanting insulting songs about England and shouting rude comments at the barman in Afrikaans. Dad's face dropped when he saw us come in and he quickly threw his cap over his pint and said he'd been sheltering from the rain until the museum opened. Mom, Wombat, and I sat in a booth and Wombat tried to order strawberries and cream for five pounds, but the waiter said the tennis special was over and brought us dry scones instead. The only tennis we got to see was a rerun of a boring game of ladies' doubles on the pub's TV. The only player I recognized was Arantxa Sánchez-Vicario, who I'm sure must be a lesbian. Her thighs are bigger than both of mine put together! She also grunts like a man every time she hits the ball. Sánchez-Vicario and her pretty blond partner embraced after they had won the match and I then had a dark fantasy about what might go on in the change room after the match.

Dad ordered a round for the whole pub, taking the money from Wombat's handbag while she was hunting for her serviette under the table. After shaking hands with everyone in the pub, he turned to me and said the South Africans had told him that living in England was worse than living in South Africa. He repeated this three times in case Mom didn't get the message.

Thursday 11th July

A long day of walking and sightseeing, including Big Ben, Houses of Parliament, Trafalgar Square, and various pubs.

Friday 12th July

CAMBRIDGE UNIVERSITY

What a beautiful place to study! I've decided that I'll have to win another scholarship and study English literature at Cambridge University. (And then after lessons I'll row beautiful women up and down the river Cam and recite love poems to them before taking them back to my rooms for some passionate kissing and fondling.)

I found Christ's College where The Guv said John Milton studied. In fact, there was a bronze statue of him in one of the quads. He may have been a great poet, but he was only the second-best-looking John Milton in Cambridge today!

Sunday 14th July

The Miltons (dressed in their Sunday best) strode into the massive St. Paul's Cathedral for Holy Communion. Wombat burst into tears when we walked down the aisle and said that this was where she got married in 1981. Mom handed her a tissue and told Wombat she was confusing her own wedding with that of Princess Diana and Prince Charles. Wombat pretended not to listen and made out she was deep in prayer. I didn't recognize any of the hymns, although I couldn't have sung even if I had.

There's a very pretty brunette staying in our hotel. We locked eyes in the lobby and she gave me a smile. I tried to smile back, but my lips were stuck to my gums.

Monday 15th July

Brunette must have checked out because there were five bald men sitting at her breakfast table this morning.

11:45 Express train to Brighton to visit Wombat's sister. Everyone was nervous. Wombat was nervous because she was seeing her sister for the first time in twenty years. Dad was nervous because Mom wants us to emigrate to Brighton. (She hasn't told us this, but Dad overheard her telling Wombat that she wanted to live in Brighton and has even started checking out possible schools for me.) Mom was nervous because Dad was looking twitchy and a bit manic. I was nervous because fear is catching and I don't like the thought of leaving my home and my country and settling somewhere cold and miserable.

12:04 Wombat and Mom have a loud argument with the train's barman because the bar is meant to open at noon.

12:07 Wombat starts knocking on the bar door with her umbrella and shouting, “The sun is over the yardarm!” The barman continues cleaning glasses without opening the bar.

12:09 Dad says, “Bugger this,” and presses an emergency button above his seat.

12:11 The conductor arrives, looking pale. He has a fire extinguisher under his left arm.

12:12 Mom abuses the conductor for not opening the bar on time.

12:13 The conductor apologizes and orders the barman to open the bar.

12:17 Sulky barman opens door.

12:18 The Miltons file into the bar with the entire carriage watching in fascination. Wombat continues crapping on the conductor and the barman.

12:22 The barman loses his patience with Wombat and tells her it’s Monday morning and suggests that she might have a drinking problem.

12:23 Wombat hits the barman with her umbrella and calls him a vagabond.

12:27 Very pale conductor calms everyone down and offers the Miltons a free round of drinks.

12:28 Dad accuses the barman of bribery and of being prejudiced against South Africans. The barman offers him a double round. Dad accepts and the three men shake hands.

12:29 Dad orders a double round of Johnnie Walker whisky for all four of us.

12:30 The barman refuses to serve me liquor.

12:31 Dad changes the order to a double round of three triple Johnnie Walkers and a tomato juice.

12:32 I tell Dad that I don't drink tomato juice. He says tomato juice is four times the price of a Coke.

12:35 Pale conductor and sulky barman have to push two tables together because our drinks don't fit on a single table.

12:40 A small group of people watch us from the door and shake their heads. A large woman with red hair turns to an even larger woman with even redder hair and says, "Course it's always the child that suffers, isn't it?" The even fatter woman nods and shakes her chins in dismay.

12:42 Dad stands up and orders us to raise our glasses for a toast. He then shouts, "South Africa one, England zero!" and sits down again and knocks back one of his triple whiskies. Wombat calls Dad "uncouth" and then sets off on a long story about the dangers of rail travel during the war. Dad takes the opportunity to steal one of Wombat's triple whiskies.

I spend the last eighteen minutes of the journey watching Miltons getting pissed with the compliments of British Rail.

THE BRIGHTON DISASTER

Bad news is that Wombat's sister, Eunice (Dingbat), is madder than Wombat. You can tell they're related because Dingbat slammed the door on us at first because she thought we were Jehovah's Witnesses. Dingbat's husband (Neville) then opened the door again and invited us in. Neville's accent was so strong I couldn't understand a single word he said. We followed Neville into the house and found ourselves in a living room that smelled of cat's pee. The culprit was a big fat red cat that lay on the couch with its legs open and a smug look on its face.

Then Dingbat became confused again and told us all to leave. Wombat told Dingbat we couldn't leave because there was an air raid under way. There was a moment's confusion before Neville took Dingbat into the kitchen and explained to his wife in a loud voice that we weren't Christians, we were Miltons. Poor Dingbat returned and started crying and apologized for not knowing who we were. Wombat eyed her sister shiftily and leaned toward Mom and began whispering rather loudly, "She was always odd, you know—I once caught her canoodling with a girl." Dad choked on his scone and Neville quickly ran off to the kitchen saying that he needed sugar cubes. We then sat down to a very awkward tea where the conversation ran dry every minute or so. Every time there was a pause, Wombat would whisper nasty comments so loudly that everyone could hear. After tea the conversation broke down completely and everyone looked around trying to think of something to say.

Then Neville turned to Wombat and said, "Look, I don't wanna mess about here, and the old girl's not been her best lately . . . so, um . . . have you brought the money?" Wombat's whole body jerked back in her chair and she grabbed her handbag. Mom looked startled and asked Neville what he was talking about. Neville looked at Wombat and said, "The money we're owed. Our inheritance, luv." Instantly Mom's lips disappeared. Wombat leaned forward and asked, "Are they begging for money?" Suddenly Neville stood up and started shouting. The next minute we found ourselves on the pavement outside Dingbat's house staring at a freshly slammed door. Mom suggested we head to the local pub for a drink to settle our nerves.

WOMBAT'S MURKY HISTORY

Contrary to rumors circulating at school, Wombat didn't kill and eat her family. According to Mom, in 1938 Dingbat married Neville, who was a plumber. Wombat and Dingbat's parents refused to accept Neville into the family because he was from the working class and their parents thought themselves to be just short of aristocracy. They forbade Dingbat to marry Neville, saying he was a working-class thug who was only after Dingbat's money and status. Dingbat didn't listen to her parents and married Neville anyway. Their parents refused to go to the wedding and disowned their elder daughter. As a result Wombat inherited everything and Dingbat didn't get a penny.

Mom finished telling the story and we all looked at Wombat, who refused to show any remorse and said that Dingbat didn't deserve the money because she didn't even bother to attend her parents' funerals. Dad shook his head and looked depressed—no doubt he was thinking about inheriting a station wagon instead of a farm. After a long silence Dad went off to book us two rooms in the hotel above the pub while Mom and Wombat drank in silence.

Mom must be serious about immigrating to Brighton, because she's set up a meeting with a real-estate agent tomorrow. Dad looked pale and ill and hardly touched his dinner.

Tuesday 16th July

Was kept up all night because Wombat kept moaning in her sleep and crunching noisily on her false teeth.

We met up with the Brighton estate agent after breakfast. Dad mumbled about the weather and sulked in the back seat of the car. Thankfully, Wombat stayed behind at the hotel because she said she had gout problems and blamed the hotel's pork sausages.

The estate agent had the ability to talk for ages at a time without stopping to take a breath. She also had a very short miniskirt that crept up her thighs every time she changed gear. Dad called her the Energizer Bunny. He nudged me in the ribs and whispered, "And you know what they say about bunnies. . . ." He then stared at her legs with glassy eyes and his mouth open. The Energizer Bunny told us that she had three places to show us that were more or less in our price range. Dad looked pale and lost interest in staring at the lady's legs.

The first place was a one-and-a-half-bedroom hovel that smelled worse than the school bogs. It was dark, poky, and miserable, with a partial view of a large rubbish dump where crows were picking around looking for something to eat. The crows obviously sit on the roof, because the window ledges were stained with white bird droppings. The Energizer Bunny did her best to emphasize the good points. (Within a mile of the shops, secure parking, and a recently renovated lift.)

Dad said the place looked like a morgue. I went to the bathroom and noticed that the toilet was leaking. The kitchen window had been boarded up and the carpets were stained and showed signs of cigarette burns. Mom looked on the verge of tears, especially when the Energizer Bunny admitted that this was the best flat of the three.

Dad and I exchanged a very low-key high five in the back seat.

Once the Energizer Bunny dropped us off, Mom looked grim and said, "Well, I suppose now you two are satisfied." We didn't say anything, but Dad looked so happy that his face was shining bright pink. The Miltons are returning to Africa and all emigration plans have been canceled!

Friday 19th July

I told the family I was sleeping in and spending the day in the hotel. The rest of the Miltons set off for Richmond to see Hampton Court, where Henry the Eighth used to hang out.

I snuck in to breakfast just before ten hoping to avoid the people who were in the bar last night. I loaded up a bowl of yogurt and tinned peaches and sat down at our table facing the wall. Unfortunately, I then couldn't see if people were gossiping about me or not. I ate breakfast at top speed and had to put up with the headwaiter, who kept coming across to chat to me. He even invited me to watch a soccer match with him in his hotel suite.

I told him I didn't like soccer and that I had plans. The real reason I lied is because his pants were pulled up far higher than necessary and he kept licking his lips whenever he spoke to me.

Made another trip to the corner shop but chickened out because it was too crowded.

Saturday 20th July

Phantom of the Opera is a sensational musical. We had seats in the third row and I didn't miss a thing. I completely lost control during the "Music of the Night," which the Phantom sings to Christine. I discovered that tears were pouring out of my eyes and I had to pretend I had an eyelash problem in case somebody was watching me. I had a sharp and sudden memory of Gecko. I remember I sang him the "Music of the Night" the afternoon before he died. He said it gave him goose bumps. Thankfully by the end of the play I wasn't the only Milton wiping away tears.

If my voice ever returns and the embarrassment of *Noah's Ark* is forgotten, then I'm going to one day play the lead in a West End musical.

Sunday 21st July

15:00 The taxi was waiting, our bags were packed, and the Miltons were ready to go home. Unfortunately, there was no sign of Wombat.

She said she was nipping out to buy some last-minute goods an hour ago and has now disappeared.

15:10 Mom decides that we can't afford to miss our flights home, so we leave messages with reception and head for Heathrow.

18:30 Mom phoned the hotel but still no sign of Wombat. Dad didn't seemed too worried at all about Wombat's disappearance and was busy spending Wombat's money like crazy in the duty-free shops. I tried to drive home how serious things were, so I exaggerated a bit and told Dad that Wombat could be lying in a ditch next to the road about to be killed by a serial killer. Dad said that was a possibility, although we shouldn't get our hopes up. He then marched over to the duty-free counter and bought himself some aftershave with Wombat's money.

Half an hour before boarding, Mom burst into tears and said she was going to stay behind in London to find her mother. Dad and I managed to talk her out of it by saying that Wombat knew London better than she knew Durban. Poor Mom eventually boarded the plane and looked miserable all the way to Athens.

Mom charged off the plane in Athens and went straight to a call box. She called the Kensington Palace Hotel and discovered that Wombat had checked out and then taken a bus to Brighton. Mom then tried to call Dingbat and Neville, but nobody answered.

Monday 22nd July

"HOME SWEET HOME"

We finally arrived back in Johannesburg Airport after nearly twenty hours of airports and airplanes. Dad was so thrilled to be home that he tried to strike up a friendly conservation with the Afrikaans security guard who was checking our passports. The Afrikaans security guard didn't seem very impressed and ordered Dad into a small booth, where his suitcase was searched.

Apparently it isn't just the country that has gone to the dogs. It looks like Frank and his new nineteen-year-old girlfriend haven't exactly outdone themselves on the housework either. Mom wrote down a list of problems:

- The pool's green.
- Blacky has dug up half the lawn in the pursuit of moles.
- Dad's rosebushes are badly dehydrated.
- Blacky has a patch of luminous green mold on his tongue.
- The bin stinks and is infested with maggots.
- Frank's nineteen-year-old girlfriend left a pair of undies down the side of the couch in the lounge. (Mom reckons Frank should be arrested for perversion.)
- The liquor cabinet is empty. (After this discovery Dad agreed that Frank had crossed the line.)

Wombat is alive and kicking. In fact, she's now living in Brighton with Neville and Dingbat. Wombat says she handed over a check for ten thousand pounds and Neville and Dingbat invited her to stay for the rest of the summer. Wombat told Mom that she couldn't die with Dingbat on her conscience and had to give over her fair share. Mom started crying, but Wombat cut her off and said they were going out for tea with the mayor of Brighton and that she didn't have time for sniveling.

Dad, who was midway through frying a massive packet of bacon for Blacky, said that Wombat actually inherited over two hundred thousand pounds from her parents and that the ten thousand pounds she handed over to Dingbat was just five percent of her inheritance excluding interest and inflation.

Friday 26th July

My report card arrived in the post.

ENGLISH	A
AFRIKAANS	A
MATHS	B
SPEECH & DRAMA	A
HISTORY	A
GEOGRAPHY	B
BIOLOGY	C
SCIENCE	E

Mom and Dad cheered loudly and called me a genius. Dad said my results called for a celebration, so he fired up bacon and eggs on the gas cooker while Mom raced to the shops to stock up on champagne and orange juice. I turned over the card and read Sparerib's comments.

John has applied himself far better over the second quarter. Notwithstanding the improvement in Afrikaans, maths, and geography and his continued good work in English, history, and speech and drama, it is of major concern that he has neglected both biology and science in his studies and as proposed matric subject choices. I advise you, his parents, to pursue this matter with him before the realignment into their matric classes in the coming term.

John is a well-adjusted boy who remains popular around the house. He does, however, tend toward extended periods of quietness and introspection and is noticeably less gregarious than he was in his first year at the school. I am pleased with his progress and particularly grateful for the way in which he has helped compatriot Vern Blackadder in his difficult adjustment to school life.

SPARERIB's REPORT (Written by Spud Milton)

Sparerib had a poor second term. Not only did he try to get Spud Milton to tell him what he wrote about in his diary, but he also tried to bully him into doing science for matric. His house continues to run amok and he has no control over the Crazy Eight, who now have a secret hideaway right under his nose. He still continues to skulk around the house like a shady detective, and there is a rumor that he likes watching boys showering while on duty.

PS Spud Milton wouldn't have to help Vern Blackadder if Sparerib had tighter controls about allowing cretins and lunatics to attend the school in the first place.

Sunday 28th July

The Guv called shortly after dawn. I heard Dad screaming with laughter on the phone and then calling The Guv a maniac. My voice was all croaky when I said, "Hello." There was a pause at the other end of the line and then The Guv shouted, "Milton the Poet!" before setting off on the Battle of Agincourt speech. He then called me a "callow youth, but sly." He announced that I'd received a merit certificate in the Alan Paton creative-writing competition. (This means I didn't make the top ten.) Before I could reply, he shouted, "All hail, Milton!" and hung up. Dad tried to get another celebratory champagne breakfast binge under way, but Mom ordered him to shave and shower because we were all going to church to give thanks. I told the folks that a merit award wasn't worth celebrating. Dad said he wasn't going back to church because it was a cesspool for communism and he was scared of being eaten by Mrs. Shingle. Mom told him he was talking nonsense, but my father was adamant that the Anglican Church is a hotbed of communism and cannibalism.

15:00 Dad staggered up the driveway and said that he had been returning the panties to Frank's girlfriend. Mom looked foul and asked him why it had taken him five hours. Dad said he had had a beer or two with Shannon's friends. (Shannon must be the nineteen-year-old.) Mom eyed him shiftily and threatened to nail him for everything he's got if he even so much as thinks of running off with a nineteen-year-old. Dad tried to put on a fake laugh and told my mother she was being ridiculous. He then went off to bed with Blacky and slept until dinnertime.

Monday 29th July

On the long trek back to school I tried to make sense of my twenty-six-day holiday that now feels like a long weekend. The bus engine screamed as we creaked up the hills and then thundered down the slopes with great shudders and rattles. I flicked on *Joshua Tree* and counted streetlamps until I got dizzy. My school uniform feels tight on me—I must be growing after all.

I dragged my bags through the great archway and into the main quad. Vern was standing on guard outside the house with Roger in one hand and a cup of tea in the other. When he saw me approaching, he let go of Roger and gave me a vigorous salute, spilling half his tea down his leg. I couldn't salute back because I was carrying bags, so I smiled and said, "Hi, Vern." Vern gave me a maniacal grin and said, "Spud." He then cackled with laughter and followed me up the stairs making funny squeals and breathing like Darth Vader. The Crazy Eight were all waiting and there were loud whistles and a few bleats when I walked into the dorm. Death Breath called lights-out and closed the door. Within seconds we were all settled in Rambo's cubicle. And then the stories began. . . .

HOLIDAY SCORECARD

RAMBO	Finally bonked his stepmom.
SIMON	Went to Spain with his family.
FATTY	Hung out with Heinz (the hot-dog king) for half the holiday.

ROGER	Came off second best in a fight with Mr. Lilly's Maltese poodle.
BOGGO	Got savagely dumped by his girlfriend Ali and says he's suicidal.
MAD DOG	Shot a wildebeest (gnu), had it stuffed, and has brought the head back to school. Mad Dog says he's hanging the head up in the Mad House.
SPUD	Wintered in England.
VERN	Reckons he had sex in the holiday. Everyone roared with laughter and demanded proof. Vern slipped his hand into his underpants and pulled out a crumpled photograph of himself with his arm around ex–Miss World Anneline Kriel. The only problem was that Vern was about eight years old in the photo and by the looks of things Anneline Kriel was completely freaked out by Vern.

We took the wildebeest head into the first-year dorm to freak out the Normal Seven. Mad Dog held the head in front of his face and made a beeline for the far cubicle, which houses two of the Darryls. After forty seconds of Mad Dog's marauding gnu routine most of the first-years had taken flight and were hiding up in the rafters. Mad Dog was about to shoot a couple of them down with his catapult when out of the third Darryl's bed appeared a black face followed by a round black body. Either there was a new first-year on the loose or one of the Darryls had returned to school in a clever disguise.

His name is Bongani Njali. Rambo told him he was the new black Darryl and rechristened him Barryl. Barryl grinned at the wildebeest head and said something in Zulu that nobody understood. His English isn't very good, so the Crazy Eight soon lost interest in him and turned our attention to Fatty and Mad Dog, who stuck Runt's head in the dustbin and then used Runt's big toe to switch the lights on and off.

Julian must have seen the lights flashing because he charged into the dormitory and said he wanted to welcome all his boys back to school. Unfortunately, he then caught sight of the wildebeest head and screamed like he was being murdered. He charged out of the dormitory shouting, "Chriiist! They've got a fucking moose in there!"

Soon all the lights were on and half the house had gathered to see the moose. Pike tried to steal the head, but Mad Dog pulled out his knife and threatened to "gut him like a shark." Instead Pike jumped on Thinny, put the wildebeest head on the poor guy's head, and pretended he was humping the creature. We stared at Pike in utter silence, watching him humping Thinny and shouting, "Ride me, horsey! Ride me!" Eventually he must have realized that he was looking like an idiot, so he started abusing Barryl instead. Barryl didn't seem to be offended and stood stock-still like a soldier. Then Pike pulled out his willy and tried to piss on Runt's duvet. He ended up having a problem with stage fright and hurled Runt's bedding out the window instead.

After all the excitement I returned to my bed and tried to sleep. Soon I heard some furious snuffling and gasping noises coming from the direction of Vern's bed. I could see Vern's duvet bouncing up and down in the moonlight. I didn't have to call the others because Vern was making so much noise that they'd all gathered around anyway. Even Roger popped his head out of the underpants drawer to see what all the noise was about.

Boggo ripped off Vern's duvet and Rain Man was caught red-handed. Vern blushed and tried to cover his very early morning glory and hide the picture of Anneline Kriel at the same time.

I lay awake for hours—definitely a little unnerved by Vern's wanking and the disturbing pervert noises he makes. I feel sorry for the girl who ever has the extreme misfortune to sleep with him.

Tuesday 30th July

The school gave Vern the "wanker chant" at breakfast. Vern blushed bloodred and chose that moment to stick a whole Vienna sausage in his mouth. Everyone roared and banged their cutlery on the tables. Julian came down from the top table and asked Vern if he was right-handed. Vern nodded, so Julian shook his left hand.

After some cunning detective work Boggo and Fatty have got the lowdown on the missing Darryl. Turns out that Darryl the third told his mom that he would commit suicide if he had to return to school. Thinny also told Fatty that the missing Darryl used to wet his pants whenever Mad Dog or Rambo entered the dormitory.

Sparerib called me in to his office after breakfast and asked if I had come to my senses and chosen science for matric. I told him I wasn't changing anything and then took great pleasure in watching his wonky eye dart from side to side in a worried manner. He told me I could still change my mind before the end of the year. I just smiled, and then he congratulated me on the Alan Paton merit certificate. All this attention for a merit award makes me embarrassed—at least if they had only announced a top three, I could have convinced myself that I'd come fourth.

Wednesday 31st July

TEACHERS FOR THE REST OF MY SCHOOLDAYS

ENGLISH .... The Guv (wicked)
AFRIKAANS .... Mongrel (could turn nasty)
MATHS .... Mrs. Bishop (wife of our deranged chaplain)
DRAMA .... Viking (the resident school Hitler)
GEOGRAPHY .... Mr. Erasmus (no nickname, but sneaky, sly, and scary)
HISTORY .... Lennox (brilliant)

It's great to have The Guv back as our English teacher. Within minutes he had a huge debate about school violence flying around the classroom. The Guv reckoned he was all for a bit of violence and said it gave you something to tell your grandchildren about. He then made me read out my merit award Alan Paton essay to the class. Everyone clapped after I was finished. I could also hear Rambo and Boggo making loud suction noises from the back of the classroom.

Friday 2nd August

I got called up in assembly to shake The Glock's hand and receive my merit award for the Alan Paton writing competition. The applause ran out of steam before I even reached the stage! Wish people would stop talking about it—if it was actually any good, I would have made the top ten.

They spelled my name wrong on the certificate. It reads J. Multan. (How can these Alan Paton people take themselves seriously if they can't even spell Milton properly?)

After I'd sat down, The Glock handed out a few ties before getting a bit carried away in his annual speech about discipline. He shouted on about the third term being called the "silly season." He then glared at us like he was sucking a lemon and said that over ninety percent of school expulsions happen in the third term. He then stared at some poor first-year in the front row and said, "Go ahead, those of you who want to test me. . . ." He paused and continued staring daggers at the first-year, who'd sunk low into his seat, before continuing in a deadly whisper, ". . . for my response will be swift and brutal." You could have heard a pin drop. The Glock showed us his big white teeth in a hideous smile and then, with a wild swish of his academic gown, the giant vampire bat left the great hall.

The Crazy Eight has developed what we call "The Glock Radar." If our lunatic headmaster rolls his *r*'s when he speaks, he is considered armed and dangerous. This means The Glock is loaded and ready to fire!

Saturday 3rd August

ATHLETICS TRIALS

It seems a complete waste of time doing track-and-field trials every year. I know I'm never going to make the school team because I'm smaller, slower, and weaker than just about everyone in my age group.

Fatty frantically dug around in his locker, looking for his doctor's slip that says he has a peptic heart murmur. Unfortunately, he couldn't find it, had a panic attack, and then sprinted off to the san like Carl Lewis. Further bad news for Fatty was that Sister Collins was off duty and a dodgy-looking matric boy with acne and greasy hair had been left in charge.

The matric boy told Fatty he had to prove to him that he had a peptic heart murmur. Fatty tore back to the house and then dragged me to the san, with Vern and Runt following convinced that there was some sort of emergency. We all arrived at the san huffing and puffing to find the matric boy lounging around with his feet on Sister Collins's desk. Fatty took some time to find his breath before he said, "This is Spud Milton. He's my witness." The matric boy looked me up and down and said:

MATRIC	You're the poof from the play last year.
FATTY	He was Oliver.
MATRIC	No shit?
FATTY	He only looked like a poof because he had to perm his hair.

MATRIC Nah nah nah . . . he looked like a sheep because he permed his hair. He looks like a poof full stop.

FATTY Okay, he looks a bit like a poof . . . but he scores a surprising amount of chicks.

MATRIC Hot chicks?

FATTY His last chick had huge tits.

I tried to jump into the conversation at this point, but the matric told me to shut up.

MATRIC How big?

FATTY I dunno . . . a grapefruit?

I suddenly had an image of Mermaid's grapefruits and started feeling a little unsteady on my feet.

MATRIC What's he got—a huge dick?

FATTY Nah, his balls haven't even properly dropped yet.

MATRIC No shit?

By now I was getting ready to stab someone with a medical instrument. The matric boy lounged back in his chair and gave a huge sigh and then looked me up and down.

MATRIC You the dude who kept jumping up and down singing solos in chapel last year?

FATTY	That was him. But he's stopped doing all that now.
MATRIC	Jeez, he really is a poof, hey?

The matric let out another huge sigh and opened a packet of jelly babies. He stuffed a handful in his mouth and then chewed for about five minutes. Poor Fatty started salivating and staring longingly at the jelly babies. The matric didn't offer us any and leaned even further back in his chair like he owned the place.

MATRIC	Look, Fatty, I'd like to help you and poof boy here, but while this san is under my control, I won't be handing out any off-sport slips. So luck for the four-hundred-meter hurdles.

I decided that I couldn't leave without saying something.

SPUD	Are you doing athletics trials?
MATRIC	You mad, poof boy?
SPUD	Why not?
MATRIC	'Cause I got an off-sport slip.

He smiled and waved a blue slip at us.

MATRIC	Now piss off and go and shit on someone else's parade.

Poor Fatty started sobbing on the bench outside the san. I tried to cheer him up, but he reckoned that if he was forced to run, he would have a massive brain aneurysm, his head would explode, and he would be left to die on the athletics track in complete agony and torment. He pointed at his massive stomach and said, "Look at me, Spud. Does it look like I'm built for sprints?" I shook my head. He nodded back at me and looked angry. "I mean, my parents are paying twenty grand a year to send me here so that I get a good education, not to break the flippin' four-minute mile."

Boggo appeared out of the morning mist dressed in tiny running shorts that made him look like giant mosquito with long white hairy legs. He nodded at us and said, "The second-worst day of the year." I asked him what the worst day was. He looked up toward Hell's View and said, "Cross-country trials. And guess what—that's next weekend." Boggo threw a thumb at the san and said, "You're wasting your time trying the san while Bernard Duffus is on duty. His nickname's Red Tape." According to Boggo, Red Tape has never issued an off-sport slip on his watch. Apparently, the highlight of his sanatorium assistant career was forcing a first-year with a broken foot to climb Inhlazane last year.

Fatty, Boggo, and I made our way to the long-jump pit, where Mongrel was repeatedly firing his starting pistol into the air and shouting: "Run, you bloody mommy's boys!"

LONG JUMP

Vern's first attempt at long jump saw him diving headfirst into the pit and then noisily chewing sand while people were trying to focus on their run-ups. Fatty's first jump fell well short of the long-jump pit and he spent the next ten minutes furiously rubbing his knee under a tree. Simon won the long jump.

HIGH JUMP

Boggo's the only person who does the scissors jump. With his long woolly legs it's hilarious to watch. Fatty mistimed his acrobatic lunge quite badly and flattened the entire high-jump apparatus. Mad Dog dived over the bar headfirst and managed to clear one and a half meters. Rambo won the high jump.

JAVELIN

Mad Dog was the best in the school last year in our age group. He can throw a javelin miles! My throw was embarrassingly short and Vern nearly killed a small boy running the 200 meters in lane six when he hurled his javelin sideways. Winner: Mad Dog.

SHOT PUT

Fatty won the shot put! I was second worst but only because Boggo fell over on all three throws and was disqualified.

HURDLES

Rambo beat us all by miles. Vern ran straight through the hurdles without jumping and Fatty was disqualified for running around the hurdles and pushing them over from the side.

100-METER SPRINT

My time was 13.45 seconds, which made me fourth, although Boggo reckons he should have beaten me but Vern kept running in his lane and making Darth Vader noises. Rambo clocked 11.8, which is point-three seconds off the school record for the under-sixteen age group.

Mad Dog won the 200 meter, 400 meter, and 800 meter. Rambo said that if he didn't smoke, he would have won the 200 meter. After our trials Fatty got a savage thrashing by Mongrel with a loose piece of hurdle. It turns out that Fatty had only run to the first corner of the 800 meters before diving down and hiding behind the high-jump mats. He then joined the group on the second lap. Bad news for Fatty was that a large crowd of people had gathered especially to watch him in case he vomited, exploded, or had a heart attack.

After his thrashing poor Fatty limped back to the house looking like he did after being stuck in the chapel window last year.

Mental note: Never begin athletics season without an off-sport slip.

Sunday 4th August

The Crazy Eight spent the afternoon attempting to stick the wildebeest head up in the Mad House. It took about two hours because Mad Dog and Rambo kept trying to creep up on us and give us frights with it. Also Fatty's plan of sticking the head to the tree with a combination of drawing pins and chewing gum wasn't as clever as it sounded last night.

The Mad House is looking fantastic. It's now big enough for everyone, it has a real Persian Oriental carpet, and what with the wildebeest head wired to the tree trunk, it makes it look like a hunter's hideaway. Rambo says he is still trying to think of a way to pump electricity into the tree so that he can bring his bar fridge to school. Mad Dog said he would try and build a wind generator. Fatty said if there was a way of catching his natural gas, it could provide electricity to the whole of Natal. Fatty then spent the afternoon trying to fart into bottles. At one stage Fatty reckoned he had turned a bottle of dam water into soda water, but nobody was brave enough to take a sip.

16:30 We found Runt snooping around in the bushes near the Mad House. Rambo was furious and demanded to know what he'd seen. Runt didn't answer and tried to make a break for it, but Mad Dog flattened him with a vicious rugby tackle. He reckons that Runt knows too much and carried him down the bank and tried to drown him in the bog stream.

19:00 African Affairs meeting turned a little nasty when Linton Austin and Luthuli almost punched each other's lights out. It all started when Lennox showed us a video interview with Desmond Tutu (Anglican archbishop and nemesis of my father). Tutu called South Africa the Rainbow Nation and said we have to celebrate our different colors together as one ray of beautiful light. Linton Austin, with his foot up on Lennox's coffee table, said Tutu was a deluded fool and that the real revolution was a class revolution. Luthuli rounded angrily on Austin and told him that apartheid has created a class divide on racial lines and race still means everything in South Africa. Linton called Luthuli "simple" and said that in thirty years' time socialists will look back and say the revolution was wasted on petty racial squabbles and not on creating a communistic state. Luthuli then called Linton a racist. Linton picked up his spectacles and his notebook and stormed out of Lennox's house without uttering a word. I kept my mouth shut the entire night, but even still it was the most riveting AA meeting of the year.

23:10 After the fiery AA meeting I headed back toward the house with my ears stinging from cold and my heart beating abnormally fast. For some reason the lights in the cloisters weren't on and neither was Pissing Pete dribbling any water into the fountain. I marched down a dark passageway that runs behind West House and tripped over what felt like a pile of books and files. I then heard a deep booming voice that shouted, "Stop! Who goes there?" I turned slowly and saw a figure holding a lantern at the end of the corridor. I felt a bit terrified, so I thought I'd better answer straightaway. I told the figure my name but simultaneously had a loud knack jump that echoed around the corridor. The figure strode toward me looking distinctly like a stick insect. I recognized the blue and red sheepskin slippers. It was The Guv. He told me he couldn't sleep, so he thought he would take a stroll and look for paranormal activity. I didn't know if he was being serious or not, so I nodded as if it was a normal thing for a teacher to be doing at eleven o'clock on a Sunday night. "Walk with me, Milton," he said. "There's more than one that drifts these halls."

The Guv and I must have covered the whole school. We didn't see any ghosts, but I did manage to tell him all about the Milton England adventure. We found ourselves on the under-fourteen cricket field where I played last year. In the moonlight it looked much smaller than I remember it. We stood chatting on the pitch and it was only after some time that I realized The Guv was quoting Macbeth while taking a pee. He says it's good luck for the coming season. When he had finished, he said, "To bed at once, young man! This late revelry leaves an old man's bones dead to the marrow." He then waved his walking stick and cried, "Exit! Pursued by a bear!"

I sprinted back to the house with the wind screaming in my ears and the freezing night air biting at my face.

Monday 5th August

WELCOME TO AUSCHWITZ!

06:30 Vern shook my hand at roll call and said it was the first of August. He then shouted, "Oi!" at Spike, who was running along the cloisters with three cups of tea. Spike didn't stop or listen. I took a look at the misery that surrounded me—everyone lined up in their trench coats, clutching at mugs of tea and breathing waves of steam into the freezing morning gloom.

Anderson kicked Barryl in the bum for being late and Emberton kicked Thinny in the knee for not showering. Anderson then moved along the lineup looking for trouble. He soon discovered that one of the Darryls was missing a shoelace. He seemed to take this personally and picked the Darryl off the ground with one hand while Emberton kneed him in the nuts. Anderson then dropped him in the gutter and moved on to J. R. Ewing's haircut. Mad Dog nudged me in the ribs and pointed at his right shoe, saying, "Check, Spuddo, guess whose shoe-lace?" Boggo turned to Fatty and said he was amazed that Anderson and Emberton could get away with concentration camp violence in the main quad. He then spread his arms and said, "Welcome to Auschwitz!" Emberton overheard him and called him a mommy's boy before thumping his head into the gutter. Boggo screamed like he had been shot and collapsed onto the floor like he had been shot (it's a plastic gutter). For some reason Mad Dog saw red and grabbed Emberton by the lapels of his trench coat and head butted him straight between the eyes. (It sounded like two planks of wood being smashed together.) Emberton reeled back with blood pouring out of his nose.

Anderson immediately canceled roll call and he, Pike, and Death Breath dragged Mad Dog up to Anderson's room while Emberton was led off to the sanatorium with a battered face. Julian also went to the san because he said he needed treatment for shock.

06:35 Anderson told Mad Dog that he was a disgrace to the house because Emberton was a senior, a prefect, and his own cousin. Our head of house then thrashed Mad Dog six strokes with his sawn-off hockey stick. We could hear the sound of it from downstairs.

11:00 Anderson and Emberton (with red nose and swollen face) were hauled into Sparerib's office. Boggo has it that Darryl (the one who was roughed up this morning) ran off to Sparerib's house and said he wanted to go home like the other Darryl. He then told Sparerib about the fighting at roll call.

11:10 Mad Dog was called into Sparerib's office. By this stage there was a fair-sized crowd milling around the quad outside our housemaster's office. Julian was practically leaning against the office door pretending to be engrossed in the sports pages of the newspaper. Boggo was pacing up and down like a nervous father in a hospital waiting room desperate for the first news from inside.

AUSCHWITZ SCORECARD

ANDERSON	Escaped with a warning
EMBERTON	De-prefected and put on final warning
MAD DOG	Put on final warning
DARRYL	Was probably given a hug and a cookie
RAMBO	Put on final warning despite not being involved

It seems these final warnings are a serious threat. They mean that even being caught night swimming could get them expelled! Emberton looked livid after being sacked as a prefect. I overheard him saying that he was going to murder the Darryl by inserting a toilet plunger up his bum and then sucking out his insides. The Darryl spent the day crying on his bed and phoning home.

Tuesday 6th August

The juniors' dance is just over two weeks away and we have to invite a date! I became so agitated when I heard the news that I had to breathe deeply and make a list. (I only really know two girls, so it turned out more like a short list.) Boggo and Fatty also looked a bit stressed, while Vern says he is definitely inviting Anneline Kriel. We have to send our invites in by next Monday or else we have to attend the dance alone, which, according to Rambo, means you're either ugly or a poof.

The second Darryl has bitten the dust. For the first time this year he was all smiles as the Normal Seven helped him carry his trunk and bags down the stairs. Anderson tried to shake his hand as he was leaving, but the Darryl was having none of it and stalked off toward his mom, who was waiting outside Sparerib's office. Poor Sparerib was trying to put on a good show for the Darryl's mom, but he was looking awkward and shifting his weight nervously from foot to foot. We were all hiding behind the house door trying to peep around the corner to see what was going on. Vern had pole position and was checking out the action from the crack in the door. Mad Dog chose that moment to make a deafening baboon call and pushed Vern through the door and into the main quad.

Sparerib wasn't impressed and called Vern over to apologize to the Darryl's mother for behaving like an animal. Behind the house door we were cracking up at Vern, who was blushing bloodred and shaking hands with everyone. Vern then stood back and furiously picked his nose. Sparerib told him to get lost, so he saluted the Darryl and strode past the Crazy Eight and spent the next twenty minutes staring at the house urinal and jotting down pages of notes in his pocket notebook.

After lights-out the Crazy Eight (including Roger) paid what Rambo calls a "hospitality visit" to the first-years. Rambo told them that now that they only have six members, they can't be called the Normal Seven anymore. Spike pointed out that the Crazy Eight only has seven members and is still called the Crazy Eight. Boggo poked Spike in the eye with a ruler and reminded him that Roger was the eighth member. Barryl then stood up and said he thought that the Normal Seven should have a new name. J. R. Ewing argued that the whole school knew them as the Normal Seven and if they changed their name now, they would lose their identity. Rambo glared at J. R. and said, "But you pricks have no identity. That's the point!" Fatty interrupted and argued that if you're famous for being boring, you're still famous. There was a lot of arguing, and eventually there was a vote. Or rather two votes. Firstly, the Normal Seven all voted for their name to stay the same, except for Barryl, who said he wanted a change. The Crazy Eight all voted for a new name for our first-years. Since we are more senior, the Crazy Eight won the election. Within minutes our first-years were rechristened the Sad Six.

THE SAD SIX

Spike
Thinny
J. R. Ewing
Darryl (the last remaining)
Runt
Barryl (the black Darryl)

Rambo tried to psyche up the Sad Six with a fiery speech about seizing the day and not being a bunch of girls. It didn't seem to help because after he had finished, they all got straight into bed without saying a word. As we trooped back into our dormitory after yet another boring first-years hospitality visit, Fatty shook his head and looked at us sadly. "You know, they just don't get it. Here we are trying to open up their horizons and it's like you've got to check if they're still breathing. I mean, what thanks do we ever get?"

Wednesday 7th August

Sparerib called an emergency house meeting and repeated The Glock's speech from last week's assembly word for word. Then he announced that various boys were on final warning and that Emberton had been suspended as a prefect. (Obviously, Emberton's sugar baron father has already been on the phone to Sparerib because earlier at lunchtime, Emberton was completely de-prefected and on the verge of expulsion.)

Between his wonky eye and his good eye Sparerib was able to glare at everyone in the common room at once. He said, "This house will be peaceful. This house will be under control. And most of all, this house will behave! Now I'm not saying it's all of you, but there are certain bad elements in this house [*lingering look at Pike*] who seem hell-bent on being revolutionary. [*Vicious look at Rambo.*] Tonight I am making it abundantly clear to those bad elements in this house who seek to undermine the good work and honest toil done by the vast majority of boys in this fine house that I will stop at nothing to hunt you down and punish you to the full extent of the law!"

There was dead silence. Mad Dog and Rambo looked at the floor. Boggo twiddled his fingers and Vern pulled out some hair with a thunk. Sparerib glared at us for some time before marching out of the common room and slamming the door. Pike bleated loudly like a sheep, but Anderson told him to shut up. Then Pike marched up to Anderson and said, "Kiss my balls, ass licker." He smirked and walked past Anderson, nudging him slightly on the way. Anderson didn't respond and slunk up to his room looking like a man with no authority.

Thursday 8th August

Luthuli charged into the dormitory to tell me that he had heard from a source on the inside that De Klerk is soon to announce a new constitution that will be one man, one vote. The Crazy Eight didn't know what to make of the head boy coming in to talk politics with me like we were best buddies. Vern seemed to be very embarrassed or feeling guilty because he put his head in his locker and pretended to be looking for something until Luthuli had left. Nobody said anything to me, but I could hear faint grumblings and insults from the far end of the dormitory.

Friday 9th August

Just had a weird meeting with Sparerib. He hauled me into his office and asked me if there was anything I knew about that he should know about. I didn't answer, and there was a nasty pause before he said, "John, listen to me. There's nothing wrong with putting things right. We've already lost three boys this year. I need to know what's going on in this house and more specifically in your dormitory." I did my best to keep my cool and avoid getting caught in the spell of Sparerib's wonky left eye. I spoke slowly in my deepest voice. "No, sir, there's nothing you should know." I marched out of his office feeling unbeatable, like a man who had defeated his torturers. Rambo was hanging around in the quad outside Sparerib's office. I gave him a thumbs-up, but he glared at me like I'd somehow betrayed him.

22:00 Fatty has invented a brilliant new game called Bread a Head.

BREAD A HEAD RULES

- The dormitory dustbin is placed on Runt's head.
- (Runt has to be used because the dustbin perfectly fits his head.)
- Runt has to stagger about and NOT fall over.
- Each player is given a slice of bread and selects a position.
- Each player is stationary and CANNOT follow Runt.
- The aim is to land your slice of bread on the top of the bin.
- The last person to land their bread on top loses. (And his bread slice is eaten by Fatty.)
- If your bread slice falls off or misses the bin, you are disqualified. (And your bread slice is eaten by Fatty.)
- The winner gets a free shot of Mellowwood brandy on Sunday at the Mad House.

Surprisingly, Boggo won the game, although it must be said it was a clever move to jab poor Runt in the stomach with his hockey stick. Runt collapsed onto his knees because he was winded and Boggo dropped the winning slice of bread onto the bin. After the competition Fatty removed the bin from Runt's head and the tape around his mouth. Runt burst into tears, so Fatty gave him a Lunch Bar and said, "Well played."

Once Runt had gone back to bed, Simon asked me why Luthuli had come by the other day. I started telling him about our AA meetings and was about to give him a crash course on South African politics when suddenly Rambo started shouting at me and telling me that my attitude sucks and that I have no guts or Crazy Eight spirit. I didn't know what was happening. There stood Vern shining his torch on me, and the rest of the Crazy Eight had gathered around and were nodding and agreeing with Rambo! I felt the blood draining from my face. Not only did it feel like I was about to be clobbered, but it seemed that everybody was united against me!

Rambo's angry face was inches from mine. He said, "We don't care what you do in your spare time or at your faggoty AA meetings, Spud. You think you're this big revolutionary intellectual hotshot dude hanging around Luthuli like he's some sort of hero." Rambo grabbed the torch from Vern and shone it directly in my eyes. "Your little secret coffee club and your up-the-bum meetings and lunches with The Guv—I mean is that ass creeping or what? And your cozy little meetings with Sparerib where you probably tell him about what I'm doing and show him your diary." I tried to tell him that I hadn't spilled the beans to Sparerib, but he hadn't finished ranting and raving about my diary. "Every single day we know you write about us and you go on about how great you are and how everyone loves you and what a great actor you are. Well, it's crap—it's all crap and we can prove it! We can prove it because we were here and we saw it with our own eyes. So write what you want, but we all know you're a phony!"

There was dead silence. I knew everyone agreed with Rambo. I could feel the horrible atmosphere in the dormitory. It was cold. In two minutes the Crazy Eight had gone from friends to enemies. Even Vern was glaring at me with something that felt like hatred.

I waited until Rambo released the front of my T-shirt. I felt relieved that he wasn't going to hit me, although this didn't make up for the sudden loss of all my friends.

I lay in bed with everything humming and spinning. When I tried to close my eyes, large yellow and red shapes rose up deep in my head. There was a pain in my stomach halfway between my belly button and my chest bone. It felt like a giant octopus wrapping its tentacles around my organs and then squeezing them slowly in one long movement. I felt so homesick.

Saturday 10th August

Feeling crap after last night, and cross-country trials made things even worse. I spent the day moping around feeling like a loser. Nobody spoke to me, and I sat alone at lunch and dinner.

Mom phoned in the afternoon to say that Dad's driven off to the Transkei after giving her an hour's warning. Apparently, a ship called the *Oceanos* sank off the Transkei coast last week and Dad and Frank have gone looking for treasure.

Still haven't got a date for the juniors' dance.

Mental note: Never assume you're a nice person just because nobody's bothered to tell you otherwise.

Sunday 11th August

SPUD'S BACK!

At least I think I'm back. Rambo said that if I drank half a cup of neat Mellowwood brandy at the Mad House that would prove to the Crazy Eight that my loyalty was back and that I could be trusted again. Rambo didn't wait for me to reply. He just started pouring. I figured this wasn't the right time to argue, so I downed the horrible liquid and then had a coughing fit.

The brandy made me very drunk and I had to be helped down the tree by Mad Dog. Boggo fed me toothpaste so that the prefects wouldn't smell the booze on my breath and Rambo ordered me to go to bed before supper and promised that the Crazy Eight would spread a story about me having a minor case of swamp fever.

On the way back to school I threw up against a tree. I remember the others howling with laughter and making funny comments. While everyone headed to dinner, I found myself in the phone room with the phone against my ear. I could hear ringing on the other end of the line. Then I heard Mermaid's voice. Two minutes later I put down the phone, staggered up the stairs, and fell into bed.

I've got a date for the juniors' dance!

Mental note: In times of sheer horror down half a cup of brandy.

Monday 12th August

The worst hangover ever. Good news is that the Crazy Eight is talking to me again and so far Mermaid hasn't phoned to cancel.

Mental note: Never touch alcohol again.

Wednesday 14th August

Order has been restored to the house after a weird week. Nevertheless, I've been keeping a low profile and have stopped writing in my diary during prep. After two days of feeling completely bulletproof, I'm now terrified about seeing Mermaid on Saturday night.

MERMAID PHOBIAS/QUESTIONS, ETC.

1. General awkwardness.
2. How do I deal with the fact that she dumped me and then ran off with a Golf-driving surfer?
3. Should I tell her that I've been stalking her since March?
4. Do I have to tell her that I kissed Amanda?
5. Should I use Simon's Ego or my Mum for Men deodorant?

I'm determined to make sure that I don't turn into jelly and then conveniently forget that this woman dumped me on Valentine's Day. (Or near enough.) At the very least she deserves a lecture on how depressed and hurt I was. Boggo reckons I should throw in something about trust and how the trust between us has been shattered. Then when Mermaid asks how she can make it up to me, I should pull down my pants and demand oral sex! I told Boggo I'd think about it.

After compiling quite a few lists, I wrote out my final list and stuck it to the inside of my locker.

OBJECTIVES FOR MISSION MERMAID

1. Get an explanation for being viciously dumped on Valentine's Day.
2. Establish what happened to the surfer boyfriend.
3. Tell her how much she hurt me. (Tears at this point will not be frowned upon.)
4. Tell her the trust is broken.
5. Forgiveness. (This is not to be given within the first hour of her arrival.)
6. Kiss (should be passionate).
7. Oral sex (depending on her response to point four).

Thursday 15th August

The tension is mounting. I've fallen behind in work for all my subjects except history. I can't concentrate for longer than about thirty seconds without thinking about Mermaid. It's been so long since I've seen her up close that I struggle to imagine what her face looks like.

CRAZY EIGHT DANCE DATES

SIMON	Vanessa Spalding (hot)
RAMBO	Vivian Grey (average to everyone except Rambo)
FATTY	No date (embarrassing)
SPUD	Mermaid (scorchingly hot)
BOGGO	Tanya (Alison's fat friend—now former friend)
ROGER	Doesn't know any female cats because he was castrated at birth
MAD DOG	No date (Mad Dog has a life ban from all dances and socials.)
VERN	Anneline Kriel (Boggo is offering 100 million-1 odds on her actually rocking up.)

Friday 16th August

Pike, Emberton, and Devries have wagered the Crazy Eight that between the three of them, they could kiss at least one of our dates tomorrow night. Boggo marched up to Pike and thrust out his hand and said, "A hundred bucks! I bet you a hundred bucks that none of you will grab one of our dates." Pike's upper lip curled upward into a smirk as he said, "I certainly wouldn't grab that humpbacked whale you're bringing." Devries sniggered and elbowed Emberton in the ribs. Emberton chortled and then thrashed his sugarcane onto my locker a few times. I met his stare and eventually he backed off.

Once the three matrics had left, Boggo told us that the bet was on behalf of all of us. He looked at us grimly and said, "So you guys better keep control of your chicks or we'll lose some serious pocket money."

Just another worry to add to the list.

Saturday 17th August

I was a nervous wreck by lunchtime. By five o'clock I was having migraines and struggling to breathe.

A team of first-years had transformed the hall from a boring old dining hall into a boring old dining hall with streamers hanging off the chandeliers. The kitchen staff had changed the tablecloths and Reverend Bishop had donated secondhand church candles for all the tables and the cloisters.

Bad news is that Pike and Anderson have been chosen as the DJs for the party. Boggo seems very worried about this. He says it is a known fact that lifesavers, doctors, and DJs get the most sex.

19:00 I stood in the main quad watching thin fingers of mist sliding over the library roof. The cloisters were lit by flickering candles in brown bags, and a crowd of terrified boys gathered around the main archway waiting for their dates to arrive. Others were leading their girls proudly (or not so proudly) across the quad in the direction of the Great Hall. I was too scared to wait at the front entrance with all the other boys, so I pretended to be entranced by the cloister candles instead. After about a minute of entrancement I decided to be brave and wait at the school entrance. Obviously my brain and my body weren't in agreement because I found myself walking back toward the house door instead.

"Hey, Spud! I heard the St. Catherine's bus just pulled in," said Boggo as he sprinted across the quad. I followed him across the quad feeling nauseous. All the boys were looking edgy, and everywhere was loud bragging, mocking, and the odd friendly beating. Cars were pulling up to the front of the school, and each time a girl would get out of her parents' car looking embarrassed. If the new arrival was beautiful, the noise would die down to a murmur as everyone stopped talking to gawk. If the bride was no oil painting, there would be loud laughter and farm animal noises.

I recognized Marge's car. It stopped directly in front of the crowd of boys. The passenger door opened and a pair of black high heels clicked onto the cobblestone paving. A door slammed and Marge drove away—other than that there was complete silence. I stepped forward and held out my hand to her. There was a flash of white teeth, a flick of wispy blond hair, and the feeling of her soft lips on mine. I led Mermaid through the crowd. Every single boy had his eyes on her. It was impossible not to.

I was soon reminded that this wasn't a dream when there was a loud shout from the direction of the vestry roof. Everyone stopped in their tracks and watched in amazement at the action happening above us and about six feet below our old first-year dormitory.

Dressed in trench coats, the Sad Six were all lined up along the vestry roof. I could see somebody pointing and directing from the dormitory window but couldn't see the mastermind himself.

Suddenly the Sad Six turned away from us and dropped their trench coats. They were stark naked and each backside had a letter painted on it. Reading from left to right, the six letters read:

MAD GOD

Unfortunately for Mad Dog, his infamously crap spelling meant that Thinny and J. R. Ewing were positioned on the wrong side of Barryl, so the joke was on him. Barryl (the letter *O*) stood out because he had white paint while the others had luminous green paint. Even worse news was that Anderson had witnessed the entire performance and had charged off to find his sawn-off hockey stick.

I could never thank Mad Dog enough. It was the icebreaker we needed, and soon the Mermaid and I were laughing and sharing stories like old times. I noticed Mermaid kept touching my arm when she was talking to me and she kept saying how great it was to see me again. So far I'd achieved absolutely zero objectives from Mission Mermaid.

I showed Mermaid to our table. I must admit it didn't look good. Vern looked completely distressed that Anneline Kriel hadn't rocked up and sat at the head of the table muttering to himself like Gollum. Fatty was finishing off the last of the garnish. (I assume he'd already finished the snacks.) Boggo's date, Tanya, was twice the size of me and had an eyebrow that stretched across her face like the Great Wall of China. Boggo didn't speak to his date and spent the entire dinner trying to edge closer to Mermaid and asked her a series of dumb questions. Whenever she said something, Boggo would stare at her breasts and pretend to be deep in thought about what the Mermaid had just said. Tanya was also glaring at Mermaid while trying to swallow an entire bread roll.

Dinner was tough. Fatty ate like a pig and dripped gravy all over his white shirt. Vern started breathing like Darth Vader again and placed his photograph of Anneline Kriel at the empty place setting to his right. Boggo waited patiently for Tanya to finish gorging herself on a chunk of rare roast beef before offering her a peppermint and a walk in the rose garden. As he was standing up, Boggo shoved a spoon in his mouth and gave us a demonstration of what he was expecting in the rose garden. Mermaid blushed and looked away. Unfortunately, this meant that she was looking straight at Vern, who seemed to be arguing with his dessert spoon. After a minute Mermaid and I followed Boggo and Tanya out of the hall and headed out through the main archway in the direction of the cricket fields.

We sheltered from the freezing drizzle under a pine tree near the cricket nets. Mermaid leaned against the tree and shivered. I stood opposite her with my hands in my pockets, took a deep breath, and asked the question:

What happened?

Mermaid stared at me like I'd just asked her to execute someone. She waved her fingers near her face as if to cool herself down, also took a deep breath, and said, "I've been practicing this for four months." I didn't say anything because I was counting back months to April. She sent me a birthday card on my birthday, so that must have been a sign. The only reason I hadn't replied in the end was because Simon said I would be castrating myself if I did. This also meant that all the time I had been hiding in her bushes watching her like a pervert, I could have just walked up the driveway and kissed her!

Mermaid talked until my face went numb with cold. Most of it I didn't listen to because at one stage she said she still loved me and I struggled to concentrate on anything she said after that.

The surfer dude in the white Golf goes by the name of Cameron. (Just the sort of name I was expecting.) When she first mentioned him, I had a vivid image in my mind of beating him to a pulp in front of the Mermaid. But then she told me that he has a karate black belt and can also throw knives and eat fire, so it's probably better that I resent him from afar.

After Mermaid's marathon apology I told her that I forgave her and said that what's past should stay in the past. Unfortunately, that set her off crying and going on about what a terrible person she was. I didn't know what to do, so I just stood under the tree and watched her sobbing in respectful silence. Eventually she stopped crying and told me I was her soul mate and that she wants to be friends with me forever.

This was bad news.

Rambo reckons that when a girl says she wants to be friends, it means she either finds you repulsive or she's found a guy who's hung like a donkey. I tried to flush the nasty image of well-hung farm animals out of my mind and racked my brains for something clever to say. All I could manage was, "Me too." I was just starting to work up the courage to move forward to try and kiss her when we were interrupted by Boggo and Tanya. Boggo looked red in the face and had a disturbing grin on his face. Tanya had wet grass stuck to the back of her pants and looked a little out of breath. I thought Boggo had approached for a reason, but instead he pinned Tanya against the tree and started kissing her right in front of us. I noticed him squinting at Mermaid out of the corner of his eye while he plunged his tongue down Tanya's throat. Boggo was also making weird groaning noises and breathing loudly through his nose, so Mermaid and I decided to make a break for the Great Hall.

Back at the dance, things were looking a bit grim. Fatty had apparently thrown up under a table after nearly choking to death on his toothpick. Mad Dog was also making loud sheep bleats and mooning people in the quad at regular intervals from the safety of the vestry roof.

"Walk Like an Egyptian" began playing, and Mermaid said she was feeling sorry for Vern and skipped onto the dance floor and started dancing with my deranged cubicle mate, who was making strange robotic movements in the far corner by himself. Vern blushed bright red and his tongue hung out of the corner of his mouth as he concentrated on his spasmodic dance moves. He looked absolutely thrilled when Mermaid began dancing with him and started inching in closer and grinning at her in a worrying fashion. Around me guys were saying, "No way! Check it out." Someone said it looked like beauty and the beast.

Suddenly DJ Pike switched on the mirror ball and Emberton darted down from the DJ booth, strode onto the dance floor, and told Vern to get lost. Emberton then grabbed Mermaid's hand and started slow dancing with her. The music abruptly changed and Pike played The Bangles' "Eternal Flame." (No doubt the matrics were hunting as a pack and they'd identified Mermaid as their target!) Mermaid seemed a little uncomfortable about being so close to Emberton, whose right hand was slowly edging down her back toward her bum. Vern didn't look too happy with developments either and started slow dancing with an imaginary partner right next to them.

Suddenly a strong hand grabbed me by the collar of my blazer and yanked me backward. It was Rambo. "Spud, wake up, you dipshit! Emberton's closing in! Snap out of it!" Then Boggo was in my face, saying, "You can't let him steal your Mermaid! Oh, and by the way, if your chick grabs Emberton, then I'm having a go after he's finished with her."

I strode onto the dance floor like I was ready for a fight. Thank God, Mermaid broke away from Emberton the moment she saw me, and soon she and I were slow dancing together. I looked into her eyes and started moving in for the big kiss, but yet again the moment was ruined. There was a shriek of static and Pike's booming voice came over the microphone. "Ladies and gentlemen! A big hand for Devries for hitting the jackpot!" A spotlight shone against the far wall of the dance floor and there were Devries and Tanya grabbing each other. Everyone cheered and Devries carried on kissing her while raising his left fist in triumph. Boggo and Rambo sprinted onto the dance floor, but it was too late. There was a shriek of static and Pike's voice boomed over the microphone again. "Sorry, Boggo, but your girl says you smell of fish paste and your dick's too small. Oh, and thanks for the hundred bucks, guys!"

So we lost our bet, Boggo lost his date, and Tanya lost her reputation.

I didn't have the guts to kiss Mermaid in front of Marge's car, so I gave her a lame hug instead. I watched Marge's car disappear into the mist and kicked a stone off the road. I should have kissed her. I definitely should have kissed her.

I felt a thump on my back—it was Rambo. "Hey, Spud, what's the point of having a hot chick if you're gonna treat her like your sister? No wonder she dumped you." I felt a familiar feeling—it was the feeling of dropping an easy catch in a cricket match.

I lay in bed, staring at the ceiling, replaying the night in my head. I had had three definite chances to make my move and had chickened out every time.

Mental note: When in doubt, kiss her.

Sunday 18th August

Woke up early in the morning feeling exhausted. I tried to go back to sleep, but Vern was making a loud whistling sound in his nose, so I gave up and headed for the showers. Because everyone was still asleep, I had a twenty-minute shower, during which time I replayed a highlights version of last night in my head. Unfortunately, my early morning meditation was disturbed by Julian, who strode into the showers wearing a bright red satin dressing gown and looking terribly upset. I said hello and then to avoid an awkward moment, I washed my hair. When I had finished a thorough washing of my hair, I opened my eyes to see Julian sobbing and holding his wrist against his forehead. I asked him what was wrong. He said, "Spud, oh, Spud, please don't make me explain—it's too difficult." I nodded and switched off my shower. Julian then called me a "coldhearted brute" and ordered me to switch on my shower again. By now I had been showering and cleaning myself for over half an hour and my skin was turning bright pink like a prawn.

"Today is my last Eucharist," said Julian. "Next Friday, I leave this school forever." I didn't know what to say, so I told him that the thought of him leaving made me very sad as well. Julian told me I had a pure soul and that I would make somebody very happy one day. He then started howling again. Thankfully, Vern arrived for a bog inspection and started accusing somebody in the toilet of bad form in the bogs and surrounds. I took the gap, switched off my tap, and made a break for it.

10:00 Pike, Devries, and Emberton marched into our dormitory and demanded their winnings. Poor Boggo was forced to hand over a hundred bucks to the man who had kissed his date! Pike told us that the next time we couldn't satisfy our women, he'd be happy to fill in for a special rate of fifty bucks. Then he turned to me and said, "So I hear your girlfriend dumped you because you're a poof." I tried to laugh along, but the sound that came out of my mouth sounded harsh and high-pitched.

17:00 Mad Dog was beaten three by Sparerib and put on absolute final warning for his bad behavior last night.

20:00 Mom phoned to say that all Dad had returned with from his Transkei treasure hunt was two speeding fines and a bout of flu.

Monday 19th August

15:30 Had an hour-long phone call to Mermaid. I can't remember what we talked about, although we did spend the last half of the conversation arguing about who was going to say goodbye first. Eventually Death Breath came into the phone room and told me to get off the phone because he wanted to phone his sick granny. Mermaid and I both said goodbye together.

Bad news is that Mermaid mentioned the *f* word again. Even worse is that she reckons she talks to me like she does to her girlfriends. She says this means we have a special bond.

Now even Mermaid thinks I'm gay!

Wednesday 21st August

Had a rather unsuccessful afternoon fumbling around in the human physiology section of the library looking for a green and white striped book on human anatomy. Boggo says there's a picture on page 124 of a brunette with a "nine out of ten" pair of knockers. Since he also rates Mermaid's boobs as a nine out of ten (and since I've never seen Mermaid's boobs), I was trying to get an idea of what I might expect to see in the hopefully not-too-distant future. I'm also making a conscious effort to be more manly.

After searching all over the Biology section, I eventually found the green and white striped book on human anatomy hiding between a manual on skin disease and a book on renal failure. Page 124 had been ripped out.

"Milton the poet!" boomed a loud voice right behind me.

The librarian (Mrs. Hall) shot The Guv a dirty look that he completely ignored. He peered at the books behind me and then frowned at me over the rims of his horn-rimmed spectacles and cried, "Biology, Milton, biology? Have you gone ball-bouncingly crackers?" There was a loud, "Shhhhhh," from the returns desk and Mrs. Hall shook her head at us and looked sour. I told The Guv that I was reading up on the plague. The Guv staggered back looking horrified and cried, "You haven't got the clap, have you?" (Not sure what the clap is, but it sounds worse than the plague.) I then asked him what he was doing in the Biology section. "Oh, the usual, Milton," he replied. "Page 124 of the green and white striped book, of course." I informed The Guv about the missing page. He shouted, "Balls!" and thumped his walking stick on the floor. Mrs. Hall then lost her temper and shouted at The Guv and told him he was setting a poor example to the boys. The Guv shouted back at Mrs. Hall and told her that her library was a complete disgrace and that the Biology shelves were in utter turmoil. He tapped me on the leg with his stick and whispered, "You see how she flirts?" He then stood up straight and said, "Monday lunch, Milton. You, me, and the EEC." With that he stormed out of the library, slamming the door behind him.

I told Boggo that The Guv knew about page 124 of the green and white striped book and that meant the book must have been around when The Guv was a student! Boggo seemed quite thrilled about it and said that this confirmed his belief that "a good pair of knockers are forever."

Friday 23rd August

Barryl arrived at my bed after lunch and said that I had to report to Julian's bed immediately. (I assumed that he meant bedroom.) I knocked on Julian's door and there was a long pause and then a loud shout of, "Come!" When Julian saw me, he placed his hand on his chest and gasped, "Oh, thank God it's you. I thought it was Anderson. He really is a giant prick, you know, and I don't mean that as a compliment."

Julian closed his curtains and then turned on me like I'd done something wrong. "Spud, you depress me, you really do." I didn't know what he was talking about, so I did my usual trick of shaking my head and looking sadly out the window. Unfortunately, the curtains were closed, so I must have looked like an idiot. Julian didn't seem to notice and carried on with his speech. "I watch you out there in the congregation every Sunday looking alienated and rejected and my heart feels like it could just burst." I nodded and tried my best to look alienated and rejected. Julian placed his arm around my shoulders and said, "Poor boy."

"So," continued Julian in a voice that didn't quite sound his own, "I have decided that in my final days as head chorister, I am going to bestow a presidential pardon on you. You are herewith christened a tenor and you are once again a member of the choir." I wasn't quite expecting this news, so as a result I couldn't think of a single thing to say. "But," said Julian with a finger pointed upward, "I have one condition, and one condition only. You are under no circumstances to sing!" I told Julian it was a crazy idea, but Julian would have none of it. He said in a year's time, when I have a tenor voice that can melt chocolate, I will get down on my knees and thank him. Then he started sniffing and going on about how much he'll miss the choir and the school. I couldn't exactly turn him down, so I thanked him and left.

There is no way in hell I'm going back to the choir until I can sing without having a knack jump or sounding like a toucan.

Sunday 25th August

I told Julian I couldn't sing with the choir today because I didn't know any of the hymns. I explained that without knowing the hymns, my lip synching would be out of synch. I then promised him I would take *Hymns Ancient & Modern* home with me and learn the songs over the long weekend. Julian sucked the whole lot in, unaware that he was being conned by a cunning Spud Milton.

Rambo, Fatty, and Mad Dog have spent the entire weekend in the Mad House. They haven't even slept in the dormitory! By the time the rest of us joined them for free bounds, they were completely smashed and had tied themselves to the tree with ropes so that in their drunken state they didn't fall out. Rambo reckoned they'd finished a bottle of brandy and a bottle of vodka and smoked two packets of cigarettes between them since Saturday morning. Rambo organized one of the grounds staff to buy the booze and cigarettes from the station café in return for a huge tip. Thankfully, there were only a few Camels left, so I wasn't forced to smoke. I noticed two big black wings hanging from the ceiling of the Mad House. Turns out Mad Dog shot a crow with his catapult. Fatty wasn't impressed with the crow's wings, though, and said they would bring bad luck to the Mad House. Mad Dog said he didn't believe in luck and that he had a drawer of crows' wings at home and nothing bad has ever happened to him.

Monday 26th August

LUNCHEON WITH THE GUV AND THE EEC

I wasn't quite sure who or what the EEC was, so I was a little apprehensive as I made my way across Trafalgar toward The Guv's house for our Monday lunch. I found my English teacher fast asleep in his rocking chair with a huge pile of books on his coffee table. I cleared my throat and coughed. The Guv didn't stir. I didn't know whether I should shake his arm or call out, "Sir." Either way I was certain to give him a fright. I decided to retreat into the kitchen and then out the back door and start again. I waited a few seconds and then knocked loudly.

"Milton the poet!" came the instant reply. Then The Guv shouted, "Speak, friend, and enter!" I made a second entry through the kitchen and into his living room. The Guv was now standing over his pile of books looking like he had never been asleep. He tapped away at the top of the pile with the handles of his glasses and said, "Milton—meet the EEC." I grinned like a cretin, not knowing what he was talking about and too embarrassed to admit it.

Turns out that EEC is actually a poet. His name is E. E. Cummings, but he writes it as ee cummings.

The Guv began by threatening to shove my head into the fire if I so much as sniggered at EEC's name. The Guv said, "For some unknown and unfathomable reason this school only allows third-years and matrics to read his work. It pains me to say that you haven't met this genius before." I asked The Guv if it had sex in it. The Guv said there was no sex in it, but he'd had a lot of sex because of it.

"The reason, Milton, why this man's poetry is deemed dangerous to young minds is because he doesn't use any punctuation."

The Guv was right. ee cummings doesn't use any punctuation at all and doesn't use capital letters for his initials or name. The Guv called him a literary pioneer and then told me that if I attempted to copy EEC's punctuation, he'd fail me and have me tortured.

After lunch he made me read out a poem called in just spring (notice no punctuation). I must admit I found it a beautiful poem but very difficult to read. Because there were no full stops, my brain wouldn't let me stop to breathe. I must have been racing along in my reading because The Guv thumped his spoon on the table and accused me of a massacre. The next time I read it through, he repeatedly pinged his fork against his wineglass to indicate where I should breathe.

I eventually mastered the EEC. The Guv's right. The man is a genius.

Inspired by the EEC, I wrote Mermaid a short love poem without any punctuation in it. I then posted it off and immediately regretted my decision. I'm not sure if the Mermaid is a poemy type of girl.

21:00 At lights-out Anderson announced that Fatty had been elected by the matrics and post-matrics to be the junior house tug-of-war captain. The big showdown takes place on Trafalgar on Wednesday, and

Fatty has to choose a team of six, including himself. Fatty held immediate trials, which resulted in Vern and me having an arm-wrestle to decide who was going to take the final place on the tug-of-war team.

The duel between my cubicle mate and me was very evenly matched. Our fists were locked in a shaky standoff, and I watched in fascination as Vern's face grew redder and redder as he strained to overpower my hand. Unfortunately for Vern, he sneezed and Fatty disqualified him on the spot. Vern was bitterly disappointed and marched off to the bogs muttering to himself and stamping his feet as he walked.

Fatty then woke up the Sad Six and organized a knockout competition to decide who was the strongest first-year. In the first round Spike dislocated Runt's finger and Darryl was so scared of arm wrestling Barryl that he disqualified himself without giving a reason. In the end Barryl easily beat J. R. Ewing in the final.

I have to take on Barryl tomorrow night at 10 p.m.

Tuesday 27th August

22:00 Our bout lasted about three seconds. Barryl shook hands with the Crazy Eight and I slunk off to my bed feeling embarrassed and, like Vern, pretended to fall asleep while everyone else discussed tactics.

Wednesday 28th August

Thanks to some heavy overnight rain, Trafalgar field was extremely soggy for the tug-of-war competition. (This was according to Boggo's mid-morning pitch report.) Rambo (despite not being captain) called the team together after lunch and changed tactics. The new tactics involved Fatty tying the end of the rope around his waist and digging his feet deep into the ground. He was the anchorman. The plan was then for the rest of our team to wait until the opposition had exerted all their energy in trying to pull Fatty out from six inches below the surface of the field and then the rest of the team would simply reel the opposition in like an exhausted fish.

Mad Dog took Fatty's old rugby boots and nailed a metal toe cap onto the front of each boot. He then sharpened each toe cap with a flint stone so that the points could dig deep into the soft ground and make it impossible to move him.

The plan worked brilliantly and completely demoralized the Larson team, who were hauled in at the speed of a water-skier rather than a fish. Unfortunately, the anchorman sank really deep into the ground and had to be dug out with the help of Rambo, Mad Dog, and a spade. Mr. Hall banned Fatty's boots for the semifinal because he had already succeeded in digging a small trench in the middle of Trafalgar, but the Crazy Five and Barryl didn't need any cunning tactics in the end. We were far too strong for everyone and won the trophy without even breaking a sweat. Sparerib was beside himself with excitement. He has been becoming increasingly worried that our house won't win a single competition this year for the first time since 1923. He gave Fatty a thump on the back and said, "We certainly took our time this year, Sidney, but thanks to you and your good men, we've avoided disgrace!"

I wish I could have joined in the dormitory celebrations. Instead

Vern and I sat on our lockers pretending to look happy and watching everyone recounting stories of the great victory of Trafalgar.

Thursday 29th August

Sparerib called a house meeting so that we could all say goodbye to Julian. The entire house cheered and applauded as Julian pretended to look shocked and then dabbed away at his eyes with an orange handkerchief. Even the Crazy Eight was united for once and agreed that school won't be the same without him.

Friday 30th August

THE END OF JULIAN

After assembly we all said our final goodbyes to Julian, who flies to London tomorrow to begin his music degree at the Royal College of Music in London. I must admit I was a little choked up as I shook his hand. Luthuli was the last to say goodbye and gave Julian a hug, followed by a thump on the back, while Thinny, Darryl, Spike, and J. R. Ewing carried his trunk across the quad for the final time. Julian gave us all a dramatic wave goodbye that looked like a bow combined with a curtsy. He then strode toward the fountain, removed his shoes and socks, rolled up his pants to the knee, and stepped into the water. He waded out toward Pissing Pete and gave him a big kiss on the lips. Pissing Pete didn't seem to mind. (If anything, his trickle got a little stronger.) Then Julian gracefully sprang out of the fountain and ran out through the archway, leaving his shoes and socks behind.

Mad Dog took one of his shoes and stuck it under a rock at the bottom of the pond. Who knows—maybe it will last there forever?

LONG WEEKEND

Back home, Dad was looking bad tempered and desperately trying to put up shelves in the garage. When I said hello, he looked at me like I'd committed a serious crime and said, "You see, thanks to you and your commie buddies and their bloody new South Africa, I can't get decent drill bits anymore!" I didn't want to get caught up in a political debate, so I apologized about the drill bits and quickly jumped on my bike and freewheeled down the driveway. Blacky chased me down the road, barking loudly and trying to bite my tires. I brought him back home and locked him in the kitchen. Dad caught me at the kitchen door and accused me of tormenting Blacky and having it in for the animal. (Clearly my father was in a foul mood. According to Mom, he's been working on the garage shelves for over a week.)

I reached Mermaid's house and suddenly felt very odd, like I should be hiding in the hedge and not standing boldly in front of the garden gate. I had already worked out my plan. I was going to march up the pathway, knock on the door, and when I saw Mermaid, seize her in my arms and kiss her passionately. I took a moment to catch my breath and tried my best to straighten my hair. I stood with my finger poised over the gate buzzer, but terror struck and my finger refused to push the buzzer. There followed a long standoff between finger and buzzer, which was eventually won by the buzzer.

I decided to think it all through and come back tomorrow.

I cycled home feeling like a coward.

WEEKEND NEWS

Wombat returned home on Monday after a long stay in Brighton with Neville and Dingbat. According to Mom, the whole thing turned sour in the end and Wombat has written them off as "low-class yahoos on the take," i.e., Wombat thinks they were trying to steal her money.

What started as a Sunday afternoon spring-cleaning session turned into a seriously intense family tree examination. Dad brought out a number of old books and yellow papers and said, "Johnny, there's more decent history in here than you get from your bloody left-wing history teachers."

While Mom's side of the family looks fairly decent, it must be said that Dad's bloodline is a bit dodgy. It turns out that Dad's famous great-great-grandfather, who went by the name of Sir Ogden Milton, was once the governor of Griqualand West and according to Dad was a great leader who used to hunt pheasants with the king of England.

It also turns out that Sir Ogden was one day marching through the Eastern Cape when he discovered a Xhosa chief crossing a river. Sir Ogden captured the chief, tied him up, and shot him three times in the head with a Winchester rifle. The poor chief's ear was then cut off and posted by ship to the king of England as a present. Dad didn't think Sir Ogden's barbarism was very serious, though, and said that in those days shooting and maiming Africans was "par for the course." After Sir Ogden the Milton bloodline took a nasty turn when a Milton married an Andrew. The name was then changed to Mildew. Dad reckons the Mildews became inbred and most of them died of syphilis.

Called Mermaid, but nobody was home. Secretly relieved.

Monday 2nd September

Finally got to see Mermaid, but I didn't get a chance to kiss her because we had to sit in the lounge with Marge and Mom. I asked Mermaid if she wanted to see the garden, but she smiled and said she was okay in the lounge.

She gave me a hug goodbye and told me to stay in touch. (Not exactly very passionate.) Unfortunately, all I could say was, "You too."

The longer I don't kiss her, the more awkward it becomes. She also didn't mention the poem. She must think I'm gay or something. Next time I see her, I'm going to jump her and stick my tongue down her throat.

Dad snapped after Blacky vomited in the pool. He chased the poor creature around the garden, hurling half bricks at the terrified animal, who eventually scampered into the lounge, hid behind the couch, and wet himself. This made Dad even more furious. He then grabbed an ashtray and hurled it across the lounge, narrowly missing Blacky by about half the length of his ear. Blacky escaped through the French doors and bolted across the lawn and out into the street. Dad shouted at

Mom for leaving the gate open and said if Blacky was run over, it would be on her conscience. Mom slammed the door in Dad's face and told him to stop terrorizing the dog and to get over his midlife crisis. Dad muttered something to himself and then stalked out into the street shouting for Blacky in a voice that sounded creepy and psychotic. Blacky didn't return.

Thanks to the Dad vs. dog commotion we ran short of time and I didn't have to visit Wombat on the way to the bus stop. I put a reminder in the memory bank that Blacky's well-timed pool vomit will be rewarded when or if he returns.

WEEKEND SCORECARD

RAMBO	Drank thirty-six beers and never vomited
SIMON	Bounced a ball on his cricket bat a record 687 times
FATTY	Contracted a severe bout of gastro after eating a sack of Israeli oranges
VERN	Built a wigwam in his garden
BOGGO	Watched videos
MAD DOG	Helped his neighbors put out a forest fire. He said it was the most snakes he's ever seen in his life.
SPUD	Discovered that he has barbarian genes in his family bloodline and still hasn't grabbed the Mermaid

I lied to the Crazy Eight and said I'd kissed the Mermaid. Rambo said this still didn't necessarily prove that I wasn't gay.

Boggo called Thinny into our dormitory and told him his mother was a sex maniac. He then went on in graphic detail about Mrs. Thinny's dark fantasies involving other women and small animals. Thinny got all defiant and said it was impossible that Boggo'd shagged his mom because he was with her the whole weekend. Boggo then accused Thinny of incest and ordered him to shag a pillow and pretend it was his mom. Thinny didn't put on a very convincing display of pillow shagging, so Boggo sprayed deodorant in his eyes and sent him back to bed.

Tuesday 3rd September

HOUSE MEETING

Emberton has been reinstated as a prefect. Anderson tried to start up a round of applause, but nobody went along with him. No doubt another million or two of sugar baron money has been deposited into the school building fund.

Vern tried to give Pike a written warning for pissing in the showers. Pike accused Vern of a false accusation and threw a bucket of water over Vern's head and then chased after him with a razor. It was quite a sight to see a naked Pike careening through the dormitories after a panicky Vern, whose brown Grasshopper shoes were making a loud squeaking noise. Pike eventually caught him at the bottom of the stairs and dragged him into the cop shop kitchen, where he tried to grill his face in the sandwich machine. Death Breath eventually broke up the action and gave Pike a warning. Pike told Death Breath to get stuffed and slunk off back to the bogs to continue his shower.

Thursday 5th September

I would rather lie in bed being pestered by a mosquito than have to decipher the degrees of a random triangle with Mrs. Bishop standing over me like a hawk. The point about triangles is that they are unexplained mysteries and are best left as such. (Examples include love triangles and the Bermuda Triangle.)

22:00 Rambo said he'd organized some brandy and cigarettes for tomorrow night's Crazy Eight mission to the Mad House. He said it was only right that we celebrate the beginning of spring with a Mad House bash. Nobody said anything, which means nobody was brave enough to say no.

Friday 6th September

22:30 With the matrics studying for their trials exams, the house was like a ghost town. Vern made two trips to the bogs and reported on both occasions that the coast was clear and that the bogs were in mint condition. Rambo gave us the signal, and we all began throwing on jerseys, tracksuit pants, and running shoes. I felt the old shiver of excitement that I always get before a Crazy Eight mission. Vern kissed Roger and shook the hand of Potato's torso before following me out of the cubicle, pointing his torch at my bum. We stumbled over J. R. Ewing as he lay asleep in his bed and crept out of the window and onto the vestry roof.

Fatty had a tight squeeze getting through the chapel window. I could see he was mightily relieved when he finally collapsed onto the chapel gallery floor. Then there was a loud hiss of, "Shhhhh!" Fatty was back on his feet and had his arms outstretched for silence. Somebody or something was kneeling at the altar. With only a single candle burning in the chapel, it was impossible to see who or what it was, but it definitely looked human. Rambo made us all lie low behind the pews and we waited for something to happen. Nothing happened.

Fatty nudged me in the ribs and whispered to me with hot breath, "My oath to God, Spud, I just saw something moving!" I stopped breathing. Fatty leaned in again and said, "Rambo, Mad Dog, guys—believe me, that's supernatural shit. It's an omen!"

There was a nervous pause and then Boggo whispered, "Good or bad omen?" Fatty squinted through the gloom toward the kneeling figure. He looked back at Boggo and said, "Dunno." There was another long pause. Suddenly Boggo got up and said he thought it was definitely a bad omen and he was going back to bed. Rambo cleared his throat to say something and instantly there was total darkness. I couldn't even see the hand in front of my face. I could hear heavy breathing to my left and Darth Vader noises to my right, so at least I knew where Fatty and Vern were.

Then out of the silence came Vern's demented voice. "Lucky I brought the torch, hey, chaps?" He then made a strange noise in the back of his throat that sounded like he was gargling on a large marble. There was a loud CLONK followed by more silence. Then we heard

Vern's voice again. "Sorry, chaps. Vern dropped the torch." Mad Dog found the torch and handed it to Rambo.

Rambo whispered, "Follow me, ghostbusters," and led us along the pew in single file. The gallery door creaked open and we made it to the staircase leading upward to the bell tower and downward to the chapel. Luckily the moonlight spilled through the stairwell windows, so we could at least see where our feet were landing. We reached the bottom of the spiral stairwell and stood waiting at the chapel door. Rambo motioned for silence and slowly opened the huge oak doors. The chapel was dark and ominous. The pale moonlight couldn't get through the stained glass windows, and every shape looked as black as coal.

Rambo flashed the torchlight over the altar. Nothing there. The mysterious figure was gone. Fatty turned to Boggo and said, "It must have been a poltergeist." Rambo hit Fatty on the shoulder with the torch and told him to shut up. "You can discuss ghosts later, you fat shit!" he hissed. "Stop farting around and concentrate. Some of us are on final warning here." Fatty fell silent and we followed Rambo down the aisle, past the altar, through the wooden door, and then down the tiny staircase and into the crypt. Rambo switched off the torch and handed it back to Vern and ordered him not to switch it on again.

The moon was brighter than we expected. Rambo whispered, "It's too bright. We have to run fast. Fatty, move your arse!" Then Rambo was running, sprinting! I battled to keep up and I could hear poor Vern snorting and wheezing somewhere behind me. Rambo didn't stop until he had leapt over both the bog stream and the barbed wire fence and was in the thick bush on the other side. We waited about five minutes for

Vern Vader and Fatty to grovel over the fence and collapse onto the grass in front of us. Rambo then split off by himself to find his connection.

Mad Dog made sure that the coast was clear before leading us on through the long grass toward the looming forest ahead. The grass was wet with dew, and my running shoes were making an annoying squelching squeak every time I took a stride. We walked at a very slow pace because the ground was uneven and Fatty was close to a heart attack.

We gathered at the foot of the Mad House tree and listened for any unusual sounds. There was nothing besides crickets, frogs, and randy bulls mooing further up the hill.

Unless you stood under the tree and knew where to look, you would never think that there was a massive tree house just twenty feet above your head.

Soon we had all made it up the tree and were gathered around the glow of Mad Dog's gas lamp, warming our hands while waiting for Rambo. After some time there was a shrill whistle from the forest below. Mad Dog whistled back and Rambo scuttled up the tree with a bag of illegal goodies. Cigarettes were lit and Mellowwood brandy was poured. What followed was a long and rather acrimonious argument about the mysterious figure in the chapel.

At one stage Simon handed me his cigarette while he poured a drink. Suddenly there was a bright flash of light.

"What the hell was that?" asked Rambo. Nobody answered. Mad

Dog turned off his gaslight and we all listened for noises in the darkness. Mad Dog said, "I don't . . ." but his voice trailed away as a strong beam of light shone up and over the floor of the Mad House. I could hear heavy breathing around me and could just make out the maniacal stare of the wildebeest head in the moonlight. There were now three distinct beams of torchlight shining around the floor and the walls. I was trembling and struggling to breathe. I hoped it was just a horrible nightmare that I was about to wake up from. But then there was a loud and distorted voice on a megaphone:

"Crazy Eight! Please come down!"

I heard sniggering and whispers of, "Give it here! Give it here!"

Then I heard Pike. "This is the forest police. We have you surrounded!"

There was more sniggering and the breaking of twigs. I heard someone snatching the megaphone and then clearing his throat before blasting forth with: "Throw down your brandy bottles and come out with your cigarettes up!" Emberton. There was more cackling laughter from below us. We heard Anderson telling the others to shut up and then he called up to us, without the megaphone this time. "Guys, I know you can hear me. Listen—you can either come down or we can come up."

Rambo was lying next to me staring up at the tree above us with unblinking eyes.

"Or if you don't choose to come down," continued Anderson, "and I don't feel like climbing up, then I think I'll go and wake up Sparerib and he can decide."

Boggo motioned to Rambo to say something, but Rambo shook his head and whispered, "He's bluffing."

Then there was a loud scream from below and some thrashing around in the grass and then Devries' voice saying that something had bitten him. Mad Dog sniggered and loaded another stone into his catty. Rambo pulled the catty away and told Mad Dog he was being an idiot.

Anderson's voice softened like he was offering us something tempting. "We have a photograph, guys. And I'm not bluffing about Sparerib. If you come down now, maybe we can resolve this among ourselves."

The game was up and we knew it. We were busted red-handed in the Mad House with cigarettes and brandy. We climbed down the tree one by one to the sound of jeering and mocking. My whole body was shaking and I was close to bursting into tears.

They were all waiting for us: Anderson, Pike, Devries, Death Breath, Emberton. All shining their torches and gloating. The seven of us marched back to the school like a herd of sheep, with our heads bowed and in absolute silence. We all knew that we were now at the mercy of these monsters that the school calls prefects, and there wasn't a single thing any of us could do about it. Because I was too shocked to realize what was happening, I hadn't really thought about what might happen to us. I just knew whatever it was, it would be horrible. I marched along staring at the Nike logo on the back of Rambo's running shoes. I think I might have been a bit drunk.

We have been confined to house bounds, which means we can't leave the house except for chapel and meals. This will last until Anderson and the prefects have decided what to do with us.

I lay on my bed with my mind doing somersaults and ideas and schemes shooting around like firecrackers. I prayed to God that Anderson would not tell Sparerib. I don't care what terrible torture he uses on us.

Saturday 7th September

While the prefects locked themselves in the cop shop for a morning of debate, the Crazy Eight hung around the dormitory discussing every possible angle of the problem. Rambo reckoned the prefects would draw the whole thing out for as long as possible. Boggo kept whining on about how his dad would kill him if he gets expelled. He said he would rather commit suicide first.

I refuse to think about my parents or my scholarship. I refuse to think about anything.

20:00 We weren't allowed to watch the movie. Not that I was really in the mood for *Weekend at Bernie's*. Although it might have been nice to think of something else besides expulsion and punishment. Pike brought around his photographs so he could gloat. He had taken a whole series of pictures this morning from inside the Mad House! Then he showed us a photo of us all drinking and smoking. You can see that everyone has a glass in front of them and you can see I'm holding Simon's cigarette and that I look as guilty as sin. Rambo and Boggo are dragging on their cigarettes and Vern is picking his nose and staring at the wildebeest.

Sunday 8th September

Mom phoned to find out how I was doing and to give me the latest Milton news. I nearly started crying on the phone but managed not to tell her about Friday night. I put the phone down, went back to bed, and started crying under my duvet. I shoved my face deep into the mattress to hide the sound.

15:00 Anderson reported us to Sparerib. Any hope that we might escape this one with just a brutal thrashing is now officially gone. Our final hope was for one last brilliant idea from Rambo, but all he could do was shrug and start packing his trunk. I flicked on my Walkman and skipped to track five on *The Joshua Tree*. I wish my life also had a rewind button.

You got to talk without speaking
Cry without weeping
Scream without raising your voice

One by one, we were called into Sparerib's office for a grueling inquisition. I wanted to shout out that the whole thing was just fun—it wasn't like we'd killed anyone! Sparerib did his best to look upset and shocked, but I knew he was secretly thrilled and excited. He's been waiting to get back at the Crazy Eight ever since Fatty was caught in the chapel window last year and Spareribended up looking like an idiot for swallowing Rambo's story at the time. (Of course Rambo shagging his wife didn't help much either.) In fact, Spareribtried to force me to blame the whole thing on Rambo! He even told me that by telling the truth about Rambo, I could lessen my own punishment and possibly save my place at the school and even my scholarship.

I shook my head and said nothing. I wasn't being brave. I just knew that if I opened my mouth, I'd start crying.

Then Sparerib handed me a printed piece of paper with a list of my crimes:

- Talking after lights-out
- Being out of house bounds after lights-out
- Bunking out (this means I went beyond the bog stream, dam, and school fence)
- Night swimming
- Smoking
- Drinking

I didn't think the night swimming would make much difference in the end, so I signed where it said *Culprit's Signature*. Sparerib told me again how disappointed he was in me and that he was filled with an immense sense of waste. I said I was sorry. Sparerib snapped back saying it was too late for sorry and told me to call in Vern.

Vern was waiting outside with red eyes and a dark patch in the crotch of his pants. He seemed to be on the verge of some sort of freak-out or epileptic fit, so I shook his hand firmly and said, "Don't worry, Vern. Everything's gonna be fine." Obviously, the handshake gave him strength because he marched into the office like he was ready to punch Sparerib's lights out.

22:00 Rambo called us to his cubicle and said, "Guys, I dunno what's gonna happen to you, but I think it's game over for me and Mad Dog." Mad Dog told him they would be fine, but it sounded hollow and he soon gave up his good cheer and went back to sharpening his hunting and filleting knife. Rambo stood on his footlocker and said, "In case this is the end for the Crazy Eight, I just want to say that it's been a hell of two years with you guys." He then started to choke up, which made us all choke up. "Anyway, it's been cool. And, hey, what can I say? The Crazy Eight went out with a bang, not a whimper!" We all shook hands and paws and returned to our beds in silence.

While the others slept, I sat on my windowsill and looked out at the main quad and Pissing Pete. The moon was out again tonight—this time not so full and not so bright. I had a head full of questions:

What happens next?

Can they really expel all of us?

If we aren't expelled, what will happen?

Will The Glock deal with us or will Sparerib?

Will The Glock say anything in assembly tomorrow?

Will I lose my scholarship?

If I do, can I still stay at the school?

Surely they can't expel Vern? He's a simpleton!

How do I break the news to my parents?

Why did I get into this mess in the first place?

Just had a thought about the barbarians in the Milton bloodline. Guess you can add another Milton name to the list.

Monday 9th September

08:00 The Glock marched into the Great Hall looking like he wanted to dismember someone. My legs were shaking like there was an earthquake under my chair. I was about to experience being on the wrong end of the Hitler that runs our school. Everybody knows the whole story by now, but The Glock shouted it out in graphic detail anyway. He made it sound so bad—really bad. He even hinted that we were performing dark rituals with animals' blood! After his tirade he finished off by reading out our names and telling us to report to his study immediately. Outside, people were shaking our hands like we were heroes. There was even a chant of "Long live the Crazy Eight!" but I could see the relief in their eyes that they weren't the ones staring down the barrel of a loaded Glock.

The Glock gave us a twenty-minute screaming-to. My legs were shaking terribly and I couldn't look at his face. He kept banging the table with his fist and ranting on about "silly season" and what our vile behavior has done to the school's fine reputation. Finally, he ordered us back to the dorm and said he had to have a meeting with Sparerib and other senior staff. We shuffled back to our dormitory like a bunch of convicts with half the school hanging around the quad like a huge flock of vultures. Boggo has packed up his trunk and bags and seems all set to leave. He reckons if you expect the worst, then you can never be disappointed.

10:30 We returned to the headmaster's study to hear the verdict. On The Glock's desk stood the bottle of Mellowwood, which was now nearly empty. (Guess what the prefects were doing in the locked cop shop on Saturday morning!) Covering just about the rest of the desk was the wildebeest head. The poor gnu, who had looked so splendid hanging on the wall of the Mad House, now looked rather idiotic sitting on a desk next to a large sign that read HEADMASTER.

The Glock stood up and placed his hands on the back of his chair and glared at us with his nasty little smoldering eyes. "Gentlemen, after discussions with your housemaster, relevant teachers, and senior heads of department, I have come to a decision on punishment for your reckless misdemeanors and complete disregard for this school and its rules." He took a breath and glared angrily at the wildebeest head like it was somehow responsible.

My mind drifted to Julian charging through the dormitory shouting, "A moose! A moose!" I wished he was here—he would have supported us and given us advice. We were lucky to have had him and

Luthuli, Earthworm, and the others. They were good people who had tried to make the house a better place.

"Your punishments are as follows: Vern Blackadder, Simon Brown, Alan Greenstein, Sidney Smitherson-Scott, and John Milton—you shall be suspended from school for a period of two to three weeks or however long your housemaster deems sufficient. In addition you shall be beaten six strokes with a light cane and be placed on final warning. You are gated until the end of the year. In other words, you may not leave the school grounds unless it is for an official school requirement. This includes the long weekend."

I hardly had time to digest the news before The Glock dropped his next bombshell.

"Robert Black and Charlie Hooper—I regret to inform you that you are no longer students of this institution. You have been expelled." The Glock's eyes flicked around the group. "Your parents have already been notified and you will both be off the school premises by sunset today."

Rambo and Mad Dog left the office without saying a word. They were too shocked. The rest of us had to line up. As usual I was the second last one ahead of Vern. The Glock grunted with every swing of the cane. He smashed harder than Sparerib and took an age between each stroke. All the while I was gazing into the demented eyes of the poor dead wildebeest. For the first time in days I've found someone who's worse off than me. The thought that I'm still alive and kicking and haven't had my head chopped off was slightly soothing, but then my bum caught fire and I found myself sprinting around the school rose garden rubbing myself like a lunatic. This time there were no cheers or people shaking my hand. I didn't feel proud. I didn't feel brave. I felt like a coward and a fool and no longer welcome here.

The scene in the dormitory was bizarre. Boggo was unpacking his trunk while Rambo and Mad Dog were packing theirs. Fatty said he was going to sue the school. I don't think Vern actually knew what was going on because he looked to be settling in for an afternoon nap. I told Rambo and Mad Dog that I was sorry. I couldn't think of anything else to say, so I went to my cubicle and started packing my own bags.

The door creaked open. It was Spareribs. Without saying a word to anyone he beckoned to me with a crooked finger. I followed him out and closed the door behind me. The door wasn't thick enough to hide Rambo's shout of "Gotcha!"

Sparerib led me to his office without saying a word. He closed the door and ordered me to sit down. He then slapped his hand against his filing cabinet, making a huge sound. No doubt it was part of his cunning plan to intimidate me with a few loud bangs before kicking off with his interrogation. I stared at him with no emotion and no sign of fear.

"Milton, for an intelligent boy you've been bloody stupid. How many times have I warned you about these influences, this ridiculous Crazy Eight gang that seems to impress everyone? Well, I can tell you, it doesn't impress me." Sparerib was so excited that he was starting to foam around the mouth. He sat back in his chair looking smug and said, "The Crazy Eight is no more. You're now just John Milton, and you're on your last chance. Now I've spoken to your parents at length and they're bitterly disappointed. They will be here within an hour."

I thought about Mom and Dad being bitterly disappointed. It didn't seem right. My folks don't deal in bitterness or disappointment. They shout and explode and throw things. But then I felt a happy thought: I may be going home in disgrace, but I'm still going home.

Back in the dormitory the realization was beginning to set in that we could be seeing Rambo and Mad Dog for the last time ever. It all seemed such a waste. A huge drama about nothing! Mad Dog was actually crying a bit and said I should visit him on his farm in the holidays. Rambo put on a brave face and said he didn't give a shit anyway and that this school was no place for born leaders and lateral thinkers.

I packed my Walkman and wallet into my bag. Eventually the time came and we all shook hands. Rambo said that he hoped that we would find out who had betrayed us and why. Fatty said he was already onto it. As I shook Rambo's hand, he squeezed my shoulder and said, "You know what? Now I'm glad you wrote it all down in your diary—because then one day maybe people will know what we did." Then Mad Dog seized me by the shoulders and said, "And you'd better make sure you write how amazing the Mad House was—I don't want people thinking it was just a kiddies' tree house or something." I said, "Don't worry, Mad Dog, they'll know it was a mansion."

We watched Rambo and Mad Dog carrying their trunks across the quad and out through the archway. Suddenly Mad Dog charged back into the quad and rugby-tackled a fleeing Darryl. He picked up the screaming first-year by the collar and threw him headfirst into the fountain. Mad Dog turned to us, barked loudly, and then sprinted across the grass and out the archway.

The Crazy Eight has gone forever.

Sunday 29th September

I'm back.

In all the rush and confusion of my suspension I stupidly left my diary back at school. I've been praying every day that it's in my classroom locker and not up in the dormitory, where it could have been found by Pike, photocopied, and shown to the world. I also had regular nightmares of Sparerib smashing open my locker with the handle of his squash racket and reading his report cards that I'd written about him. My hands trembled quite badly as I turned the combination lock backward and forward and then backward again. The locker door popped open and there lay the most beautiful thing in the world. My shiny red diary. I checked if anyone was watching and then danced a jig and screamed silently with relief. (Unfortunately, for some unknown reason I'd also left an apple in my locker, which was now badly decomposed and covered in two weeks' worth of fruit flies.) I read back over my last few entries before I was suspended but then started depressing myself, so I stopped and turned over to a clean new page.

Mental note: Whenever in doubt, just turn straight over to a clean page.

21 DAYS OF HELL (No-Lights Package)

My twenty-one days at home were no picnic. In fact, it was more like a Nazi concentration camp, with my mother shouting orders and blasting me for the slightest thing I did wrong. She even banned me from seeing the Mermaid. (Foolishly, she didn't ban my afternoon bike rides—so Mermaid and I met up every Wednesday and Sunday for twenty minutes in the park near her house.)

Worse news is that I still haven't kissed the Mermaid! It's now become so normal not to kiss her that it would be weird if I did. Last week I plucked up the courage to hold her hand, but Mermaid giggled, squeezed my hand, and then let it go. She says I'm the best friend she's ever had, while I get more desperate and pathetic every time I see her. I'm too scared to ask her if she still wants to be my girlfriend in case she decides to dump me again.

I've never seen the folks so angry as the day they picked me up. Dad wasn't really that mad—he was just pretending to be angry because Mom had obviously told him to be angry. I could tell by the way his eyes kept darting across to Mom after he'd finished every line of his long lecture on bad behavior. Mom, on the other hand, was truly livid and remained truly livid for twenty-one days. She seemed to take the whole thing very personally and snapped at anyone who crossed her path. Things got even worse when Mom blamed Dad for my "drinking problem" and then banned alcohol from the house during weekdays. This meant that Dad stayed out in the garden watering his roses until nine o'clock every night. On the weekends the folks got snot-flying drunk and had nasty fights about who was to blame for my irresponsible behavior.

Wombat advised Mom to send me to Boys' Town and said I was practically a criminal. She stared at me like I was a lowlife scum and said, "He's definitely looking more like his father by the day." She then asked Mom if it was too late to give me up for adoption. Mom gave it some thought and then said it would be too complicated. Wombat looked at me full of distaste and said, "I suppose you're right. I mean, who's going to take him anyway. He'd be like Oliver!" Wombat's the kind of granny who kicks you when you're down and praises you when you're up. I now understand why Dad has repeatedly tried to kill her.

Mental note: Beware the Wombat who kicks you when you're down.

On the plus side I did manage to get through piles of work. In fact, I think I might well be far ahead in most subjects.

The Guv called me every three days or so to chat and find out how I was doing. He told me not to feel too bad about things because one day I'd be remembered as a hell-raiser. I'd always thank him for his advice and he'd say something like, "Advice is free, Milton. It's just sex one has to pay for!" The problem is that when it comes to The Guv, it's very hard to separate the genius from the ridiculous. This gets even more difficult when he's been drinking. He ended the last call on Friday by shouting, "Let them eat caviar!" He then slammed the phone down but obviously missed the cradle because I heard a screech and a shout and then a door slam.

Monday 30th September

Not much has been said about the whole Mad House debacle. Boggo says he spoke to Rambo in the holidays and apparently Rambo's dad has set his lawyers on the case because he plans on suing Sparerib. With only five of us in the dormitory, everything feels weird and a bit boring.

Sparerib called us into his office after lunch and told us this was our last chance to make a fresh start. He said we needed to prove to ourselves and to him that the school's good faith in us is justified. (Glad he thinks suspensions, expulsions, and brutal beatings are showing good faith.)

We were attacked in the night by intruders who set on us with pillows and laundry bags stuffed with shoes and books. By the time I woke up, I was surrounded by attackers and the only thing I could do was cover my head and take a pounding. Fatty managed to break away from our attackers and switch on the lights. The poundings thankfully stopped as the attackers backed off. The five remaining members of the Crazy Eight staggered to their feet and looked on in horror as the gloating victors marched triumphantly out of our dormitory and straight into the first-year dorm. We had just been thrashed senseless by the Sad Six!

Our humiliation is complete.

Wednesday 2nd October

Pike came over to gloat at roll call. He and Devries have now christened us the Faggoty Five. Even Darryl and Runt were laughing at us without showing any fear.

Fatty made a bid to take control of the dormitory. After prep he moved his stuff into Rambo's cubicle and took over Rambo's old bed. He tried to christen us the Fatty Five, but Boggo refused and argued that this excluded Roger, who was still a member. Boggo then suggested our new name should be "Boggo's Boys." We all laughed and Simon said it sounded like a gay porno movie. Simon then tried to show his power by ordering Vern to shine his cricket boots, but Rain Man gave him the middle finger and marched off to the bogs with Roger trailing along behind.

Thursday 3rd October

We all gathered in the tiny telephone room while Boggo phoned Rambo to ask for guidance. When Rambo heard about us being beaten up by the Sad Six, he didn't laugh like we thought he would. In fact, he started screaming at Boggo and calling us all a bunch of fags and a disgrace to the Crazy Eight. Rambo ordered Fatty and Boggo to seize joint control of the dormitory and immediately take revenge on the Sad Six. He then said something strange. He told Boggo to tell the rest of us to answer truthfully should anyone ask us about Eve. Not sure what's going on, but Rambo's definitely up to something.

Mad Dog called five minutes later and abused us for being dominated by the Sad Six. He reckons he's missing school except for work, chapel, prep, and Sparerib. He then said he wanted to speak to Runt. I found Runt hanging around the urinal and dragged him into the phone room and handed him the receiver. Within thirty seconds Runt was crying and saying, "Please don't, Mad Dog, please don't!"

It's amazing that Mad Dog can terrify first-years from a thousand miles away. It's also a bit embarrassing that we can't do it ourselves.

Boggo and Fatty psyched us up for a vicious return attack on the Sad Six. Fatty explained the whole thing through, but unfortunately Vern didn't realize that it was just a rehearsal and charged into the first-year dormitory screaming like a madman. When he realized nobody was behind him, he stopped dead and his hand shot onto his head. He then screamed loudly and galloped back into our dormitory, dived onto his bed, and pulled the duvet over his head. Fatty and Boggo agreed that the element of surprise was gone and we'd have to save the brutal attack on the Sad Six for next term.

Friday 4th October

After breakfast Simon was hauled into The Glock's office. He came out ten minutes later and said that The Glock wanted to see me. My internal organs did a 360 and my leg started shaking again. I didn't have a clue what I had done wrong this time, but my brain had clearly decided that this was the end for me.

The Glock has now hung the wildebeest head on his office wall. I bet he tells parents he shot it himself. It would definitely sound better than saying that he'd expelled the hunter who killed it and then stole his trophy!

Thank God, I wasn't in trouble.

In fact, it turns out that Sparerib could be in trouble.

THE GLOCK'S QUESTIONS

- Do you feel that Mr. Wilson victimized Rambo?
- Has Mr. Wilson ever encouraged you to incriminate Rambo unjustly?
- Do you believe Rambo was unfairly placed on final warning?
- Did Rambo have a non-platonic relationship with Mrs. Wilson?
- Would you be willing to swear to this before God in a court of law?

I said yes five times.

Then I told The Glock that Gecko had caught Rambo and Eve last year having sex in the cricket pavilion. The Glock went bloodred and his eyes bulged. He mopped his brow with a white handkerchief and said, "Well, in that case, er . . . send in Gecko immediately." I reminded the bumbling psychopath that Gecko was dead. The Glock didn't seem too fazed and said, "Oh, all right, well, send in Blackadder. He's still alive, is he?" I nodded and went off to find Vern.

Vern refused to speak to The Glock and climbed into his trunk and pulled the lid down over his head. We tried to persuade him to come out, but he was convinced The Glock was going to cane him again. I was getting a bit desperate because no doubt The Glock was fuming in his office and tapping his watch and perhaps even looking around for his big cane. Eventually, with the help of Fatty and Boggo, we carried Vern and his trunk down the stairs and all the way to The Glock's study. We left Vern in his trunk outside the door in the passageway and told The Glock's secretary to tell him that Vern Blackadder was waiting for him outside his office but inside an army trunk.

Mom phoned for a Milton catch-up. Thankfully, I think she feels that her point has been well and truly made and apart from the odd sniping comment, it looks like she's forgiven me for bringing shame on the family. Much to my father's relief, the booze ban at home has been lifted and Mom even allowed Dad to book us a three-night holiday in the game reserve so that we can all unwind after what she said had been "a traumatic month."

Sunday 6th October (one month since the big bust)

MILTONS' UMFOLOZI GAME RESERVE ADVENTURE

09:00 Milton departure.

09:25 Dad did a dangerous U-turn on the freeway near Umhlanga Rocks because he'd forgotten the meat in the freezer. He blamed Mom for not reminding him.

10:00 Just as well we returned home because Dad had also left his bird books, torch, checkbook, gas cooker, Swiss army knife, and mosquito spray behind.

10:20 Dad led a loud chorus of "Yellow Submarine" as we roared down Broadway and veered onto the freeway. Unfortunately, none of us knew any more than the first line, so after repeating it about five times the singsong ran out of steam and Dad turned on the A program on the radio instead.

13:30 Dad shat all over the security guard at the Umfolozi gate because the road from Mtubatuba was full of potholes (most of which Dad succeeded in hitting). The security guard didn't really seem to know what was cracking and kept saying, "Okay, okay," and then, "All right, all right." Eventually, Dad gave up and returned to the car in a sulk.

13:40 Before driving into the reserve, my father gave us a long lecture about how we were now entering the animals' world and that the only things we should leave behind were our footprints.

13:45 Our first animal sighting was a large troop of baboons sitting in the middle of the road. Dad got so excited that he wound down the window and made loud baboon noises to try and get the apes to do something interesting. The baboons didn't look very impressed and carried on with their daily chores of looking for ticks and sleeping on the road. Dad threw a handful of peanuts out the window to try and encourage some funny baboon action—they ignored Dad and his peanuts. I asked Dad if calling, feeding, and scaring baboons was not against the rules. He snapped back, "Oh, so now you're an authority on rules, hey?" I sat back in my seat, stared out the window, and said nothing.

We arrived at the camp, which is stationed on top of a steep hill. Dad crunched his empty beer can on his forehead and told us to enjoy the natural beauty while it's still around. He then spotted a crow sitting on a dead branch and shot it with an imaginary gun.

We took an afternoon drive around the Sontuli loop. According to my father, the Sontuli loop is the best game-viewing section in the world. The loop runs along the Black Umfolozi River and Dad kept showing us where the great floods of '87 had reached up to. We didn't see any predators—unless you count a sleeping crocodile.

ANIMALS SPOTTED BY MILTONS

Impala
Nyala
Wildebeest (made me think of Mad Dog and Rambo)
White rhino
Giraffe
Baboons
Monkeys (Mom had a giggling fit because of their bright blue balls)
Crocodile (sleeping, maybe dead)
Fish eagle
Vulture
Warthog

Dad told us stories late into the night about his days growing up on the farm in Namibia. Most of them involved meetings with leopards, lynxes, and deadly snakes. I sipped on my Coke, watched the fire, and thought that it must have been cool to be growing up in the 1950s.

Monday 7th October

Still no predators. Dad stormed into the camp office and asked the game ranger where he was hiding his lions. The game ranger thought Dad was joking and grinned at us without answering.

The best spotting of the day was a huge owl sitting on a telephone wire in the camp.

At last we saw a hyena. Unfortunately, it was charging into the bush with a roll of Milton sausage in its mouth. Dad charged after the animal with a Castle Lager in one hand and his cooking tongs in the other. He swore at the fleeing scavenger, but it was too late and half our dinner was gone.

Tuesday 8th October

Still no big cats.

Dad fed the camp warthog a slice of toast and the thing nearly took his finger off. Dad reckons the animals in the park are becoming angry because people aren't sticking to the rules. He blamed the Frogs (French) and the Krauts (Germans).

18:00 In a last-ditch effort to find a big cat, we set off on a night drive with a truckload of Krauts and two Frogs. Unfortunately, the only cat we saw was a small spotted genet, which, although very pretty, can't really be considered Big Five material.

Dad had to stop the night drive so that he could take a pee. The game guide wasn't very impressed and made Dad stand in the middle of the road and instructed one of the Krauts holding the searchlight to keep it fixed on my father in case a lion attacked. Poor Dad then became very nervous and stood for ages in the middle of the road without anything happening. Eventually Dad let out a huge groan and had an exceedingly long and loud piss that left a mark on the road that looked suspiciously like the map of Africa.

Wednesday 9th October

Dad had us up at first light for one last shot at the Sontuli loop. After we'd been driving for about an hour, something spotty caught my eye against the blur of green.

When I pointed the leopard out to my parents, all hell broke out. Dad cheered so loudly that the leopard fell out of the tree and disappeared into the bush. Dad then raced the station wagon along the dirt road with his head out the window. Suddenly there was a flash of spots and the leopard crossed the road in front of us in two leaps and disappeared into the thick bush on the other side. We waited another twenty minutes, but the big cat was gone. Dad reckons that he definitely got an award-winning photograph of it as it sprinted across the road.

Dad was so proud about the leopard sighting that he had to stop every car on the way back to camp to tell them about it.

For the first time in ages I was toasted at a Milton meal. Thanks to my sharp-eyed spotting, my shares with the folks are back up to the old levels. I even sang "The Final Countdown" at full volume with the folks screaming along with me. It was the first time I've sung anything in months, and my voice sounded deeper and didn't knack-jump.

Got home and ran a bath. I didn't stop singing for half an hour. Spud Milton's singing career soon to be back in business!

Friday 11th October

Went to the beach with Mermaid. She spent the entire time talking to surfers and lifeguards. Some of them asked her if I was her younger brother. She told them I was an old friend.

Think I must sign up for the school gym. I have the body of a ten-year-old. Maybe I should write to Rambo and ask him for some muscle-building routines.

Unfortunately, Dad's photograph of the leopard crossing the road wasn't as good as he thought it was. In fact, the leopard wasn't even in it! All you could see was a photograph of the dashboard and the bonnet of the station wagon. It must be said that after looking at the photo more closely, you saw a disturbing number of red lights flashing on the station wagon dashboard and both the rev counter and the heating gauge were in the red for danger parts. Dad was adamant that you could see a flash of the leopard's tail in the top-left corner of the photo, but I reckon it was the yellow rim of Mom's plastic wine goblet.

Sunday 13th October

Spent the morning bowling to Mermaid in the Crusaders cricket nets. She looked very sexy wearing my pads and a rather short denim miniskirt. She laughed at my ball box and said it looked like a miniature birdbath. I told her it was too small for me now and handed her the thigh pad.

I bowled Mermaid twenty times in half an hour, which either means she's useless or my bowling is brilliant. She's still better than Vern, though, who runs away from the ball and only hits it once it's come to a standstill.

I tried to practice my batting, but Mermaid's bowling/throwing kept going off the pitch and into the side netting. We eventually called it off when a big crowd of men came out of the bar and stood behind the nets to watch my batting.

We returned home to find Mom lounging on her sun bed with a gin and tonic in one hand and her flyswatter in the other. Dad was blowing into the fire and cursing the quality of charcoal in the country. Mom and Wombat were obviously in the middle of a conversation about Frank and his nineteen-year-old girlfriend. It soon became clear that Wombat was under the impression that Mermaid was Frank's nineteen-year-old "floozy." She glared at Mermaid and then turned to Mom and said, "She looks like a slut. You can tell by the skirt." Luckily Mermaid is used to Wombat's general madness. She smiled at me after I'd apologized for about the fourth time and said, "At least she hasn't gone on about my boobs yet." We then had an awkward moment when Mermaid caught me looking at her boobs. I should have kissed her, but the Miltons were watching.

Mental note: Never have a platonic relationship with a gorgeous woman. Rather get dumped on day one than have to put up with a life of confusion, frustration, and kissing your pillow.

Monday 14th October

WEEKEND SCORECARD

FATTY	Been working on unraveling the Mad House conspiracy
BOGGO	Says he's clinically depressed and thinking of leaving the school
VERN	Showed us photographs of his holiday to Cape Town. (Unfortunately, Vern was only about six years old in the photographs and missing his front teeth.)
ROGER	Has dumped Vern and has started sleeping in my locker
SIMON	Says he's going to be promoted to the first team from tomorrow
SPUD	Saw a leopard in the game reserve and developed a dark fantasy about the Mermaid in cricket equipment
RAMBO	Expelled
MAD DOG	Expelled

Vern didn't look happy about Roger giving him the cold shoulder. He accused me of doing voodoo on his cat and told me he would be watching me closely.

Wednesday 16th October

Viking made our whole drama class stand on the front of the theater stage and scream as loudly as possible for as long as possible. He said he had the feeling that some of us had unresolved issues. (He was looking directly at me when he said it.) I must admit a good long maniacal scream made me feel at least thirty percent better.

Thursday 17th October

The Guv is outraged that both his opening bowlers have been expelled. He was even more furious when he discovered that his captain and best batsman had reported to the first-team practice instead. He announced that he couldn't be expected to operate under such sordid circumstances, called off the practice, and announced his retirement from coaching cricket. We didn't know what to do, so we hung around the nets and waited. The Guv returned about twenty minutes later with a hip flask and a large cigar.

The Guv studied the eight of us in dismay and said the only two possible ways we could keep our unbeaten record were divine intervention or seven weeks of extensive flooding. He then told us to get practicing while he went off to unearth rough diamonds at the under-15B net practice.

He returned ten minutes later with three players and said, "Gentlemen, meet your new teammates. They may not look like much, but the rest I dare say were even worse." He lit his cigar and said, "God, it's a dry, featureless desert out there." He then slammed his shooting stick into the ground, perched himself onto the seat, and shouted, "Come on, men, stun me!"

The new players are:

Shamus Walsh—medium-pace bowler—nickname Anus
Martin Lewis—medium-pace bowler—nickname Stinky
Danny Davids—short and fat opening batsman—nickname Devito

Friday 18th October

Simon has been selected for the first team. Even Sparerib looked thrilled. There must have been a problem with our team sheet because my name was typed out first, which means I should be opening the batting. (If this isn't an error, I'm heading to the san for an off-sport slip.)

Fatty tried to break his own farting record. Unfortunately, the whole thing was a letdown when Fatty called off the attempt at the last minute because of indigestion.

It's official! The Sad Six are no longer frightened of us. J. R. Ewing wanders through our dormitory like he owns the place and Pike comes in every night to take brandy orders from the bar. We have almost daily meetings about how we're going to get revenge on Pike, Emberton, and the Sad Six, but nothing ever happens.

Tuesday 22nd October

Went to spy on the Sad Six. Runt was lying in bed listening to his Walkman. The rest of them were nowhere to be seen. After a year and a half of watching Rambo at work, I decided to take the initiative. I marched up to Runt, ripped his earphones out of the Walkman, and tried to lift him up to his feet with one hand. I didn't lift him up, but I did manage to rip his T-shirt and then uppercut him sharply on the chin. It was an aggressive start and I decided to keep him under pressure and speak in a commanding, Rambo-like manner.

SPUD	How did you know about the Mad House?
RUNT	I followed you one Sunday, but I didn't see anything.
SPUD	Who did you tell?
RUNT	No one.

The way Runt said, "No one," made me think that he had definitely told someone and possibly everyone. Unfortunately, then Vern arrived and gave Runt a written warning. Runt took the blue warning without seeming too concerned about it and placed it in his locker on a huge pile of other blue chits. I decided that with Rain Man now scribbling a series of written warnings with his tongue hanging out, my investigations were going nowhere.

I told Runt I would be watching him closely and stormed out of the dormitory like I was furious.

Friday 25th October

Death Breath handed me a green envelope at break:

Dear Spud (or no longer),
You naughty boy! I heard you guys got suspended. Is it really true that you built this incredible tree house where you drank, smoked, and read poetry? Very Dead Poets Society. *Everyone at school is talking about it.*
Oh—and why did you never take me there?
CU soon?
Amanda

Saturday 26th October

According to Boggo, Mad Dog has been phoning every day for the last four days. He says he's wickedly bored and having six hours of home schooling six days a week.

Monday 28th October

I wrote a letter back to Amanda giving her the rundown of the Mad House debacle. I also let her know that I was no longer a spud, although it seems that the nickname has stuck.

I told the others that we are now famous in all the girls' high schools in Natal. Everyone got really excited until Simon pointed out that we were gated until the end of the year and by next year everyone will have forgotten about what happened.

Fatty has been pestering Emberton for a month now about telling us the truth about the Mad House and who ratted on us and why. He decided to target Emberton because he's a greedy sadist with low intelligence and the easiest prefect to bribe. Eventually, Emberton agreed to spill the beans in return for the following items.

EMBERTON BRIBE DEMANDS

A block of cheese (Gouda)
A tin of hot chocolate (large)
A large Whole Nut chocolate (Cadbury's)
Spud's girlfriend (the one with the big tits)
A latest release CD from a band called The Rampage
$30 in cash
Simon's hair gel

We also have to call the idiot sir for a week. We all coughed up ten bucks and Boggo cycled off to the trading store to make the purchases. Everyone said the reference to Mermaid was a joke, but I spent the rest of the day feeling a little concerned that I may have just sold my girlfriend into slavery.

Friday 1st November

22:00 Fatty called the dormitory to a meeting and lit up his candles.

Turns out that the prefects received a tip-off about the Mad House before the July holidays. Nobody knows who leaked the information because it was written on a piece of paper and anonymously slid under Anderson's door in the middle of the night. The traitor had even drawn a map to guide the prefects to the exact spot. Anderson discovered the Mad House, and he knew immediately that we were using it as a hideaway den for drinking and smoking. They had reported it way back then to Sparerib! Sparerib apparently told them to wait until they could catch us in the Mad House with booze and to make sure Rambo was there at the time. According to Emberton, Sparerib made it clear to all the prefects at the beginning of the year that he wanted to get rid of Rambo and that they would receive special privileges if they assisted.

I told Fatty that I'd interrogated Runt and that I was convinced it was Runt who had blown the whistle on us. Boggo agreed and said Mad Dog had made a blunder in not drowning Runt in the bog stream the day we found him snooping when he had the chance.

Boggo was in the middle of explaining how he was going to torture Runt when the door creaked open and a large shadow stood on the threshold in the doorway. With expulsion looming over us, we all dived onto our beds and pretended to be asleep. There was a long silence. Finally Vern shone his torch on the shadow.

"Rambo!" shouted Vern.

"Oh my God!" gasped Fatty.

"You're both right," replied Rambo, and dragged his trunk into the dormitory.

Rambo wasn't impressed with Fatty taking over his cubicle and gave him thirty seconds to pack up and get lost. Fatty did it in twenty-seven.

Rambo has done it again.

THE OFFICIAL STORY

The school's board of governors agreed that Rambo had been wrongfully expelled because he shouldn't have been placed on final warning in the first place. The board also believed that there was evidence of bad blood between Rambo and Sparerib and that the decision to expel Rambo had been hasty and not fully researched. Rambo has just been beaten six by The Glock and is now, like the rest of us, officially on final warning.

Mad Dog's expulsion will not be changed because he was on absolutely final warning and hasn't passed an exam in two years.

THE LOWDOWN

Rambo says his dad's ex-girlfriend's sister is best friends with Derrick Watts from *Carte Blanche* on TV, the program that does investigations into dodgy things. Rambo apparently threatened to go on live television and admit to having an affair with a teacher (Eve) at our prestigious school last year and say he was unfairly expelled by Sparerib because Sparerib wanted revenge. (That was the point when The Glock called us in before the holidays to ask us those questions.) The board of governors realized that the whole thing could get messy and public, so they decided to let Rambo come back provided he tell nobody about the Eve affair nor the circumstances of the whole case. They made him sign a confidentiality document and have made it clear that should he step out of line again, he will be instantly expelled with no second chances this time.

But the lowdown gets even better! Apparently Sparerib threatened to resign as housemaster if Rambo came back to school, saying it would compromise his principles! Rambo says that Eve has finally admitted to Sparerib that they've had an affair. Rambo says Sparerib has been pretending that he never knew.

Rambo then made us swear an oath of secrecy. Nobody had a Bible, so we all swore on Vern's dictionary.

"Right," said Rambo as he pulled off his tie, "I believe it's time to take out the trash." He pulled a squash racket out of his kit bag and led us into the first-year dormitory.

The Sad Six were all sitting around chatting on J. R. Ewing's locker. When they saw Rambo striding toward them with Vern's torch in one hand and a squash racket in the other, they looked utterly horrified. Rambo smashed J. R. Ewing on the head with the racket. J. R. fell off his locker and onto his bed, clutching the top of his noggin. Rambo then picked up the final Darryl with one hand and threw him headfirst into the locker. The others cowered against the back wall pleading for mercy. Rambo told them to shut up before saying, "There's bad news and there's even worse news. The bad news is that I'm back. The even worse news is that I'm coming back here tomorrow."

Saturday 2nd November

Rambo kept his promise, and tonight he led another attack on the Sad Six. This time he drenched Barryl's bed in water and suspended Runt from the rafters with four school ties and a backpack.

In fact, Rambo's attack was so ferocious that soon the entire Sad Six confessed to being the Mad House rat and begged for mercy. Rambo then asked them which one wrote the letter and they all put their hands up again. In the end Rambo couldn't be sure who was guilty and who wasn't, so he thrashed them all with his squash racket.

Just to rub it in, Fatty let off a disgusting fart as we were leaving. The Sad Six spent the next half an hour outside on the vestry roof waiting for the vile smell of sulfur to fade.

Sunday 3rd November

We all went back to the Mad House during free bounds because Rambo wanted to see what was left of it.

There was nothing there. Even the beautiful big tree was gone.

We looked around in the grass and bushes and found nothing. It suddenly felt like the Mad House was a dream that went bad and had maybe never really existed in the first place. The only thing that made it real was that Mad Dog was no longer with us.

Rambo led us to the workshop and found one of the groundskeepers working under his car with a huge spanner. The man had gigantic teeth.

The man seemed quite thrilled that he'd met what he called "the gang that built the Royal Hotel of tree houses." He asked Rambo who had built it, and without missing a beat Rambo told him that he had crafted the entire thing himself. The man with the giant teeth shook his hand and said, "Nice work."

Apparently The Glock had ordered the tree chopped down so that there would be no copycat tree house builders. The groundskeeper's teeth gleamed in the afternoon sun as he explained that he had used the wood to build a kids' playhouse for the staff with young children.

The Crazy Eight—from Mad House to playhouse.

Tuesday 5th November

DARRYL'S BIRTHDAY

In what must rank as one of the worst birthdays ever:

J. R. Ewing, Barryl, and Thinny threw him in the fountain.

Pike, Devries, Emberton, and Anderson bogwashed him.

Darryl then puked on Anderson's shoe and was beaten four with the sawn-off hockey stick.

Boggo's opened betting on how long Darryl will last at the school.

Gone by the long weekend:
1-1
No return after long weekend:
2-1
Gone before the Christmas holidays:
5-1
Will last until the end of matric
1,000,000-1

Further bad news for poor Darryl is that it was Rambo who put down fifty bucks on him not returning from the long weekend.

20:00 My father called in a state of great excitement. He says the South African cricket team under the captaincy of Clive Rice is going to play three one-day internationals against India next week. Dad said, "Johnny, we're going to give those curry munchers a bloody good thrashing." He then said he could smell burning coming from the garage and hung up.

Simon had already heard the news. I could tell by the way he was marching around the cloisters pumping his fist and shouting, "Baby!"

Wednesday 6th November

Mad Dog has phoned me two days in a row now. He keeps asking me what's going on at school. I told him about Darryl's birthday and he roared with laughter. He then said, "What else?" I told him that I had no more news and then he accused me of trying to hold back stuff to deliberately make him feel worse. I told him I had to go, but then he started begging me to stay on the line. Luckily I saw Rambo having a piss and handed the phone over to him.

As a joke Rambo pretended that he didn't know who Mad Dog was. Poor Mad Dog was beside himself with agitation and kept listing a whole series of stories to jog Rambo's memory. Rambo kept Mad Dog going for ages before telling him he needed help and hanging up. Rambo strode past me and snorted, "From Mad Dog to lapdog!" The phone rang again. I told Runt to answer it and if it was for me to say I was at the sanatorium.

It was Mad Dog again, looking for me. Runt did as I ordered. He then put down the phone and dropped to his knees and started doing press-ups. I asked the idiot why he was doing press-ups in the phone room. He said Mad Dog had ordered him to drop for fifty. I told him that Mad Dog had been expelled and was nearly a thousand miles away. He did them anyway. Then Vern pitched up after one of his urinal inspections. He skulked into the phone room like Runt and I were doing something highly confidential. He then slid onto his stomach and started doing press-ups along with Runt.

I left the two cretins to their workout and headed to the common room for an episode of *Santa Barbara*.

Thursday 7th November

Sparerib has resigned as our housemaster. He made the announcement at the house meeting and it was immediately followed by loud applause and whoops of joy. Sparerib thought we were cheering for him and became weirdly emotional. His good eye filled with tears and he kept shaking Anderson's hand.

Somebody stuck a piece of paper on the house board. It read:

Full-time score: Rambo 2, Sparerib 0

Friday 8th November

SPEECH DAY AND LONG WEEKEND

Being imprisoned like criminals for the long weekend meant that Speech Day had no light at the end of the tunnel. My heart sank when I saw Mom leading Wombat by the hand up Warrior's Walk. Dad lagged behind and seemed to be furiously rubbing his right shoe against the trunk of a plane tree. I greeted them at the school entrance and asked Mom why she and Wombat were wearing hats. Mom said they were wearing hats because they were embarrassed because their son was an alky. She then ordered me to show Wombat to the ladies' room.

Unfortunately, the ladies' room is on the other side of the quad, so I had to make the deadly crossing in full view of the house. Wombat moved her handbag onto her other arm and eyed me shiftily. She then asked me how long I had been a criminal. I didn't want to make a scene, so I told her I'd recently taken it up. Suddenly there was a loud bark from a window above, followed by a shout of, "Hey, Milton! Nice babe, but I thought you were gay?" Wombat darted into the loo and locked the door behind her as if I was going to attack her. She then took ages, which meant I had to greet hundreds of parents as they filed past on the way to the amphitheater.

When Wombat eventually reappeared, she accused me of hanging around the ladies' toilet and of being a pervert. I led Wombat back across the quad toward Mom and Dad. There was a loud growl from above and then a shout of, "Give her one for me!" Other parents had stopped in the quad and were looking around in confusion for the loud, booming voice.

Dad obviously didn't get all the dog poo off his shoe because a nasty smell lingered around us for the long three hours of Speech Day. The people closest to Dad's feet had to move after twenty minutes. Dad didn't seem to notice that he was responsible for a large gap that had suddenly opened up around him and merrily cheered along as each prizewinner was announced.

This year's speaker was even more boring than last year's. And that's quite an achievement considering Lance Ranger's granny passed out from boredom during last year's speech. The Guv was wearing his dark shades and showed very few signs of being awake during the three hours of torture.

I received the English and history prizes. I was also given a certificate for academic merit. Vern was awarded the Van Vuuren trophy for commitment to the school. For once Vern didn't do anything deranged, although it did take him quite a long time to find his seat again. (His mother ended up waving him to it like an airport signaler.)

Next year's head boy is first-team lock Rich Beamon (nickname Fuse) from Barnes House. The parents applauded loudly as he received his blazer and badge from Luthuli. Nobody seemed overly concerned that just two years ago, Fuse was suspended after he attached a first-year to a piece of rope and then dragged the poor slave around Trafalgar with one of the school tractors.

Perhaps there's hope for me yet.

Dad put his arm around me during lunch in the quad and told me that he was still proud of me. I thanked him and told him he had dog turd on his shoe. Dad disappeared into the crowd and then returned within a minute. He showed off a clean shoe and the bottom of his right pant leg, which was soaked.

Let's hope Pissing Pete was the only one to see my father washing off dog turd in the school fountain.

Mom and Wombat both started crying when it was time to go, although I think this wasn't because they were sorry to be leaving me but because Mr. Hall had announced that the bar was closed.

The Crazy Eight watched all the other boys driving off with their parents for the long weekend. Pike said goodbye to us repeatedly and howled with laughter every time he said it.

Worse news is that Anderson and Death Breath are staying behind to study for exams. Our head of house has made it clear that if we so much as leave the house after 5 p.m. every day, we'll be expelled.

Sunday 10th November

SOUTH AFRICA VS. INDIA

05:00 All six of the Crazy Eight risked expulsion by creeping out of the house and then sprinting across the quad, across another quad, up the stairs, and then into the AV room. Boggo had bribed the Barnes AV representative to lend him the keys for the week in return for two porn mags and a starkers picture of Kim Basinger. Boggo said this was the reason why we had to pay five bucks each to watch the cricket.

After a fog delay, Andrew Hudson and Kepler Wessels strode onto Eden Gardens in front of ninety-two thousand people, none of whom were shouting for us. Kapil Dev took the ball and had Andrew Hudson caught behind off the third ball of the match.

After about two overs of play Fatty asked us when we were going to start cooking up the rice. When we told him that Cook and Rice were South African cricketers, he said, "Bugger this," and went back to bed.

Despite Allan Donald taking five wickets, South Africa lost their first ever One Day International. I didn't care because it was just so wonderful to see my country playing international cricket again.

13:45 When we got back to the house, Anderson demanded to know where I'd been because my mother has been disturbing his studying with nonstop phone calls. He gave me a number to phone and told me to do it immediately. I started to get the feeling that something really bad had happened. There was something about the way that everyone was looking at me that made me feel like they knew something that I didn't.

I stopped breathing when a woman's voice said, "Hello, St. Augustine's hospital." My voice shook as I asked for my mother. There was a pause, followed by the click-clacking of her sandals in a corridor. She said Dad may have had a heart attack but that he's going to be fine. I asked her what caused his heart attack. "Hudson and Wessels," was her reply.

According to Mom, Dad was so furious with Hudson's three-ball batting performance that he punched a hole in the bathroom door. She reckoned Wessels's terribly slow batting finally drove him over the edge and he had a stabbing pain in his chest and collapsed on the floor. Mom called an ambulance and Dad was taken away on a stretcher still shouting on about Kepler Wessels being an Australian spy, deliberately trying to sabotage our cricket team with his slow run scoring.

I put down the phone and took myself off for a stroll in case I burst into tears. If the third term is "silly season," then the fourth term is the dying season!

15:00 Dad didn't have a heart attack. The doctor said it was an anxiety attack, and Dad has been discharged with a packet of assorted tranquilizers.

20:00 Dad called to say that he's suing Hudson and Wessels for distress and hospital charges. He started shouting about the umpires being cheats before Mom was able to get the phone away from him and send him to bed.

Mom said Innocence has threatened to throw the television in the pool if Dad persists with his maniacal behavior.

Everyone was talking about my dad's heart attack, although nobody asked me if he was all right.

Monday 11th November

WEEKEND SCORECARD

RAMBO	Broke into Pike's room and booby-trapped it
VERN	Got busted wanking seven times (three red-handed)
SIMON	Bounced a cricket ball on the side of his bat a record 113 times
ROGER	Tried to shag my toiletry bag. (And by the smell of things he may have pissed in it!)
SPUD	Spent a good portion of the week-end on the phone to Mad Dog
BOGGO	Busted Vern wanking seven times (three red-handed)
MAD DOG	Expelled (spent a good portion of the weekend on the phone to Spud)
FATTY	Ate a third of Vern's Adidas rugby boot after being dared to by Rambo. (He swallowed the tongue and laces but said Vern's sole tasted funny.) He also gave us all a tarot card reading.

Although Fatty definitely has links with the supernatural and could be an alien, I'm not so sure his fortune-telling skills are up to snuff. Half the time he seemed to be guessing, and I noticed during my reading that he kept looking at his watch. He said the exact timing of the reading was important to tell the future. I reckon I was just unlucky that my reading started fifteen minutes before lunch.

TAROT CARD READING

RAMBO	Will die at twenty-three after a gunfight with a Mafia boss outside a nightclub in New York.
SIMON	Will captain Transvaal at cricket. Unfortunately, his career will be cut short by a freak injury. Will also discover he's gay after his twenty-first birthday.
BOGGO	Will fall in love with a beautiful prostitute and live happily ever after. (Sure, I've heard that one before.)
SPUD	Will become famous and wealthy after his diaries are secretly published.
VERN	Will be bald by twenty and in a mental institution by thirty.
ROGER	Will die young after choking on a fur ball.
FATTY	Will achieve a doctorate in archaeology and claim the first official sighting of the Loch Ness Monster.

There was much applause from Boggo as Darryl dragged his trunk through our dormitory. Boggo then started singing, "Fifty bucks . . . ," over and over and dancing a jig on his locker. Rambo handed over the cash and then strode off to maim Darryl.

22:00 There was a loud scream from the bogs. We raced down to find Pike foaming at the mouth and writhing around on the bathroom floor in agony. Rambo had replaced Pike's toothpaste with Deep Heat.

Rambo's also sewn sardines into the lining of Pike's mattress and sprinkled itchy powder in the crotch of three pairs of his underpants.

Revenge is very sweet.

Tuesday 12th November

South Africa lost again, although thankfully Hudson was dropped and Wessels batted faster this time. There were no calls from home.

Rambo reckons that since the Sad Six has been thrashed, Sparerib retired, and Pike is in the san with a genital rash, the only further outstanding revenge target is Anderson.

Thursday 14th November

I've finally decided that enough is enough and it's time for make or break.

Dear Mermaid,
How you doing? How's school? When do your exams start? Had a

really boring weekend here at school with not much to do and prefects lurking around and looking threatening. Has your mom decided what you guys are doing in the holidays? Not sure what we are doing either, although there has been talk of a family reunion in Namibia. Anyway, I just wanted to wish you well for your exams and to say hi. Afraid I don't have too much news because we are still being treated like criminals and have no contact with the outside world.

Lots of love,
Johnny

PS Do you want to be my girlfriend again?
PPS I've been wanting to ask you this since the dance.
PPPS What do you think?
PPPPS Please reply soon.
PPPPPS Sorry about all the PS . . . ing.

21:15 Roger was sleeping on my pillow while I lay sprawled out on my bed reading a book on restoration theater and stroking the purring animal with one hand. Then out of the blue Vern attacked me. I heard Boggo shout, "Fight, dudes, fight! Check, Spud and Rain Man are having it off!" Vern was screaming loudly and trying to bash my head into the wooden partition. I kicked him solidly in the balls and was able to get out of his grip and thump him on the head with *The Guide to Restoration Theater*. This stunned Rain Man momentarily and I was able to catch him in a deadly Milton headlock. (If my arms were slightly longer, I could have got him into an unbreakable half nelson.) Vern struggled and screamed, but I held him until his body suddenly fell limp and the idiot collapsed onto the floor and pretended he was dead. Everyone started laughing and mocking Rain Man, especially when his left eye opened slightly to check out the crowd. Obviously this was Vern's cretinous way of saving face after he lost the fight that he started in the first place. Fatty stepped forward and shouted, "Hey, guys, Vern's dying! I've got to give him mouth-to-mouth." Before Fatty could move a step, Vern came back to life. He fluttered his eyelids and pretended that he had just come out of a coma and had completely lost his memory. Simon asked him his name. Vern pretended he didn't know. Rambo then grabbed Vern's left hand and said, "Hey, Vern, why are you wearing my watch?" Poor Vern couldn't argue as Rambo ripped off his watch and stuffed it into his pocket. There was nothing Vern could do other than watch his possessions being stolen and handed out. Eventually all his clothes, possessions, mattress, duvet, and pillows had been dragged off and hidden. Vern sat on the hard wooden planks of his bed and muttered angrily to himself. Rambo shouted from the far end of the dormitory, "Hey, Vern! I think you learned a couple of lessons here today. Never enter a fight unless you know you can finish it and never play the martyr unless you enjoy being walked on." Vern jotted something down in his notebook but said nothing.

Despite the fact that Vern cold-bloodedly tried to slam my head into the wall, I still felt sorry for him curled up on the wooden planks and sniffing and sighing to himself. I stole Mad Dog's old mattress and gave him my blanket and laundry bag, which he could use as a pillow. Obviously Roger has forgiven his master for whatever he'd done wrong because he settled down on Vern's chest with some loud purring and intense head butting.

Mental note 1: Never enter a fight unless you can finish it.

Mental note 2: Never play the martyr unless you enjoy being walked on.

The dreaded Hudson has returned to the South African team, but to everyone's relief, he wasn't called on to bat. At last South Africa won a game, and Dad sounded delighted over the phone. He reckons because of his fine performance today, he's decided not to sue Wessels, although he's still planning to write a snotty letter to Hudson. Apparently Blacky barks every time Richard Snell runs in to bowl. Dad says this is because Blacky can smell a weirdo from a hundred paces.

Friday 15th November

Today's the anniversary of Gecko's death. I told the others, but none of them seemed to be particularly interested. I took an afternoon stroll around the grounds and found myself passing the dam and climbing up the old hill to Hell's View. The view looked different from how I remembered it. Why is it that time travels so fast these days? I surveyed the green fields of the school below and the redbrick buildings that looked like plastic dummy models made by a nerd with too much time on his hands. Suddenly a wave of sadness overtook me. I wasn't thinking about Gecko. I was thinking about my life. Everyone said school would get better as you went on—why do I get the feeling that this year has been considerably worse than last year? I decided that things had reached the point where a list needed to be written.

1991

POSITIVES

- My marks have improved.
- Nobody's died (yet).

- Traveled overseas.
- Pike's leaving.
- My balls dropped.
- Sparerib has retired as housemaster.

NEGATIVES

- My good name has been ruined after being caught drinking and smoking.
- Lost my singing voice and was kicked out of the choir.
- Now have a dodgy friendship with Mermaid.
- Mad Dog was expelled.
- Julian/Luthuli leaving.
- Vern has become more bizarre and tried to kill me last week.
- My acting career is on the rocks after my disastrous performance as the Dove of Peace.
- My (ex)housemaster hates me.
- Cricket team has gone to the dogs.
- With South Africa now returning to international sport, my father may not make it to forty-five.
- My grandmother thinks I'm a criminal.
- My mother thinks I'm an alcoholic.

Clearly it hasn't been a good year because it took ages to find the positives and the only reason I stopped writing negatives was because I ran out of flat ground to write on. I'm sure if Gecko was alive, he would have added a number of things to the positives list to at least even them out with the long list of negatives. I tried to remember his face, but all I could imagine was his pale hands with the nails bitten off and the pink skin around the edges of his fingers nibbled away.

Huge black thunderclouds were building up over the Drakensberg Mountains. I remembered that Fatty said November was the worst month for killer thunderstorms, so I galloped down the hill and didn't stop until I was back in the house. For some reason I then felt much better about life and for the first time in months, I was ravenously hungry.

Fatty made us stay up until midnight listening to his humming and weird chanting. Gecko's ghost didn't respond.

Wednesday 20th November

Rambo and Boggo tied a piece of fishing line at knee height across Anderson's doorway. Our head of house stepped out of his room just before roll call and did a spectacular cartwheel down the stairs. Boggo told Emberton that he'd seen J. R. Ewing messing around outside Anderson's door, and within minutes J. R. was beaten three with Emberton's sugarcane.

Friday 22nd November

Still no news on who our next housemaster will be. Sparerib is hardly ever around the house anymore. Anderson makes up for this by being everywhere at all times.

Saturday 23rd November

Kings College smashed us to pieces.

Even more embarrassing was that Amanda made a surprise appearance and stayed for the entire massacre. (This means she saw my bowling and batting disasters.) Her hair was gleaming golden red in the sun, and with her dark sunglasses and short skirt, she looked like a movie star. Like Julia Roberts, in fact.

I skipped lunch and sat with Amanda under a large jacaranda tree. She casually told me that she'd broken up with her boyfriend and then just as casually asked me to go away with her and her friends to Leisure Bay in December. I remember making a Dad-like whistling sound and then stumbled quite badly over my words. Amanda laughed huskily and said, "I'm not asking you to marry me, you moron. It's just a weekend down the coast." I tried my best to act cool, so I said, "That will be cool." Amanda arched her left eyebrow and asked, "You're not still pining after that bimbo, what's her name again . . . Whale Girl or something?"

"Mermaid," I corrected her.

"Whatever," she replied.

"Of course not," I lied.

Counting down the days until the end of term. I've decided to stop pining for the Mermaid. Not only is it driving me crazy, but even if I do miraculously get her back, she's only going to dump me for a blond surfer with big biceps eventually.

Besides, she wants to be friends anyway.

I didn't get a chance to chat with Amanda after the game because The Guv was in a mad rush to buy wine before the shops closed at 5 p.m.

Sunday 24th November

Luthuli interrupted our last-minute cramming for exams to say that he was leaving. It took me a moment to realize that he meant that he was leaving the school forever. He shook all our hands and wished us well for the future. I wish I had been brave enough to tell him how much he inspired me to be a freedom fighter and how much I respected him, but the others were watching and I couldn't find the right words, so all I ended up saying was, "'Bye."

And then, as quickly as he had arrived, Luthuli was gone and everything felt slightly unreal for the rest of the day.

Monday 25th November

Freddy Mercury, the lead singer of Queen, died yesterday of AIDS.

There was mourning in the common room. Pike and Anderson were both in tears, while Death Breath was blasting "Who Wants to Live Forever" from the huge hi-fi in his room.

Upstairs, Emberton, Rambo, Boggo, and Fatty were having an argument about AIDS. Fatty said it was going to become like the black plague that wipes out half the world's population. Rambo said it was just a homo disease and that this meant Simon probably wouldn't survive until matric. Emberton snorted with laughter and thrashed his sugarcane into Boggo's locker. He then told us that AIDS stood for Arse Injected Death Sentence, but nobody believed him.

15:00 The entire school is bizarrely quiet except for the music of Queen, which was blaring from all over. I could hear sobbing from outside Death Breath's room as he blasted repeated versions of "The Show Must Go On. . . ."

Looks like the dying season has struck once again.

Thursday 28th November

Exams end!!! (Scholarship should be safe for another year.)

Friday 29th November

It came in a red envelope.

Dear Johnny,
Thanks 4 the letter. Sorry I haven't replied faster but have been caught up with exams and needed to think about stuff. I'm sorry if I gave you the idea that I only wanted to be friends with you. I thought you didn't want to be together with me after what happened before. I also felt like you didn't trust me and were keeping me at arm's length because you just wanted to be friends. I just want you to know that I would love to be your girlfriend again. I've been counting down the days until you get home—by the time you get this, it will be only a week to go.

Love,
Mermaid

PS Please come away with us to Sodwana. It's on the North Coast. My dad isn't coming, so there shouldn't be any fighting this time.
PPS I'm so excited. Yay!
PPPS I can't write poems like you, so this is my poem for you . . .

Inside the envelope was a blank tape. I borrowed/stole Boggo's old radio/tape deck and headed for the dam, unsure of what was about to be revealed. I wasn't so sure I wanted to know. All I remember was running very fast and not blinking much. I found a secluded spot and pressed play.

There was one song on it. "Eternal Flame."

Whoever is writing the script for my life must be a depraved and sadistic swine. I think Depeche Mode hit the nail on the head when they sang:

I think that God's got a sick sense of humor
And when I die
I expect to find him laughing!

Mental note: If two beautiful women come into your life, you can bet your dog it will be at exactly the same time.

Saturday 30th November

FINAL MATCH AGAINST ST. JULIUS

Play was delayed because a lime green station wagon slid down the bank and onto the cricket field. The idiotic driver (who shall never be named) was trying to park his vehicle under the shade of a small tree and reversed over the edge, slid down a steep, muddy bank, and ended up on the field boundary. The deranged driver (with his equally deranged wife shouting and waving her arms about) then made another three attempts at driving up the bank, all of which resulted in another dramatic slide back down the slope and onto the field. The grass on the bank was ruined with ugly tire marks, and the gathered crowd of about forty people laughed and cheered along with each disastrous attempt. Eventually it took the whole team and the school tractor to haul the station wagon up the slope to safety. The deranged driver then kicked the car several times, smashing out a taillight in the process.

We won by five wickets. The Guv told us that we'd covered ourselves in glory and said that apart from the fourth-term meltdown, it had been a splendid season all around. He then told us that he'd lost all his mirth and headed off to drink with the crazy people in the lime green station wagon.

Sunday 1st December

Spent the afternoon under the pine trees discussing my love life with the rest of the Crazy Eight.

ADVICE FROM CRAZY EIGHT

RAMBO Bonk them both.

BOGGO Choose Amanda and leave Mermaid to him. Option B, organize and film a threesome.

FATTY	Choose Mermaid. Fatty says he's scared of Amanda.
VERN	Mermaid.
SIMON	Cheat on them both.
ROGER	Amanda (Vern translated).

Simon and Rambo reckon I'll get away with having two girlfriends. Boggo said I had to choose one because the truth will always come out. I thought about making a pros and cons list, but I made that list with Gecko last year and Amanda won.

"I THINK I'LL HAVE TO THINK IT OUT AGAIN. . . ."

Had our final AA meeting of the year. It all felt a bit weird without Linton Austin and Luthuli. Thankfully, Lennox put on a video about Sir Ernest Shackleton's assault on the South Pole and nobody had to say anything about politics. It was also a relief not having to take notes and read out the minutes. Next year I won't be secretary again.

Tuesday 3rd December

The matrics performed the haka (which is a New Zealand Maori war dance) in the main quad after their final exam. Afterward the house gathered to say goodbye (and good riddance) to the class of 1991. Emberton tried to break my wrist when he shook my hand. Anderson didn't look any of the Crazy Eight in the eyes, and Death Breath is still looking terribly grief stricken about Freddie M. even though it's been over a week since the news.

When Pike shook my hand, he said rather ominously, "Ciao, Milton, see you in six weeks." I asked him if he was coming back for post-matric, but he just grinned and refused to answer. No doubt a final attempt to ruin my holiday.

Anderson is staying on until Friday to keep discipline in the house. The third-years are suddenly all racing around looking powerful and important. Rambo reckons they're all making a last-ditch attempt at pushing for prefect.

17:00 I was setting off along the cloisters to fetch my trunk from the storeroom when I noticed Sparerib carrying a huge pile of papers and stationery from his office. I lagged back so that I wouldn't have to speak to him, but he then dropped half his stuff all over the cloisters and in the gutter. The wind was blowing the papers everywhere and I felt obliged to help him out. I knelt down to pick up some textbooks and met Sparerib's face, eye to wonky eye, just as he pounced on some flapping papers. He suddenly seemed to me to be a different human being. Like he was twenty years older. He was pale and sickly and sad—but I mean really sad, like it was impossible that there was anything that could cheer him up ever again. He said, "Thanks, John, let's take them back to the office. I'll bring my wheelbarrow when the wind dies down." I headed back into his office and dumped the stuff on the floor near the cupboard where he keeps his canes.

Sparerib placed the rest of the papers and books on his desk and continued looking away from me and out the window, which looks onto his house. Suddenly I realized that his shoulders were shaking and then a low moaning sound escaped from his lips like an animal in pain. I didn't know what to do, so I started a very steady reverse creep back toward the office door. I was just inches away from freedom when the wind slammed the door shut with a huge bang. Spareribs turned around and his eyes were red and stained with tears. "John," he said in a broken voice, "what . . . what should I do?"

Here was my housemaster with tears running down his cheeks asking a rather small and insignificant second-year what he should do. I didn't know what to say and I couldn't use my old trick of shaking my head sadly and looking out the window because Sparerib was staring at me with tears streaming out of his wonky eye, demanding an answer to what seemed like quite a serious question. Thankfully he spoke again because so far, I hadn't come up with anything helpful. He said, "What do you do when you're a small wooden raft surrounded by a . . . a seething sea of complete madness?"

He seemed to be asking this question more of himself than of me. But I felt like I finally had the answer to his question. I cleared my throat and said, "You keep a diary, sir."

Sparerib glared at me like he was about to start shouting, but then his face seemed to almost shatter into a smile. He started laughing loudly, although tears were still streaming down his face. It seemed unnatural for Sparerib to laugh. It made you think that he might be on the verge of a sudden seizure.

But his laughter died as quickly as it had begun and his face returned to looking desperately sad again. He studied me for some time before saying, "Thank you, Milton." He then dismissed me with a very formal nod.

I left my housemaster's office for the last time and realized that I didn't hate Sparerib anymore. Perhaps it's because for the first time he didn't seem to hate me. Maybe it's just that I feel sorry for him now. This doesn't mean that I necessarily like him. . . . We'll call it a truce.

Wednesday 4th December

Dear Mermaid,
I can't wait to see you too and I'm thrilled that you are my girlfriend again. And yes, I would love to go to Sodwana with your family. It may just save me from another nasty family reunion in Namibia. I can't wait to see you and miss you lots.

Love,
John

PS I am going to Leisure Bay with some school friends for a boys-only weekend next weekend.

My hands shook as I posted the letter. I get the feeling that I may one day regret writing that PS.

QUESTIONS

What am I doing?
Does this mean I have two girlfriends?
Where the hell is Gecko!

Thursday 5th December

22:30 There was a loud scream from the first-year dormitory followed by a thump and then silence. Then I could hear footsteps in the doorway and then the creak of floorboards. Somebody or something was approaching. Rambo leapt on the intruder and tried to wrestle him to the ground. In the end the intruder wrestled Rambo to the ground and then growled like an animal. Vern's torch illuminated a figure dressed in black with a baseball cap pulled down over his face. There was a loud swoosh and suddenly a hunting and filleting knife was gleaming in the torchlight and an old friend's face was revealed. Mad Dog was back!

There was chaos when it was discovered that the Dog had appeared out of nowhere. After massive hugs and a long and vicious session of backslapping, Mad Dog said, "Jeez, guys, I spent two years thinking about how to break out of this place and now I'm breaking in." Mad Dog told us he had caught the bus to Mooi River and hiked the rest of the way. His folks think he's visiting a friend in Pinetown.

I knew I should have refused to go, but with Mad Dog having traveled over a thousand miles to join us on a final night swim, pulling out would have been impossible. Vern conducted a thorough search for Anderson and discovered that he was at the Leavers' party in Pietermaritzburg. Rambo gave us the all-clear and we all filed into the first-year dormitory.

Mad Dog was amazed that the final Darryl was still at school and congratulated him for showing courage and sticking it out. He then dangled the poor slave out the window until he'd wet his pajamas.

Once in the chapel I started getting flashbacks to the Mad House night. It seemed like it had happened so long ago. In fact, with Mad Dog around it felt like the night had never really happened at all.

Mad Dog led the charge across the field and vaulted the fence. He smashed his way through the bush and long grass before leaping into the dam with a gigantic splash. Boggo told Mad Dog to keep the noise down. Mad Dog started climbing the big tree and shouted, "What they gonna do, Boggo—expel me again?" He then threw himself off the branch and his powerful body swooped through the air like a giant bat before gracefully arching itself into a slow backward flip and crashing into the dark water below.

Rambo made us all jump off the high branch as a final salute to Mad Dog. Climbing up a tree in the darkness is no easy feat, and this time there were no nails and planks to help us up. Vern reached the branch but then got scared about jumping off and started reversing along it back toward the trunk of the tree. He was muttering loudly to himself when suddenly there was a snap followed by a screech. Vern hit the ground and rolled down the bank and into the water. Rambo pulled him out of the water with one hand and plonked him down on the bank. Vern gave us all a thumbs-up before having a nasty coughing fit. Miraculously, the only injury he had was a bitten tongue.

Once everyone had swum out to the middle and back, jumped out of the tree, and been dunked at least twice, it was decided that it was time to head back to school. Mad Dog said goodbye to everyone and said he was leaving. "Where you sleeping?" asked Boggo. Mad Dog pointed in the direction of the forest and said, "Where do you think?"

Vern (who had spent the entire night swim with his tongue sticking out) started sniffing and rubbing his eyes. Fatty shook Mad Dog's hand and asked, "Why did you come back?" Mad Dog shrugged and said, "For this."

We watched Mad Dog run off into the bush and then followed Rambo across the field toward the school buildings that looked like giant ships anchored in a dead calm sea of darkness.

Friday 6th December

D-day.

The sky is always brighter on the last day of term. The turtledoves call louder than usual, and there is a strange feeling of harmony that fills the school and everyone in it. Even the final assembly is a celebration rather than a horror.

The Glock gave out a record amount of ties, badges, blazers, and certificates and did a lot of general handshaking. In fact, he gives out so many awards that if you don't get one, you feel like a complete loser. When he announced our new housemaster for 1992, Rambo's head sank into his hands, Fatty looked terrified, while Boggo shook his head like he had just been dealt a killer blow. Simon looked grim and Vern looked utterly crazy with one hand on his head and his tongue lolling out the side of his mouth like Blacky. For once I was the only one smiling.

Our new housemaster is Viking.

God help all of us.

After saying goodbye to the Crazy Eight and the Sad Six, I packed up the last of my things and ran down to The Guv's house to say goodbye. He was listening to loud classical music and striding around his lounge conducting the music with wild swishes of his walking stick. "Beethoven, Milton!" he shouted over the loud din. "Sheer majesty and grandeur! A celebration of life and genius." He turned the music down before rounding on me with his stick. "I suppose you've come to say your goodbyes, young Milton?" I nodded and wished my English teacher a happy Christmas, but his thoughts were already elsewhere.

"Does time fly for someone of your age?" I held up my diary to him and said, "One year, sir." He grinned and said, "Ah, your true account, lest he returning chide." Without missing a beat, I replied, "On his blindness, sir." The Guv chuckled before announcing that "in the land of the blind the one-eyed man is king." I couldn't help laughing at The Guv glaring at me over his spectacles with one eye. He then shouted, "Exit!" I turned to him and shouted back, "Pursued by a bear!" I left by the kitchen door to the sound of Beethoven winding up again in the lounge.

Dad arrived in a foul mood. He said the station wagon was out of whack and he's just had the bloody thing serviced. Dad was wearing his blue running shorts (pulled up way too high), flip-flops, and a bright yellow T-shirt on which was written: UP THE BANANA BOYS. I ordered my father not to get out of the car and nearly broke my back loading my trunk into the boot.

The engine took a few turns to catch. Dad shouted, "Come on, you slut!" just as Mrs. Hall was making her way across the driveway. She shot a savage look at my father, who then shouted, "You biscuit!" before revving the engine like a drag racer. I pretended to be digging in my bag for a pencil and kept my head under the dashboard. Dad then put on the Carpenters tape way too loudly and I heard a loud chorus of laughter and the name "Spud" being shouted out. I kept hiding my head and counted down the seconds to my freedom.

TOWN HILL (THE END . . .)

It began with smoke pouring out of the engine. Dad said it wasn't a problem and that the car did that from time to time. Next there was an ominous whine from somewhere beneath my seat. Dad put it down to the Carpenters rather than the car. The station wagon died with a massive shudder and the green machine staggered into the emergency lane. Dad smashed his hand onto the dashboard and then ripped out the Carpenters tape and hurled it into the fast lane of the freeway, where it was immediately run over by a navy blue BMW.

We certainly weren't on top of the world looking down on creation. More like halfway down Town Hill looking like a long walk home. (That's when I realized that we'd broken down no more than a mile from where we'd broken down on the way up to school.) Dad sat dead still with his head on the steering wheel. He seemed to be muttering, "Not again," over and over to himself. I must admit this so-called coincidence pointed to a sign from God. I have no clue what the sign meant, but there had to be a good reason for the bizarre coincidence of breakdowns.

Dad and I bolted across the freeway and through some bushes on the other side. We followed a narrow road up a hill and found ourselves at the gates of the Town Hill Psychiatric Center. Dad's left eye was twitching and he spoke in a strangely high voice when he said, "You'd better hold the fort. I'll go and find a phone and call your mother." He looked at me sadly for a moment and then pushed through the gate and loped up the pathway toward the entrance.

Dad approached a silver-haired man dressed in a long white coat standing at the bottom of the steps with a clipboard. I watched him hold out his hand to introduce himself and heard him shout, "I've just had a breakdown!" The man nodded and made a note on his clipboard. Dad turned to me and shot me a thumbs-up. I returned it with a double. Then the man in the long white coat put his arm around my father's shoulders and led him slowly up the stairs.